Praise for *Transcendental*

"*Transcendental* shows exactly why Gunn attained Grandmaster status in the first place."   —*Locus*

"Gunn has issued a novel that equals or tops his earlier landmark, earning, I think, a permanent rank in the extended canon of our genre. It is wise, exciting, clever, surprising, hip, and au courant (or perhaps timeless is a better word). Its technical craftsmanship is subtle and awe-inspiring."   —Paul Di Filippo

"The narrative promise of the novel is largely deferred to future installments of what will most likely be a trilogy. But the stories, which compress thousands of years of multiple alien evolutionary timelines into a few tales, are a wonder to those interested in world-building and the slow but transformative force of the imperative to survive and thrive. Darwinists, take heart: This book is for you."
                                                     —*Kirkus Reviews*

"Gunn keeps the action dancing nimbly through uneasy alliances, abrupt betrayals, and sudden violence as the ship sails through the starless void toward its destination."   —*Publishers Weekly*

"A fascinating tale . . . Riley's journey alone is reason enough to read this book. James Gunn's *Transcendental* is one of my recent favorites. It's definitely worth a look."   —*Amazing Stories*

"*Transcendental* is possibly [Gunn's] finest novel to date, with an awe-inspiring, thought-provoking, and suspenseful plot and a cast of characters intriguing enough to please both longtime sci-fi fans and newcomers."   —*Bookgasm*

Books by James Gunn

*A Tor Book

TRANSCENDENTAL

JAMES GUNN

TOR®

A TOM DOHERTY ASSOCIATES BOOK

NEW YORK

TRANSCENDENTAL

Copyright © 2010, 2013 by James Gunn

Several chapters of this book were previously published, in somewhat different form, in *Gateways,* edited by Elizabeth Anne Hull, Tor Books, 2010.

Edited by James Frenkel

A Tor Book
Published by Tom Doherty Associates, LLC
175 Fifth Avenue
New York, NY 10010

www.tor-forge.com

Tor® is a registered trademark of Tom Doherty Associates, LLC.

The Library of Congress has cataloged the hardcover edition as follows:

Gunn, James E., 1923–
    Transcendental / James Gunn.—1st ed.
        p. cm.
    "A Tom Doherty Associates Book."
    ISBN 978-0-7653-3501-2 (hardcover)
    ISBN 978-1-4668-2081-4 (e-book)
    1. FICTION / Science Fiction / Space Opera. I. Title.
    PS3513.U797 T73 2013
    813'.54—dc23

                                                        2013023856

ISBN 978-0-7653-3503-6 (trade paperback)

Tor books may be purchased for educational, business, or promotional use. For information on bulk purchases, please contact Macmillan Corporate and Premium Sales Department at 1-800-221-7945, extension 5442, or write specialmarkets@macmillan.com.

First Edition: August 2013
First Trade Paperback Edition: September 2014

Printed in the United States of America

0 9 8 7 6 5 4 3 2 1

TRANSCENDENTAL

CHAPTER ONE

The voice in Riley's head said, "You almost got us killed."

Riley looked around the waiting room. Terminal was the jumping-off place for anyone wanting to go farther out. There wasn't much farther out, but he and an odd-assortment of passengers were heading there in search of something he was pretty sure didn't exist.

The debris from the barbarian Minal attack had been cleaned up, but the reason for the attack was unclear. Maybe it was the weather here on the equator, first freezing cold, then wet and hot.

"April is the cruelest month," his pedia said, "breeding lilacs out of the dead land, mixing memory and desire, stirring dull roots with spring rain."

His pedia said things like that, and other things he found more comprehensible and less benign. "What is 'April'?"

"A thousand years ago people on Earth used that word to designate a time of renewal when plants started to grow again after their winter death," his pedia said. "When humanity ventured out among the stars, they brought words along that had little meaning there. Except war. That means the same everywhere."

"I was born on Mars."

"Thanne longen folk to goon on pilgrimages," his pedia said.

Riley ignored it, as he often did when it gave him nonsense from its immense mass of stored information. Maybe it was talking about the pilgrimage he and the others were soon to embark upon if the authorities here ever let them board the climber.

A few hours ago the barbarians who lived in the wild mountains attacked Terminal City and battled their way almost to the spaceport. They killed hundreds of civilized Minals and a few outworlders as well, including a couple of humans. Riley himself had dispatched half a dozen of the barbarians when they approached the barricaded port, shooting them in their vulnerable underbellies as they reared up to launch their spears and arrows, and killing the last one with his knife when it fought within reach.

Riley had questioned Minal officials, but their answers were the equivalent of a human shrug: none of the Minal knew what the raiders wanted, or they were reluctant to speculate, or the Minals and the outworlders had reached a communication impasse. To add to his woes, after the attack was over and a semblance of order restored, the Minal officials had been unable to explain why passengers in the spaceport had been forced to wait as much as forty-eight hours for their transfer to the ship orbiting above, or when they might be able to depart.

The attackers took no booty and no slaves as they withdrew, only their wounded. Maybe they wished to delay the pilgrimage or to kill the pilgrims. Maybe the officials and the barbarians were working together. The announcement of the pilgrimage had aroused almost as much opposition as the rumors of transcendentalism itself.

Riley looked around. The waiting room was small—no more than twenty meters square—and cluttered with refugees from dozens of alien worlds. They had been living here in the waiting room and some of them had slept here, and their trash had piled up under the seats, the pedestals that passed for seats if you were built differently, and the supports used by some species. The odors of strange spices and fetid emissions were a miasma on the air currents; the way it smelled depended upon your origins and your organs. The far wall was transparent except for a cloudy portion in the lower left-hand corner where a barbarian arrow had nicked it and a couple of bullet holes had not been repaired. Through the holes seeped the decay of the Terminal tropical jungle. Beyond was the spaceport out in the bay with its standard space elevator like an almost-invisible black beanpole ascending into the clouds above; a climber waited at its base. Beyond that lay the Terminal jungle, green and orange and blue masses of vegetation ending at the mountains that entirely surrounded this basin except on the ocean side. Behind the mountains the reddish Terminal sun was setting in a gulf between the clouds. Afterward would come the Terminal night, far blacker out here in this remote region of the spiral arm than that on Mars.

Riley turned his attention back to the waiting room and its occupants, trying to identify who was a pilgrim and who was here on some other business. Playing this kind of game forced him to pay attention to details. No matter what the people who had implanted his pedia thought, he was no superhero. He was a survivor, and he had survived so far by paying attention. Most creatures didn't. Most creatures died sooner than they should.

That heavy-planet alien standing on a tripod of its two trunk-like legs and its thick tail: it had been a stalwart in the fight against the barbarians, hurling them aside with ease and sustaining cuts that seemed to heal as they were being sustained. It was not paying attention now, with two of its eyes closed and its short proboscis swaying. Riley didn't think it was a pilgrim: heavy-planet aliens already thought they were perfect. It was probably a trader or an envoy, or maybe even a vacationer enjoying the exhilaration of low-gravity worlds.

A tank with treads, like a motorized coffin, stood in front of the window—a poor location for a creature whose fragile life-support system needed this kind of protection. The tank was decorated with engraved designs that Riley would have liked to examine more closely, but alien sensitivities were unpredictable. He had no desire to cause interspecies conflict, but the tank, for that's what it most closely resembled, piqued his curiosity, if for no reason other than its unusual exterior. The tank had no windows, no obvious means of observing the outside world, as if the outside world was irrelevant or the occupant, if there was an occupant at all. It was impossible to discern anything at all about the interior of the tank. For all he knew, the tank itself might itself be the alien creature; or, if there was an alien within, it might already be dead or near-dead and being sustained by some high medical art.

On the other side of the window stood a tall, spindly creature, its head, like a yellow flower in the heat of the day, nodding forward on a stem-like neck. Several extensions protruded from its body, like stems; fluids could be observed coursing through them and up the torso that was scarcely larger than the extensions. Riley would have thought it no good at all in a fight, but during the barbarian attack, he had noticed it slicing the armored neck of a barbarian with one swing of an arm.

A couple of small, wiry humans sat together. One was dark-haired, the other, blond. Riley couldn't be sure what gender they were. Maybe they weren't sure, either. Riley judged them to be members of the space crew. They moved a bit sluggishly on-planet, but they had acquitted themselves well against the barbarians, acting decisively, efficiently, and cooperatively.

The next person he saw was a small alien who reminded Riley of pictures he had seen of weasels—a pinched muzzle of a face, if it was a face, and small, shifty eyes, if they were eyes. It had fought like a weasel, darting in and out to deliver fatal blows with a knife. It might be, he thought, another space crew member, or maybe a pilgrim. He inspected and catalogued others before he came to the woman. She sat on a pack of belongings to his left and to the right of the weasel-like alien. There were thirty-seven in the waiting room, not counting the Terminal officials—a couple other human males; a barrel-like Sirian with small, hooded eyes and a round hole for a mouth; an Alpha Centauran with a feathery topknot, a fierce-looking beak, and vestigial wings; and several whose home world he could not identify. He had saved the woman until last. She sat like a cat, relaxed but lithe, as if she could spring into action at a touch. She had dark hair and blue eyes, a combination that was striking even if she wasn't beautiful—her features were regular and her eyes were large, but they moved restlessly; moreover her mouth was too firm and her chin too set. But somehow she seemed just right for what she was and Riley thought he would like to know her, and maybe he would. She was a pilgrim, he thought, and she had accounted for as many barbarians as he had.

He was still pondering her status, when the heavy-world alien woke up, or perhaps had not been asleep after all. It clomped across the floor to the platform that served the quadruped Minals for a desk and said something that Riley's pedia translated as "My name is Tordor, and we will leave now!"

Tordor would be someone to watch.

Within minutes the announcement came over the P.A. system in Galactic Standard that the climber would depart in half an hour. It was more like an hour.

The climber was primitive, no more than a huge metal box with grippers, as befitted a frontier planet. On more advanced planets, climbers offered private rooms, food, and windows to view the planet below or the starry sky above, and sometimes canned entertainment on viewers of various sorts. Here pedestals and seats lined the walls, with a single window on each side; otherwise the walls were bare. A cubicle at one end provided privacy for creatures that required it for elimination or ingestion, and a large open area in the middle left space for creatures that rested lying down. Dispensers at the end farthest from the privy offered several kinds of fluids but no solid food. Instructions told travelers to bring their own nourishment, and to provide their own protection against thieves and predators.

The climber was a cattle car and the passengers were cattle. The trip to geosynchronous orbit would take seven days; it had started an hour ago with a subtle jar and a grinding noise from the grippers. If the waiting room had been odorous, the climber was worse. It smelled already. More than half of the creatures from the waiting room were crowded in, including the heavy-planet alien. It stood in front of Riley.

A series of grunts came from it that Riley's pedia translated as "I am Tordor. That is not my real name, which is not suitable for your voicing system. I am designated after my planet of origin, in the galactic custom."

"Tordor," Riley said. "Good work back there." Tordor could take that as either a compliment on his fighting during the barbarian attack or his ultimatum to the officials.

Grunts: "You, too." The barbarian attack, then; the ultimatum was SOP. "Protective association is wise."

"I agree. But how do we trust each other?"

Grunts: "We enlist others. You pick one. I pick another. Two each. One from each always on guard."

"Good," Riley said. He approached the woman. "My name is Riley. This is Tordor. We're forming a protective association for the trip up, and you're invited to join."

"I'll take care of myself," she said. Her voice was low but confident.

"And a good job you'll do, too," Riley said cheerfully. He led Tordor to the two space crew types, who introduced themselves as Jan and Jon, although it wasn't clear which was which. They accepted.

Tordor picked the flower-headed alien. It produced a swishing sound by swinging its stem-like extensions. His pedia identified the swishing sounds as language but could not interpret. "It is from Aldebaran," Tordor grunted. "Self-identified as flower child four one zero seven. It accepts." Tordor went on to the coffin-shaped vessel, which had trundled onto the climber under its own power, and stood silently near one end. "This creature does not identify itself," Tordor grunted, "and spurns our offer of association."

Tordor completed his part of the group with the bird-headed Alpha Centauran. Neither Tordor nor Riley proposed approaching the weasel, but Riley suggested keeping an eye on it, and perhaps on the Sirian as well.

At the end of thirteen hours they had climbed more than sixteen hundred kilometers. In the last hour, standing at the window, he had watched the sky turn black and the stars appear—paltry as they were. He saw Terminal become a partial sphere and felt gravity slowly drop to what felt like about 50 percent. The loss of weight improved his energy levels and his spirits, which always were depressed by the thought of trusting his life to a meter-wide film or the centimeters-thick window through which he gazed. He looked around and saw that even the pachyderm-like Tordor moved with something approaching grace.

They conversed briefly about organization and the deficiencies of bureaucracies.

"Hierarchies are far more efficient," Tordor said.

"Democracies encourage progress," Riley said.

"Progress is bad," Tordor said.

"The galactic powers agree," Riley replied.

"No more wars," Tordor said.

"We can agree on that," Riley said. The wars had nearly destroyed the galaxy before the various sapient species had decided to make a peace that allowed no one to gain an advantage on pain of everyone else ganging up on them. Tordor, from a heavy planet with a hierarchical organization based not on birth but on seniority, believed in stasis, in keeping everything, people, culture, politics, the way they had always been, maybe because Tordor's culture thought it would survive the centuries and others would fall.

Tordor was a pilgrim; Riley had been wrong about that. But Tordor didn't say why.

By the time Riley felt it wise to get some sleep he had gotten acquainted with Jon and Jan. Jon was the dark-haired one, Jan, the light-haired. They were space crew hired to serve on the starship *Geoffrey*. Riley didn't like the name of the starship; he never liked ships with people names, even if they were human names.

Previously the brothers? Sisters? He couldn't tell . . . had worked on a freighter, but some months earlier they had jumped ship. He had been right about them, anyway, although he had never heard of anyone jumping ship in space; it didn't seem possible unless they had been given planet leave, and who would give or accept leave on a planet as barren of attractions as Terminal?

Neither Jon nor Jan volunteered any information about gender, and Riley didn't ask. Before they arranged sleep times, the members of Riley and Tordor's protection association agreed on a rotation for keeping watch. Riley took the first one and woke Jan for the second. Before he went to sleep, with his head upon his single bag of belongings and his hand upon the gun tucked under it, he told Jan to keep his—or her; he still wasn't sure which—back against the wall and to watch everybody, Tordor included.

He awoke suddenly with his hand around the wrist of the weasel-faced alien.

The weasel made a gesture that could have been a shrug of apology and retreated to a corner. Riley looked at his hand. It was still holding the weasel's arm. The end of the arm—it was not quite a hand—had a knife in it. The other end wasn't bleeding, as if the blood vessels had immediately shut down. Riley looked behind him. Jan was slumped on the bench, asleep or unconscious. The flower-headed alien stood on hairy, rootlike feet a couple of meters away, its head drooping.

Riley dropped the arm with the knife still clutched in what passed for a hand and got to his feet. Jan was still breathing. Riley felt his pulse and smelled his breath. Jan had been administered a subtle soporific, Riley's pedia told him; it would degrade into harmlessness in an hour.

He shook Jon awake and pointed to Jan. "He'll be okay," Riley told Jon. "No thanks to you," he told the flower child. It did not acknowledge his words. Maybe it too had been sedated, but Riley's pedia provided no insights into alien physiologies.

By this time Tordor had opened his eyes. The large alien took in the scene with a quick swivel of its head. "So," he grunted. "It begins."

Riley picked up the arm and carried it across the floor to the corner where the weasel-faced alien crouched. "I think this is yours," he said.

The weasel accepted the arm and laid it at its own feet. It said something that sounded like modulated whistling. Riley's pedia didn't interpret, but Tordor grunted, "It says it saw your guards asleep. It feared someone would do you harm."

"Tell it I regret detaching its arm," Riley said.

"No matter, it says," Tordor reported. "Arms easy, life hard."

Riley laughed. He was beginning to feel a sneaky admiration for the weasel's bravado.

When he got back to his sleeping place, the dark-haired woman was sitting nearby. "It could have killed you," she said.

"You saw it?"

"I don't need much sleep. I see a lot of things."

"And you didn't think it was worth warning me?"

"It was none of my business. If it killed you, it would be because you weren't tough enough to survive. And if you're going to be a pilgrim, you'll need to be tough. Only a few of us will survive."

What makes her so sure about that? He kept his question to himself.

"Who said I was going to be a pilgrim?" So she was a pilgrim, as he had thought, and if he could keep her talking, he might get a better idea of where she fit in with this pilgrimage crowd.

"You're here," she said. "It didn't intend to kill you."

"How do you know?"

"It had the opportunity before you awoke."

"That's what it said. It said it was protecting me."

"It was the only creature that approached you."

"Thanks," Riley said. He didn't want her to think he needed help in figuring out what the weasel wanted. Neither did he tell her that his pedia had awakened him as the weasel approached and that he had pretended sleep until the last moment.

But he didn't know what the weasel wanted. He thought about it as he and Jon tried to revive Jan. Whoever had put Jan to sleep also may have had something similar for the flower child, but that implied a level of preparation that challenged belief. Of course the flower child could be part of the conspiracy, and could have administered the knockout chemical to Jan and only pretended to be asleep.

When Jan stirred, stretching and yawning and apparently feeling no aftereffects of the drug except guilt, he/she/it had no memory of anyone approaching or any sting of injection or an odor other than the universal stink. "I'm sorry," it said.

"They were ready for us," Riley replied.

"They?"

"Whoever they are."

"It won't happen again," Jan said, and Jon nodded in agreement. "We'll be ready for them."

"Get some sleep," Riley said.

"It's still my watch," Jan said.

"I don't feel sleepy," Riley said.

When he sat down on the bench Jan had vacated, Tordor was rocking back on its tail a meter or so away, but its eyes were open, looking at Riley.

"What did you mean," Riley asked, " 'So it begins.' "

"Long journey," Tordor grunted. "Many perils. Many die. Many wish pilgrimage to fail."

"Many forces," Riley said. "Many motives." His pedia processed the words as a series of Tordor-like grunts, which led Riley to respond in the same sort of clipped syntax as Tordor. The pedia needed time to translate languages with which it was unfamiliar.

Tordor waved his proboscis in a gesture that swept the room.

"Right," Riley said. "Who are pilgrims? Who are anti-pilgrims?" Maybe, he thought, there are no legitimate pilgrims at all. Maybe they were all attempting to sabotage the pilgrimage. That would be an irony even the transcendental gods could enjoy.

They conversed for another hour, partly keeping awake, partly feeling each other out. As best they could in their limited common vocabulary, they discussed the reasons why this new religion might create universal fear.

"Surely," Riley said, "every creature, every species, wants to be more than it is."

"Not so," said Tordor, "since only a few could transcend—if transcend possible at all—and leave other species behind."

"We have a myth," Riley said, "of the hero who ventures into a region of supernatural wonder, encounters fabulous forces, wins a decisive victory, and comes back with the power to bestow boons."

Tordor replied, "We have story like that but ours is leader blessed by the gods who pass their god-gifts to leader's tribe."

Riley studied the elephantine alien. "And yet you venture forth."

"My elder commands," Tordor grunted.

They fell silent, and soon Tordor had rocked back upon its tail and closed its eyes. Riley looked around. The flower child was standing straighter now. Perhaps it was conscious again, if it ever had been unconscious. Jan and Jon were asleep at his feet. The weasel-like alien was huddled in the far corner, his abandoned arm at his feet, apparently unmissed, but the knife the arm had held was gone. The coffin-shaped alien had moved a meter or so during all the activity. Riley had not seen it in motion. The woman sat on a bench a few meters away, her legs drawn up against her body with her arms folded across them and her eyes looking at Riley. When their gazes met she didn't look away.

And Riley knew that in his bag was an innocent object he had not placed there. The weasel had put it there before the attack, and the attack, if that was what it was, had been a diversion.

*　*　*

soporific

Riley awakened to a sense of danger. He had fallen asleep sitting up, in a chair, his bag under his feet. He hadn't intended it, but three days of alert readiness, except for that brief hour or so before the weasel approached, had caught up with him. Or maybe he had succumbed to the same strange soporific that had affected Jan. Now his pedia had awakened him again. Jon and Jan were asleep nearby. The flower child's head was drooping once more, and the Alpha Centauran was crouched beside the frame, his top feathers alert. Tordor was still asleep, rocked back on its tail. The woman sat in the same position, her knees drawn up. She still looked in his direction.

Something was wrong.

The woman felt it, too. Her arms clasped her legs tighter. Her eyes were wider, and her expression seemed to ask, "What woke you? What is about to happen?" Or maybe she had a pedia of her own.

Nothing had changed. No, the alien coffin had moved again. Now it was against the far wall. But that alone was not alarming.

Then he understood. The speed of their travel had increased. Not enough to change Riley's feeling of gravity but enough for his pedia to detect, as well as the small increase in the noise of the ancient motor powering their ascent with the aid of the focused laser beam from beneath.

Something exploded! The climber was beyond the atmosphere, and no noise reached them, but Riley felt the impact on his feet and his buttocks. His bag rose in the air and thumped back to the floor as the climber began to gyrate and its passengers were tossed from side to side like bags of grain.

Riley reached out to grab Jon and Jan and tugged them to the bench. "Hang on!" he said. He turned to help the woman, but she had her legs under the bench and her hands gripping the edge as she dodged flying bodies.

The space-elevator ribbon had parted—or had been parted. But the climber wasn't falling. It was being pulled upward like a weight on the end of a long string. The release of the ribbon's tension had imparted a wild swing to the climber, and the counter-balancing weight on the other end was plunging them toward outer space.

At least they were not falling. That was hopeless doom. But being flung into space in their barren box was only doom delayed.

The flower child stood in its frame, alert and swaying. The Alpha Centauran grasped the frame for support. The weasel flew past toward the other end, followed by its arm, but it swung itself around like an acrobat so that its legs could absorb the impact. The alien coffin seemed to have anchored itself against the far wall.

Riley dodged Tordor as the other hurtled past, and into the wall beside him. The heavy-planet alien was too big and too dense to try to stop. But Tordor braced itself on its legs and tail, facing the wall.

The violent motion began to slow as the pull from above dampened their gyrations.

"Something wants to stop this pilgrimage," Tordor grunted.

"Something seems to have succeeded," Riley replied.

"Who'd want us dead?" Jon asked.

"Yeah," Jan said.

"Maybe it's one of us," Riley said. "The alien in the box over there, the woman, Tordor here, me . . ."

"The ribbon was cut below," Tordor grunted.

"A mistake?"

"A miscalculation?"

"Who is to say?" Riley responded. He did not tell Tordor about the change in the rate of the climber's ascent before the explosion. If that had not happened, the ribbon would have parted ahead of them instead of beneath. Someone knew enough about the climber's motor and how to change its speed, and about the explosive charge and when and where it would be set off.

"What's going to happen to us now?" Jan asked.

"Yeah," Jon said.

From his feeling of weight, Riley judged that their speed was increasing. "We're going to fly into space with enough velocity to leave this system. Of course that will take a millennium or so, and by then we all will be dead. In fact, even if we brought a lot of provisions, our food won't last for more than seven days, and air and water not much more than that."

"Gee," Jon said. "I never knew one of these strings to fail."

"Yeah," Jan said.

"It didn't fail," Riley said. "It was blown apart."

"Golly," Jan said.

"Yeah," Jon said.

"We're going to go on a pilgrimage, all right," Riley said, "but it wasn't the one we intended." He looked at the woman. He knew she had heard the conversation, but she didn't say anything. She had straightened out her legs, though. Her feet were on the floor and her hands held the edge of the bench.

Riley continued to look around the room, to take stock of the effects of the explosion. Two aliens had been killed in the gyrations of the climber, a third had broken a leg, and a fourth had lost a tentacle. The half-dozen informal self-protection groups combined efforts to treat injuries and ration supplies and protect individuals from predation. Clothing and other materials were shared with those who suffered from the increasing cold.

Through all the mutual aid, Riley kept thinking it was all useless, like maintaining law and order when the wave front of a supernova was scheduled to arrive in a few days.

Seventy-one hours of desperate fatigue and soreness later Riley felt a thump and the increased weight of deceleration. Creatures fought for a place at the windows, but only blackness, without stars, could be seen. An hour later, he heard more thumps, followed by the sound of the release of the airlock door beyond the privacy room. The fetid air inside the climber was invaded by the only slightly less fetid air of a spaceship.

"Boys," Riley said to Jon and Jan, "we've been saved."

They emerged, one by one, into the airlock of a ship. A party of space crew greeted them with food and drink and blankets, and received Jon and Jan with particular warmth.

Riley recognized one of them. He wore the insignia of a spaceship captain.

"Hello, Ham," he said.

"Up to your old tricks, Riley?" the captain said.

"Thanks to you," Riley said.

CHAPTER TWO

The *Geoffrey* accelerated as soon as the passengers in the elevator car had been retrieved and the car had been jettisoned to resume its interrupted journey into deep space. As he was directed down the narrow passageway into the decontamination chamber and the isolation of the passenger quarters, Riley asked a crew member what had happened to the carbon-fiber cable on which the car had climbed.

The crew member shook his head. "That stuff don't wear out, and you can't cut it."

Riley was too tired to ask the crew member about it, and he had no more opportunity to talk to the captain before getting to the decon. Passengers' quarantine was standard: exotic bacteria, viruses, and fungi lurked inside bodies for weeks, and some alien physiologies were always deadly to the unprepared. And passengers offered nothing to a voyage but trouble: the less the crew saw of them the better for the welfare of the crew and the vessel.

Riley was desperate for sleep, but he knew that was something he couldn't do at least until he got to his quarters and had a chance to check his pack for a certain item. In the meantime, he'd simply have to stay vertical and alert through the decon process . . . and once he and the other passengers were in the passengers' lounge, the joys of acceleration.

Acceleration was jerky, which spoke of old engines, the maintenance of which had been sketchy at best, or perhaps of a crew that
was still learning its ship. Maybe both. There would be no Jumping-
Off nexus this close to a system, so acceleration, at a constant one-
earthgravity, would last at least one hundred hours and give
planet-acclimated passengers a chance to adjust to the environment
of space and the fragile tubes that flung themselves through it.

Riley endured acceleration, with its unexpected moments of free
fall, as he always had, with grim contemplation. He took his mind
off the unsettling sensations by reviewing the past seventy-two
hours. His pedia helped him recall the waiting room on Terminal,
and he identified an alien or two he had overlooked: a caterpillar-
like creature that lifted its forward section cautiously to look around,
and in the far corner an aquatic alien in a cloudy tank bubbling with
gas.

He reviewed the events in the climber, adding details to his picture of events: who was where and when and what they were doing.
He could not tie any movements to the point at which the climber
had accelerated, or the point at which the cable had been severed,
although the coffin-shaped alien had been closest to the wall that
housed the controls.

"Insufficient information," his pedia said. Riley sometimes hated
his pedia, but he hated even more its confessions of imperfection.

Until he found some privacy, he would have no opportunity to
explore his pack and see what the weasel had left or planted on him.
First he had to keep track of his fellow passengers . . . the pilgrims.
The passenger compartment was divided into living zones adaptable
to the requirements of the various kinds of creatures who sought
passage. Some required special atmospheres or special diets, or
special configurations of accommodations; the steward had to be a
person of many parts.

The crew was no problem. Providing similar amenities for the crew who had to work the entire ship would have been impossible. Human vessels were manned by humans, or by humanoid species that could tolerate human environment. And the *Geoffrey* was a human vessel.

The aquatic alien, its writhing tentacles breaking the murk of its aquarium, disappeared shortly after boarding. Other exotic aliens followed. The rest, including the coffin-shaped alien, were gathered in the passengers' lounge. His contemplation was interrupted by a familiar grunting.

"Saved by higher power," Tordor said, leaning back on his tail to brace himself against acceleration.

"At least one closer to the controls," Riley replied.

"And for greater purpose," Tordor said.

The enigmatic woman looked scornful. Riley turned to her. "Where do you think we're heading?"

"Toward transcendence," she said.

"Where is that?" he continued.

"Wherever you find it," she said.

"Better question," Tordor said, "what direction?"

"Only the captain knows that," Riley said.

"You speak like man who understands."

"You, too. You know your way around a ship."

Tordor waved his proboscis in a movement that Riley's pedia interpreted as "of course." "We leave Terminal," he said.

Riley nodded, hoping that nods were part of Dorian gesture vocabulary. To gather at Terminal for a journey inward made no sense. They were headed farther out along this arm of the galaxy, and there were few stars farther out.

The *Geoffrey* was a war-surplus vessel, a cruiser much like the one aboard which Riley had served part of his service time. A lot of warships had been converted to civilian use after the Galactic War. War surplus meant the ship was armored around the flight deck and engine room, and some of its weapons array might still be operational. It also meant that passenger quarters were primitive.

Of course all accommodations on spaceships were primitive. The romantic notion that spaceships had staterooms like surface ships, or even the modest efficiency compartments standard on over-populated planets, misunderstood the price of space in space. Privacy was costly, and the cost was comfort. Each humanoid passenger was assigned a cubicle in a wall of cubicles, like drawers in a morgue; a built-in metal ladder allowed access to those above waist level.

Each cubicle was two meters long, one and a half meters wide, and one and a half meters high. Each was equipped with air, temperature, and humidity controls, that sometimes worked, an adjustable mattress, a shelf for personal items, a cupboard at the far end for clothes, and a light. An overhead viewer could be positioned for viewing from a half-sitting or lying-down position. The ship's computer offered fictional and nonfictional materials, views from the ship's front, back, and sides, revealing the great emptiness of space, and basic information about the ship, its layout, and its operations. Riley scanned the information that would, he knew, become part of his pedia's memory. He might have to know his way around as well as any crew member.

The cubicles were no place for claustrophobes, but then neither was space itself.

Before the discovery of the JumpingOff places, the cubicles had been equipped for long sleep as well; the connections and outlets had never been removed. Everybody who had been through the old ways blessed the unknown human genius who had deciphered the galactic network map. Going into long sleep was painful and waking up was even worse, but not as bad as not waking up, which hap-

TRANSCENDENTAL   29

pened two times out of ten. Nobody would have put up with it except that casualties in ships that saw action in the Galactic War averaged 50 percent of the crew—each time a ship went out.

The alien compartments were different. They weren't more spacious, but some were arranged vertically or slanted, had an adjustable mixture of atmospheres, and an adjustable wavelength of light. Everything about them was temporary, obviously thrown together in a hurry after the passenger manifest was received. Some were still under construction.

Riley felt a fleeting moment of relief that he didn't have to trust his comfort, much less his life, to that kind of ramshackle accommodation. His cubicle was one from the top, third from the left, in a stack of sixteen. As soon as he entered his cubicle and disabled the viewer, he opened his pack and stowed away his few belongings, piece by piece, inspecting each of them, until he was left with the empty pack. He went over it millimeter by millimeter. Finally, under one magnetic closure, he found what he was looking for: a mere metal sliver, an electronic bug of some sort, or perhaps a concentrated explosive, or a poison timed for release.

He left it as he found it, made sure the door to the cubicle was locked, and said "sleep" to his pedia. He figured he'd have no trouble sleeping, too. After the seemingly endless hours of trying to stay alert, especially in the long period after the explosion, he might sleep forever . . .

The passenger lounge became a gathering place of social significance. It offered cramped closets for elimination and slightly larger closets for cleansing with recycled fluids of various kinds.

Any passengers who wore clothing and couldn't manage the contortions necessary for dressing in the confines of the cubicles had to dress in the lounge. But passengers thrown into intimacy for long stretches of time lost most semblance of modesty, even if that was part of their culture.

The lounge also served as a dining hall where various kinds of food were available from wall units, when serviced properly. Some popular items soon were depleted, or weren't replaced, or were hoarded by crew members, and eventually it came down to a choice between eating what was available if it wasn't poisonous—or starve. Shelves and stools slid out from the walls for species that sat.

In spite of its many purposes the lounge was not large, perhaps twenty meters square, and when all the passengers gathered little empty space remained. Some species, though, hibernated during long passage or were culturally antisocial or xenologically impaired, and no more than a dozen were present at one time, except at story periods. The telling of stories or personal accounts was traditional for long trips; the viewer fictions paled by comparison.

The *Geoffrey* had been old by the end of the war. Now it was even older and more dilapidated. The narrow corridors had been worn bare at shoulder level. Many of the doors stuck, including cubicle doors, and even the emergency doors separating the various compartments of the ship, which were intended to snap shut at the first indication of a drop in air pressure. The cruiser bore a general air of defeat, like a ship that had barely escaped destruction in an ambush but had been consigned to a used-vehicle orbit rather than being rehabilitated. Perhaps it had.

Riley used his time in the lounge to move among the others, picking up more of their language for his pedia and engaging them in conversation when languages permitted, trying to place them in the galactic chess game in which he found himself an unwilling player. What kind of piece were they? How did they move? Whose invisible hand moved them? What was their color?

He felt good about Tordor but questioned whether his judgment was influenced by the alien's solidity and air of blunt honesty. The weasel was on the other end of the spectrum, not simply because of his appearance of sly subterfuge but because he *felt* untrustworthy. Riley had learned early in his experience with aliens that appearance meant nothing, but he had also learned to trust his instincts. Now his instinct told him that he should trust nothing, and, most of all, not his instincts.

"You must trust nobody but me," his pedia said.

Nor his pedia.

What he wanted to do was to circulate among the passengers, engage them in conversation, and find out, directly or indirectly, why they were on this pilgrimage to nowhere. He would have found that difficult, but not impossible, with human companions, but in his experience, most aliens did not strike up conversations or ask revealing questions, even if they could communicate with other species at some primitive level.

His pedia was no help. Either it was not equipped to make such judgments, or withheld them, either through its own volition or because of some built-in block.

He settled for talking to the woman. "We're going to be stuck with each other for months, maybe years. We might as well be friends."

She shrugged. "Until our interests diverge."

"And what interests are those?"

"Survival now. Reaching our destinations. Then—who knows?" Her face, passive until now, broke into a smile that dazzled Riley.

"We might as well introduce ourselves. I'm Riley."

"Asha," she said.

"And why are you on this crazy journey?"

She swept the room with her arm. "For the same reason as all of them—to escape the inescapable, to find the unfindable, to achieve the unachievable."

"You like riddles."

"Me and the sphinx," she said, and would say no more.

He got even less from the aliens he tried to engage in conversation, and decided to return to his cubicle for contemplation. But that was not to happen.

The crew had its own quarters and lounge. They were even more off-limits to passengers than the passengers' quarters were off-limits to the crew except for repairs or replenishing. That was why the discovery of a crew member's body in a passenger cubicle was a shocking event. The crew member was Jan. The cubicle was Riley's.

The head of security appeared first. He was a small, waspish humanoid alien—an oxygen-breather who nevertheless carried a vaporizer that he resorted to regularly like a Victorian dandy with his perfumed handkerchief—who did nothing but check to make sure that Jan was dead and that no weapons were visible. The medical officer was human. He came right behind the head of security. He climbed into the cubicle and examined the body without moving it. Then came the captain. Riley saw him from a distance as he entered the passenger quarters. The captain climbed the rungs of the ladder, looked in at the body, climbed back down, scanned the motley crowd of aliens and the two humans, and disappeared the way he had come. As far as Riley could discern, the captain's facial expression had not changed. The head of security ordered two human assistants to remove the body and carry it on a litter out the door into the crew's quarters where, Riley guessed, it would undergo an autopsy for cause of death. From his own discovery of the body and its unnatural rigor, he thought he knew what it was. Once the cubicle was empty the head of security crawled up into it, closed the door, and spent several minutes inside before emerging and leaving the passenger quarters. No one had said a word.

The passengers who were still gathered around his cubicle looked at one another in silence, looked at the cubicle, and looked at Riley. Riley shifted uncomfortably. Finally, the annoying human woman broke the silence.

"Somebody doesn't like you," Asha said.

"Or you don't like somebody," Tordor grunted.

Riley thought he detected Dorian humor.

He shrugged. "Nobody would mistake Jan for me," he said, "and if I wanted to do away with someone, I wouldn't leave the body in my own cubicle."

Nothing happened for twenty-four hours. Riley knew what was going on: the captain had convened a court of inquiry. He would preside, as regulations required, unless his duties demanded his presence elsewhere, in which case he would delegate his place to his second-in-command, or if some emergency required them both, his head of security. The first sessions of the court would meet in the crew's quarters.

While that was going on, the other passengers approached him individually. Some of them offered their sympathy, as if Jan's death had been a personal loss to Riley, or as if the loss of any human affected the entire species. Others, if Riley and his pedia interpreted them correctly, congratulated Riley, as a member of the human species, for a good death and a happy translation to a better life; or for Jan having been reunited with the great soul of his people; or for being fortunate enough to have escaped into the Great Nothingness from an existence schooled in pain; or they expressed the hope that Jan would be reborn into a superior existence or a superior universe; or, best of all, that in his demise he might have achieved the transcendence they all were seeking.

Their intentions were something else. Riley knew that while they were mouthing all the right words, they were evaluating Riley's relationship to the dead man and his possible relationship to the death itself, but, more important, how this event would affect the pilgrimage and Riley's place in it, and whether Riley's potential weakness would make him an easier target for elimination or would, at the least, remove him as a rival for leadership; or if, indeed, he had killed Jan and could avoid punishment, whether he was more of a threat than ever.

As to what he might be threatening, Riley was no closer to figuring that out, except for knowing that it wasn't Jan that his presence might be threatening.

The appearance of the court of inquiry cut short Riley's reevaluation of his new situation. The court was less than impressive. In the limited confines of the passengers' lounge, the captain sat on one of the stools that extended from the wall, removed his pedia from his wrist, and placed it on the table that slid out from the wall, as if to say, "Everything said before this court will be recorded and analyzed and subject to penalties for perjury or obstruction."

The captain was a large man with short legs, almost as if he had been cut down to fit into spaceship dimensions. His heavy black eyebrows met over his nose, a nose that overshadowed a dapper mustache—all this in defiance of fashion and genetics. His dominant feature, though, were his eyes; they were blue, and fierce like those of a desert Arab.

His second-in-command, an athletic blond human, sat on his left, his head of security, the waspish humanoid, on his right. A couple of humanoid guards stood on each side of the entrance and summoned witnesses one by one. The captain saved Riley for last. Riley thought it was a psychological ploy, though it might have been merely an investigator's strategy.

At last Riley stood in front of the captain, rejecting the easy comfort of a nearby stool.

"Riley," the captain said, "this is a serious business."

"Death is like that."

"You found the crewman?"

"As you know."

"Describe the circumstances."

"I was returning to my cubicle at the end of my twelve-hour wake cycle—"

"You spend only twelve hours awake?"

"I like to spend a few hours alone before my sleep cycle, and a day isn't very long to recover from days without sleep. When I opened the cubicle door, I saw the body. I recognized the crewman as one I had shared the cable ride with—Jan, he called himself."

"And then?"

"I sounded the alarm."

"You didn't check to see if the crewman was dead?"

"I've seen many dead men."

"You didn't touch him?"

"I didn't need to. I could feel death's icy breath."

"He was frozen," the captain said.

"So I assumed," Riley said.

"It seems likely that the deceased sneaked into the passengers' quarters when nobody was in the sleep area, crept into your cubicle, and was surprised by a quick freeze from the long-sleep nozzles."

"Possible but unlikely," Riley said. "The cubicle was locked and with a combination that I reset. The long-sleep nozzles were inactive. I checked. And Jan had no possible reason to seek me out."

"He also had no reason to jump ship at Terminal nor to sign aboard the *Geoffrey*."

"No apparent reasons."

"What are you suggesting?"

"Obviously he had reasons. Some obvious—he didn't like his previous berth, the crew or the captain didn't like him, he was in trouble for infractions of rules or laws, or he simply wanted adventure. Or perhaps some more subtle—he was paid or persuaded by someone else to join the *Geoffrey* for a purpose yet undisclosed, he was a convert to transcendentalism, he had some personal reason to seek transcendence . . ."

"Enough," the captain said. "This board is adjourned until further notice."

The captain paused at the door, after motioning the others to leave before him. "If this is some kind of double-reverse trick, Riley, or we find evidence that you had a hand in Jan's death, this trip will be your shortest."

"Captain," Riley said, "I'm as innocent as you."

But the captain was long gone.

The lounge filled with passengers as soon as the captain's court had left. Even the aliens from the other environmental venues—the flower child, the aquatic alien, the caterpillar—joined the group.

"The court decided . . . ?" Tordor asked.

"Nothing," Riley said.

"You tell?"

"Nothing. I had nothing to tell them. You?"

"Also."

"And them?" Riley indicated the rest of the group.

"Them, too."

Surprisingly, the weasel stepped forward. His arm was half regrown. He spoke in hisses that suddenly Riley's pedia changed into language. ". . . beginning," the weasel concluded. He peered up at Riley.

"The captain and his crew not trusted," Riley's pedia backed up to retrieve. "This death only beginning."

"That is only a suspicion," Riley said, his pedia translating the speech into a series of modulated hisses that surprised even Riley as they emerged from his limited vocal apparatus. "And the death is of a crew member, not a pilgrim."

The Sirian moved into the little group. "I overhear," it said. Riley's pedia was much quicker at picking up the guttural language. "We depend upon crew and officers to take us where we wish to go. They can take us wherever, sell us, remove us one by one and keep the money each of us has paid for this journey."

The flower child spoke like the rustling of leaves in the wind. The pedia was silent. Tordor translated. "It says, 'This gathering has many talents—captain, crew, navigator. If must, can run ship.'"

"Passengers must trust their ship and its crew," Riley said. "This is no different. The person killed was a crew member, not a passenger, and his death may have had many purposes, but one of them was not to threaten this pilgrimage. Perhaps to threaten a pilgrim."

Riley's pedia chose Dorian to translate, and from Tordor the statement spread around the room. Some seemed to be in agreement; others seemed disturbed.

"You," Asha said, turning to Riley. "You're the pilgrim?"

"That's possible."

"Then another logical conclusion might be that you are a nexus of violence," Asha said. "Beginning with the attack on the Terminal waiting room to the cutting of the vator cable, to this murder in your cubicle. With the first two, the focus could have been any of us, but now, with Jan's death, you are clearly the nexus. You may be the lightning rod that brings down destruction on all of us."

The others, in their own ways, indicated interest.

"You and the captain think alike," Riley said. "But lightning rods also have the property of guiding electricity harmlessly into the ground. While I'm alive and attracting attacks, the rest of you are not—unless you get too close, as in the climber."

"Or," Asha said, "you may have begun a process to eliminate everyone who shared the cable ride with you, once the attack on the cable failed."

The others gave him more room. No one translated Asha's remark, and Riley didn't know whether they all understood, but somehow he thought they did. His pedia was silent. No doubt they had pedias of their own.

"On the other hand, Jan's death in my cubicle may have been intended to divert suspicion from someone else," Riley said.

The others seemed to digest that information.

"Maybe I'll be able to tell you more soon," Riley said. "The captain said he would reconvene his court when he had more information."

He nodded at Tordor and touched Asha on the shoulder as if to say that he forgave her channeling the distrust of the captain and the crew toward fear of him. He climbed the ladder into his cubicle. It was still chilly, but he was used to death and cold. Suddenly superstitious, perhaps, he stuffed a sock into the long-sleep nozzle and went into what he hoped would be a short sleep.

The sleep was even shorter than he planned. Only three hours had passed when someone banged on his cubicle door. Riley opened it with his toes and peered past them at the ugly face of the head of security.

"The captain wants to see you."

"The desire is mutual," Riley replied.

"Huh?"

"I'm coming." Riley had lain down fully dressed. He slid from his cubicle and climbed down the ladder. "Lead on," he said.

The head of security tried to take his elbow but Riley's look said that he would be touched only at the other's peril. The other led him down passageways familiar in their contours and appearance but new in context until they arrived at a small room that had a table and attached benches and food dispensers in the wall. His pedia identified it as the crew's mess. On the far side of the bench sat the captain. He was alone.

"Sit down, Riley."

Riley sat opposite the captain. "What's up, Ham?"

"You'll call me 'Captain.'"

"As you prefer."

"Jon has confessed," the captain said, "that he and Jan had been paid to kill you in a way that would look like an accident."

"Why would they do that?" Riley said.

"That's what I'd like you to tell me, because it seems likely that Jan was trying to rig the long-sleep nozzles to kill you when he was overcome."

Riley was silent.

"Or," the captain continued, "you discovered him, rendered him immobile or unconscious, and turned on the long-sleep nozzles yourself."

"How would I do that?" Riley asked.

"We've been around a long time, you and me," the captain said. "We've learned a lot of ways to kill."

"I had no reason to kill Jan," Riley said, "and he had no reason to kill me. I'd like to speak to Jon."

"You can't."

"Why not?"

"He's dead."

CHAPTER THREE

The two humanoid security guards escorted Riley back to passenger quarters. They wanted to take hold of his arms, but Riley glanced at each, and they stopped. He didn't know their species' capabilities but his look said he was confident that he could handle either one of them, or both if necessary. Security guards, whatever their species, believed in their invincibility, but Riley's air of confidence made them hesitate and decide not to take the chance. His choice was simpler: violence would serve no purpose except to relieve the frustration he felt at the Jan situation—now the Jan and Jon situation. The captain would answer no questions about Jon's death, and Riley had to accept the captain's statement or cause a confrontation long before such a tactic would be useful.

But he could not be sure that Jon was dead. Being dead was a convenient way of avoiding difficult questions. Or if he was dead, how had he died and why?

The guards watched him enter passenger quarters before they closed the airtight door behind him. Riley heard the lock engage. He didn't like that, either, but it, too, was something he had to accept, at least for now.

"What cannot be cured must be endured," his pedia said. It was full of homilies like that as well as information that sometimes was valuable.

The prospect of his cubicle was particularly unappetizing right now. When he got to the lounge some kind of ritual observance was in progress. The lounge was filled with participants—worshippers, perhaps, including the aliens for whom the humanoid oxygen environment was deadly or unpleasant—not only the flower child and the caterpillar but the aquatic and the coffin-shaped alien. Those who had heads and necks were looking upward toward the inner skin of the ship that served as a roof to the lounge and a protection from space and the stars. Or prevented passengers from observing the infinite and the eternal. Or joining them.

The only person not participating in whatever ritual was unfolding was Asha. She, like Riley, was an observer. She stood just inside the port to the lounge, arms folded below her breasts. The worshippers were all facing toward the forward wall, but no one stood there. Apparently, the ceremony required no minister. He wouldn't find out from that who had called them together.

A mixed murmur emerged from the group. The alien words were so intermingled that Riley's pedia had difficulty distinguishing any meaning, and then it singled out one particular stream of words for translation: "I am insignificant but I will be greater. My imperfections will be stripped away. As the pupa emerges from the larva, the adult will emerge from the pupa. No longer a child. Fully developed. Transformed. Perfected. The Transcendental Machine awaits my coming. The universe awaits my emergence."

Riley looked at Asha. She shrugged.

At that moment, as if in response to the mongrel chant, the ship lurched. Riley looked up as if he were one of the worshippers. The spaceship skin above seemed to evaporate, letting in the chill of space and the terror of black infinity. The passengers floated like jellyfish in a sea of night. Riley felt his body turn inside out, as if he had been imprisoned in his own flesh and now all his organs had been liberated. He was paralyzed for an eternity, hurting in every fiber of his body. In front of him the worshippers seemed frozen. Those who had faces expressed mingled ecstasy and horror.

Then the moment passed. His body felt normal again, and the ship's hull closed around him. The worshippers moved and lowered their heads. Some of them started to wail.

After a moment, Riley realized he knew what they had all experienced: it was a Jump from one nexus to another across a fold of space. For a few seconds, or an eternity—time had no meaning during the Jump—they had been outside their known universe of time and space, a state as truly alien as it was possible to be. Too bad, he thought, they had to come back to the same universe in the same old imperfect shapes. Maybe this was where the concept of transcendence had arisen—from the potential of the place Outside. But that had happened only after the beginnings of interstellar flight.

Throughout the history of humanity, Riley thought, a few individuals, liberated from their everyday existences—by drugs or contemplation or divine intervention or madness—had achieved transcendence. They touched the infinite and brought back a sign—a feather, a stigmata, an engraved stone, a vision—and they tried to share it, with varying success, with those less able to fully access the direct experience. Sometimes, a few of those who were themselves unable to experience transcendence understood and responded with superhuman feats. Or created a religion.

"Religion," said his pedia, "is the opiate of the masses."

The glow always faded, the inspiration always became corrupted by everyday reality, the dream always became ritual, nothing lasted. Until now, with its promise of something real, a machine that offered transcendence. Not the feeling of transcendence or the illusion of transcendence but transcendence itself—real, observable, repeatable—but perhaps just as remote, as far from human grasp, as paradise itself.

"A Jump," he said to Asha.

She nodded as if the event were too commonplace to deserve comment.

"Who started the ceremony?"

She shrugged.

"You don't know or you don't care or no one started it?"

"The last."

"That's odd," Riley said.

"It's an odd religion," Asha replied. "Everyone is his or her own messiah."

"Including you?"

She shrugged again.

"For someone who has ventured her life on an unlikely mission, you don't seem to be much involved."

"And you, too much," she said.

As the worshippers scattered, Tordor stopped in front of Riley. "You are back," he said. His syntax was improving—or rather the pedia's ability to translate Dorian. "No guards."

"Jon confessed to a plot, the captain said," Riley said. "Before he died, the captain said."

"Ah," Tordor said. It was a sound that suggested a familiarity with the ways of the powerful.

"How did this ceremony happen?" Riley asked.

"Ah," Tordor said. It was a sound that suggested a basic inability to understand the ways of sentient beings.

"You seem to have an insatiable curiosity about your fellow travelers," Asha said.

"When your life may depend upon your companions, it pays to learn as much about them as possible," Riley said, "including whether they are likely to answer some mystical call when you need them most. Or perhaps will sacrifice you to gain an advantage."

"If I may guess," Tordor said, "murder, anxiety, ritual comfort."

"What?" Riley asked.

"He's answering your original question about how the service got started," Asha said.

"For you, as well?" Riley asked Tordor.

"Ah," Tordor said. "Worship with others, eat with others, fight with others."

"Another avenue to group solidarity," Asha said. "You might consider it," she said to Riley.

"He can belong," Riley said. "I'll try to understand. We'll see whose method works the best." He turned to Tordor. "But what brought them together?"

"No one," Tordor said. "Everyone."

"He means the call to worship was spoken by none, understood by all," Asha said.

"I know what he means. I just find it hard to believe." Riley looked back at Tordor. "Who was the first to come in?"

Tordor swung his proboscis toward the weasel and the Sirian. "They here. Then—" He gestured toward the coffin-shaped alien, the flower child, the caterpillar, the aquatic, and then the others. "When all here, worship as one. No one first."

"Did you hear a call to worship?" Riley asked.

"No call," Tordor said.

"You?" Riley asked Asha.

She shook her head. "Why do you care?"

"I want to know what everyone else knows. Clearly everyone else knows a great deal more about transcendentalism than I do. If I didn't hear a call, and you two didn't hear a call, and all these did, then that may mean I don't know enough to be on this pilgrimage."

"That thought has crossed my mind," Asha said.

"They know more than they should?" Tordor said. It seemed to be a question. Did he mean "too much"?

Riley shrugged, not knowing whether Dorians understood that gesture, either, and changed the subject. "You noticed the appearance of this part of space during the Jump?"

"Dark," Tordor said.

Riley nodded. He turned on the vision plate that occupied almost an entire wall of the lounge. An interrupted Sirian myth play resumed. Riley quickly switched to the ship's forward view. Only a few faint stars appeared. He switched to a side view and then the other. Even fewer and fainter stars. The rear view, however, showed a vast river of stars. Clearly the ship was heading still farther from civilization.

"Where are we going?" Riley asked. "Do either of you have an idea?"

"Toward transcendence," Asha said. A brief smile curled the corners of her lips. She had said that before.

"There?" Tordor asked. He gestured with his proboscis toward the forward view that Riley had returned to.

"Ah," Riley said. It was a sound that suggested Tordor was right and those poor faint stars ahead were unlikely to nourish sentience much less some kind of technological civilization that could produce transcendence for its own species, and perhaps—though even less likely—for other species.

"You know the captain," Tordor said. "Competent?"

"I would have said so," Riley said, "but now I wonder. People change. People get cautious. People get frightened. Sometimes . . . people get bought."

"If transcendence is real and has escaped discovery until recently," Asha said, "it must be in an unlikely place."

"If it is real," Riley said.

"Why are we all here, if it is not?" Asha said.

"Wager lives, family, fortune," Tordor said.

"He means—" Asha said.

"I know what he means," Riley said.

"The question is whether you mean what he means," Asha said. "Whether you believe."

Riley shook his head. "I believe in what I can see and touch. What is knowable."

"Then why are you here?" Asha asked.

"To be convinced," Riley said. "This myth is exploding across the galaxy like gamma rays from a supernova. Some of you—maybe all of you—believe. If it's true the reality is too important to miss. So I'm willing to gamble a couple of years of a not-particularly-satisfying existence to find out the truth about what a lot of otherwise smart creatures think is real."

"You talk too much," said his pedia.

"Maybe more," Tordor said.

"Maybe I'm willing to bet it all," Riley said. "Maybe I'm not a total agnostic." He laughed. His pedia wasn't fooled. Neither were Asha or Tordor.

"Or maybe you hope to transcend your not-particularly-satisfying existence," Asha said, "or, like the captain, maybe you have still another motivation."

"Which brings us back to the captain," Riley said, "and the question of where is he heading, and why? And can he be trusted?"

"And who's going to find that out?" Asha asked.

She and Tordor both looked at Riley.

"Ah," he said. It was a sound a man makes after he has drawn the short straw.

The lock surrendered to Riley's pedia without foreplay. The built-in alarm took longer. Asha and Tordor looked at Riley with greater respect, under the illusion that his skill alone was responsible.

Riley eased open the door. No guards. That established a baseline for him: the captain's overdependence on electronics. In the old days Ham always had trusted his A.I.s too much. Riley looked back and held up his hand toward Asha and Tordor with his five fingers spread. He eased the door shut and trotted down the passageway toward the captain's quarters following the guide laid out in his mind by his pedia. The captain's quarters were always close to the control room, and on this old cruiser that had to be centrally located, as far from potential combat damage as possible, and protected, like the control room, by armor.

Outside the passenger quarters the odors were different. Preoccupied with the Jan mystery and the questions the captain would ask and the answers he might provide, as well as the increasingly annoying intrusions of his pedia, he hadn't noticed it in his earlier excursion. The passenger quarters smelled alien; the mingled scents of a score of different creatures from a score of different worlds overpowered the smell of human and humanoid effluvia that had circulated through the ship for years until the air renewers gave up. Outside, on its separate air-renewal system, human sweat, respiration, and other emissions dominated. Riley wondered how he had ever endured it.

"Humans have a unique ability to adapt and ignore," his pedia said.

The engine vibrations were pervasive and loud enough to cover his light footsteps, but not enough to conceal the unwary sounds of a crew member approaching.

He dodged into a cross passageway and waited until the footsteps had passed. The trip didn't take long—nothing on a ship was far from anyplace else—but he had to avoid discovery, and as he neared the nerve center of the ship, crew density increased.

As he approached his goal, an alarm went off—a siren and blinking red lights. He turned his back to the passageway as if he were swinging toward the passenger quarters. Crew members pounded by him toward the compartments he had just left. When the movement ceased, he turned once more and found himself in front of the captain's cabin. The control room would still be manned, but the captain's cabin would have all the information available in the control room and maybe more.

The lock on the captain's cabin opened even more quickly than the one on the passenger quarters. His pedia improved with experience. Riley slipped inside. The cabin was empty. Cabin, of course, was a euphemism for a room that was small even by spaceship standards, big enough for a bunk that folded into one wall, a desk and chair that folded into another, a basin and toilet unit that folded into a third wall, and a fourth wall dedicated to dials and gauges.

Riley looked at each dial and gauge in turn. He was no navigator. He had piloted a two-man fighter during the war, but he had been ferried to each engagement by a warship, along with a dozen other fighters, and any navigation necessary aboard the fighter was done by computer. But his pedia recorded and analyzed everything he looked at.

"According to these, we have passed the last known nexus," his pedia said, "and we're heading farther out along this spiral arm than my charts record."

"If it isn't listed," Riley thought, "it isn't known."

"You should not rely on my infallibility," the pedia said. "My memory is not infinite. But you may be right. Anyway, we can learn nothing from this. We must get back before we are discovered."

"What about the captain's log? Surely he makes entries there."

"The captain's log is virgin."

"That breaks every regulation."

"Unless he records in another log."

His pedia? Riley thought.

"Maybe. If so, he has it with him. The only electronic activity in the cabin is the repeaters, and I have observed that humans are never without their imperfect pedias. We must get back."

Riley searched the compact, impersonal cubbyhole. The bunk bed and the cupboard behind hid nothing other than neatly stacked clothing. Ham had always had a neatness fetish. The lavatory and toilet had only dispensers for soap and depilatory and disposable towels; their surfaces were spotless. The desk had only a voice-activated minicomputer and an electronic tablet, both built in. Both, his pedia assured him, had never been used. That was unlike Ham. When he had been the navigator on Riley's fighter, he had fondled his gadgets as if they were women's parts.

The cabin not only was bare, it was barren. Except for the anonymous clothing in the cupboard, the cabin looked as if it had never been occupied. Riley surveyed the room in frustration, knowing that, as his pedia kept reminding him, his time was almost up.

Behind him the airtight door opened.

"Is this what you're looking for?" the captain said.

Riley turned. The captain was holding out his wrist pedia.

The captain was accompanied by the two humanoid guards who had escorted Riley back to passenger quarters.

"Very likely," Riley said.

"I should have you thrown in the brig," the captain said. He looked speculatively at the two guards.

"Where I could conveniently expire, like Jon?"

"It would be far easier to simply eject you from the ship."

"But you won't."

"Old friends?"

Riley shook his head. "You've got an unruly and maybe rebellious group of passengers back there."

"Who staged a fight to create a distraction for you."

Riley nodded.

"The woman seemed to be holding her own with the pachyderm creature."

"She's handier than she looks."

"What's going on, Riley?" the captain asked. "Why are you giving me all this trouble?"

Riley looked at the two guards. The captain motioned with his head. "Wait outside," he said.

As soon as the airtight door closed behind them, Riley said, "Jan's death was only the precipitating factor. This trip isn't going to go well unless your passengers have confidence in your ability to take us to our destination."

"If there is one," the captain said.

Riley leaned back against the cabin wall and folded his arms across his chest. "There better be one."

"Unruly passengers are easily handled. When you control air, food, and fluids, rebellion stops quickly."

"The Space Authority would never let you have another ship if you returned without your passengers."

"What makes you think I want another ship?"

"Moreover, these are exceptional creatures," Riley said. "They made it this far and survived a sabotaged vator—"

"With my help."

"And, as you can see, your locks and alarms are inadequate. I think it's time you made the passengers full partners in this project."

"What does that mean?"

"They need to know where you're going and what your motives are."

"The second part is easiest," the captain said. "I'm sure you haven't forgotten our last mission together."

"How could I forget?"

"The fighter was blown apart, but somehow we both survived," the captain said.

"I didn't know you had survived until you rescued us from the vator."

"I was in reconstruction for three months in a different hospital ship."

"They put you back together pretty well," Riley said.

"What you can't see are the mechanical parts and the A.I.s."

"I'm grateful for that."

"Why did you leave me there, Riley?"

"I was unconscious for thirty days," Riley said. "And when I woke up, they told me you were dead. They didn't have to rebuild me, like you, but I spent nearly a year in the hospital."

"Maybe they wished I was dead," the captain said. "Or maybe

they lost me in the system. The man who came out was not the same man who went in."

"Which man am I speaking to?"

"Some kind of composite creature who would like to be Hamilton Jones again," the captain said. "That's what the Transcendental Machine offers me."

"You're right: that's an answer to the second question," Riley said. He wasn't sure it was the truth, but it was an answer. "What about the first?"

"As to that," the captain said, "I know only a little more than you do."

"How can that be true?"

"The ship was hired from the corporation. The payment was substantial—they could have bought this sorry vessel for less, but the price included the captain and funds for hiring a crew."

"Who rented the ship?"

"Commercial transactions are often anonymous, or hidden behind a series of go-betweens; this one, though, was concealed better than any my employers had ever experienced."

"I understand why no one would want it known that the ship had been hired to seek out the Transcendental Machine, but why wouldn't your employers demand that kind of information?"

"The money was solid. My employers were satisfied. They were paid enough that they didn't care if the ship ever came back, and I was satisfied to be a part of it once I found out where we were going."

"And where was that?"

"Ah," the captain said. It was a sound that suggested the gulf between goals and destinations.

"You mean you knew that we were supposed to seek out the Transcendental Machine but you weren't given directions."

The captain looked at Riley as if surprised at Riley's ability to riddle his meaning. "Exactly. What I got was a pedia that opened to a new nexus only after the previous one had been passed. Ordinarily I would have kept it all in here." The captain tapped his skull. "My add-ons have unusual abilities. But this wrist pedia is all I have."

"Surely you can break through any firewalls."

"Ordinarily I would say you were right," the captain said. "I'm very good at programs, and my add-ons are even better. But this one was created by a master—maybe the most advanced programmers I've ever encountered. Or—"

"Or what?"

"Or my pedia is being updated after each Jump."

"But that would mean—"

"Yes, the person or creature who has the directions to our destination is on board."

CHAPTER FOUR

Riley returned to the passengers' quarters without an escort, feeling liberated while reminding himself that freedom was relative for a person living inside a metal can surrounded by vacuum, light years from help of any kind.

Asha, Tordor, and a few of the other pilgrims were restoring order to what had been a scene of battle. Asha was unmarked but Tordor had a bruise on the side of his sturdy head. Asha fought well, it seemed, even in staged events.

"Thanks for giving me cover," Riley said.

"Is nothing," Tordor said, but looked at Asha.

"We had to make it convincing," Asha said. "But what of your expedition?"

"Return without guards," Tordor said. It sounded like a question.

"I bring good tidings," Riley said. "That's an ancient human saying," he explained for Tordor's benefit. He announced to the aliens within hearing range, "The captain wants to speak to us—not as an investigating officer, as before, but as a fellow voyager on this trip into the unknown."

The weasel looked up from a corner by the food dispenser. The Alpha Centauran turned from its contemplation of a crystal it held. The Sirian opened its hooded eyes.

The word would get communicated, Riley knew, through the variety of mechanisms and languages represented among this group of aliens. Without further announcement, the pilgrims began to gather, some from the separate environments maintained for them, some bringing their environments with them. Even the coffin-shaped alien. They were together in whatever their cultures considered appropriate by the time the captain arrived, this time without his humanoid guards, as if announcing his new status as a pilgrim like the rest of the passengers.

He walked to one end of the lounge in the characteristic glide developed by longtime spacers. He stood silent for a long moment, his hands clasped behind his back, his head cocked as if listening to inner voices. Maybe he was listening to his add-ons, Riley thought. He hoped that the captain didn't know about Riley's.

"This trip has had a troubled start," the captain said. "But perhaps no more troubled than most voyages." The message spread around the lounge in a mixture of modulated sounds, hoots, hisses, whispers, gestures, and light flashes, and perhaps other means imperceptible to human senses. "But this voyage is unprecedented. We are following a will-o'-the-wisp, a phantom that appears and disappears, leading us deeper into the swamp of space.

"We all have our reasons for following this phantom," the captain continued, "including me and members of my crew, and we need to work together and trust one another if we are going to have any chance of reaching our goal. We are all pilgrims here, all looking for transcendence, venturing our lives and our dreams, our everything, on a fable that has captured our imaginations because it represents the goal of all existence: to evolve, to achieve our ideal forms, to transcend our limitations."

Riley felt proud of Ham and his humanity. His eloquence was

unexpected—and perhaps wasted on aliens who had it all filtered through inadequate pedias.

"For that reason we are relaxing the customary rules of travel that restrict contact between passengers and crew," the captain continued. "We cannot allow passengers unrestricted access to other parts of the ship—the crew cannot perform their jobs with strangers wandering among them—but we will allow a representative to occupy an adjunct position with the crew and serve as your spokesperson and representative, and report back to you."

Something that resembled a murmur arose from the passengers. Such a representative would be useful to the passengers in many ways, some unimaginable at the moment, but he or she or it also might acquire power that would be meaningful as the end of the voyage approached, as transcendence became reality, as perhaps only one might be chosen.

Riley was the logical candidate. Everyone knew it. He was human; he could go anywhere without comment, without environmental aids. He was experienced. He had negotiated their new status.

Ham could have made it so much simpler if he had named Riley as the adjunct. But Ham couldn't do that, Riley knew. If named, Riley would have become the captain's choice and the captain's confederate; the captain would have gained nothing in soothing passenger unrest—and the representative would lose any power to shape attitudes and events. Riley would have to compete with all the others. He glanced at Asha and Tordor. Both were looking at him with expressions he could not read, and neither could his pedia.

"I will entertain questions," the captain said.

"How choose?" Tordor said.

"That's up to you."

"What of those who aren't chosen?" Asha said. "What will they have gained?"

"Information from one of their own," the captain said, "and, as captain, I will keep all informed of developments that affect the group, like conditions if they change or departures from routine or Jumps as they approach.

"And one is approaching very shortly, and I must leave to prepare the ship. You will be notified before it happens."

"What of the crew member who died?" someone called out in an alien hiss.

"What of Jan?" another whispered.

"And the other—Jon?" came a grumble.

The captain was already heading for the hatchway. "I don't have time for further questions now. Decide upon your representative, and I will talk to that person."

After he was gone, all of the voyagers began to talk at once. "Like the Tower of Babel," Riley's pedia told him.

The passengers shifted into small ad hoc groups, like dust specks on a pond. Only these specks were noisy. The babbling that had followed the captain's departure intensified. Riley's pedia picked up snatches of remarks: " . . . traitor . . . danger . . . opportunity . . . trap . . . who . . . who . . . who . . ." Riley wondered if his pedia could overload, and what would happen if it did.

"How choose?" Tordor asked.

Riley looked at Asha. "Humans have elections. One person—or in this case one being—one vote. The being with the most votes wins. Or if you want a majority rather than a plurality, you have a second vote between the two top vote-getters."

"Democracy is not a universal practice," Asha said.

"Agreement," Tordor said.

"He means 'consensus,' I think," Asha said.

"But how arrived at?" Riley asked.

Asha gestured at the other passengers. The noise was getting deafening. "I think that's what they're doing. When they've reached a decision, they'll let us know."

"No campaigning?" Riley asked. "No promises? No racial slurs?"

"No bribes," Asha said. "No buying votes. No promises. No success and no failure. Whoever is chosen gets dismissed the same way, sometimes fatally."

"Is choice," Tordor agreed.

The process took less time than Riley expected. Within minutes the weasel approached Riley and Tordor. "You," he said and pointed toward Tordor with his half-grown arm.

Tordor raised his proboscis in recognition. He looked at Asha and then Riley. "So let it be," he said. He blew a surprising blast of noise from his long nose. As the other passengers turned toward them and quieted, he said, in language that Riley's pedia began translating in greater fluency, "Beings, you have chosen me to be your representative, and I will do so to the best of my ability. I go now to begin the process." He turned to Riley and said in a voice that only he and Asha could hear, "You are the better choice, but the galactics would never choose a human. The memory of the war is too fresh and the belief in the unpredictability of humans too ingrained."

He turned and ponderously marched to the hatchway. He pounded on it. It opened, revealing a portion of the passageway outside and a humanoid guard beyond before the hatch closed again behind him.

Riley looked at Asha. She shrugged. "Galactics seem to have long memories as well," she said.

Riley looked back at the hatch. "What does Tordor expect to accomplish?"

She looked at Riley as if evaluating the implications of his question. "I guess we'll have to wait and see."

"I'm going to talk to the galactics," he said.

"That might be misinterpreted. In fact, it's sure to be misinterpreted."

"That's basic to the process," Riley said and moved off to the group that contained the weasel, the Sirian, and the Alpha Centauran. All the members of the group guardedly turned toward him. "Their posture suggests the possibility of violence," Riley's pedia said. Riley held his hands in front of him, palms up. "I join you in your excellent choice of Tordor as representative," he said.

The galactics relaxed.

"Tell me how you chose him," Riley said.

"Some choices are not choices," the weasel said in his characteristic whine.

"So obvious they require no thought?"

"These persons have learned to live in peace by thinking clearly."

Riley again felt surprised at the eloquence of the alien, so different from the lingua galatica pidgin he had grown used to. Either the aliens were becoming more adept or his pedia was becoming more skillful as examples accumulated; or perhaps the aliens had been concealing their sophistication behind a pretense of patois. "Without emotion?" he asked.

"With logic."

"Forgive a poor, hotheaded, ignorant human," Riley said, hoping that irony didn't translate, "but perhaps you could tell me why you are here on this pilgrimage."

"In this matter, this person can speak only for itself," the weasel said. "This person comes from an ill-favored planet where life is hard and cunning is essential. Logic tells this person that evolution has pushed its people into blind alleys. Transcendentalism offers these persons a way out."

"And you?" Riley asked, turning to the Sirian. "If you will forgive my inexperience?"

The Sirian opened its eyes. "Inexperience is correctable; ignorance is teachable; effrontery is unforgivable."

"I am a poor, ignorant—" Riley began again

"My native world is the daughter of two suns," the Sirian broke in, as if to cut off a repetition of Riley's self-abasement. "And thus my people are drawn in two directions—one hot blue and near and one yellow and distant. We live in the near blue but we long for the remote yellow. Somehow this dichotomy must be resolved."

Riley would have turned next to the coffin-shaped alien, hoping to get beyond the enigma of its existence, but the ship's communicator announced the next Jump, and a moment later the illusion of transcending reality began again.

Tordor returned an hour later, escorted by two battered guards. Tordor was unmarked but indignant. "You may expel me from your company," he said, "but you will have to deal with me before this voyage is over."

As soon as the guards had left and the hatch had been locked behind them, Riley spoke. "I gather that you did not get along."

"They would not talk to me," Tordor said loud enough for everyone to hear. "They would not answer my questions. They would not let me go where I needed to go. Finally I confronted the captain, and he refused to discipline his subordinates. I could not do my job."

In a lower voice that only Riley and Asha could hear, he added, "The captain agreed that I was not the right representative."

"What shall we do?" asked the weasel.

"We will have to make a more practical choice. This being"—
Tordor pointed at Riley— "is the captain's species and shares the
captain's language and experience. He can come and go freely and
learn what we cannot.

"Because he is human we distrust him. His kind has not yet
earned our respect, much less our trust. We do not know what they
may do, or why. But I have learned that we must trust if we are to
earn our reward. And so I ask that you name this being your representative."

The passengers milled around before the weasel turned toward
Riley, Tordor, and Asha once more and the weasel-like alien said,
"We agree."

Tordor spoke only to Riley and Asha once more. "It had to be this
way. First they must see that their choice is impractical. Second they
must learn to accept what they cannot change. It is a difficult lesson
for beings who have governed the galaxy since humans were living
in caves."

To the other passengers he said, "These humans are barbarous
beings. We must watch them closely and control their choices. For
that reason I, your first choice, will monitor everything that this being does and report to you what he does not."

"And I," Riley said, "am a poor, ignorant human, untutored in
the ways of the civilized galaxy, and I must ask your forgiveness in
advance for any errors in judgment or information I might make,
while pledging myself to consider the well-being of all over my own
personal benefit."

The other passengers muttered among themselves at the far side
of the room, next to the food dispensers, but were not upset enough
to mount an insurrection. "Well said," Tordor remarked to Riley.

"They do not believe you," Asha said, "but they respect your willingness to placate them with fine words."

"I have a lot to learn," Riley said with uncharacteristic humility.

"The admission of ignorance is the beginning of wisdom," Tordor said.

"We humans have a similar saying," Riley said.

"Rational beings are the same everywhere," Tordor said, "adrift in an enigmatic universe. Otherwise they could not communicate."

Riley wondered again at Tordor's newfound eloquence.

"I will put that into action," he said, and ventured once more into the gathering of aliens. The group dispersed as he approached, as if trying to avoid contact with the barbarous human. He noticed again what a variety of sentient beings they were, some dressed in what seemed like rags, some adorned in what passed for finery, many of them unclothed and with curious appendages dangling; small, large, humanoid, and vaguely repellant because of the resemblance that had gone awry, utterly alien and repellently horrid. . . .

"Judge not!" his pedia said. Riley told himself that he must be just as repellant to some of the others, maybe more so. He would have to work even harder to make himself accept these creatures as fellow galactics.

"I desire to serve this group as I desire to help myself," he said to the coffin-shaped alien, but the alien was as perversely silent as Tordor's universe. He turned to the Sirian.

"The path into darkness is strewn with pitfalls," the Sirian said. Riley had to remind himself that for Sirians, under the glare of their overpowering primary star, night was a time not only of rest, but of nirvana.

"We do not expect much," the Alpha Centauran said. "Surprise us."

That would not be hard, Riley thought. This pilgrimage was full of surprises, with, he had no doubt, more to come.

He turned and threaded his way through the odorous and cacophonous gathering and went through the hatch into the corridor of the working ship. This time the lock surrendered without a struggle.

No guards waited outside the hatch. A crew member in patched one-piece coveralls glided past without giving Riley a glance, as if Riley, in similar coveralls, was just another member of the crew. Either the word had gone out to give him the freedom to do his job, or the crew had gotten used to him.

Riley hoped the condition of the coveralls did not reflect the condition of the ship. They had a long way to go, and alien territory to explore.

"Here there be Tygers," his pedia said.

Riley shook his head and started toward the ship's control center, noticing for the second time the place along the corridor, about shoulder height, where the finish had been worn from the paneling and, here and there, where emergency equipment lockers had been emptied and not refilled.

By the time he passed the captain's quarters, deserted now, Riley felt depressed. Not only had the *Geoffrey* seen better days; it might not see many more.

The control center seemed as shabby as the rest of the ship. Half of the gauges were broken, and the other half flickered erratically. The captain sat in the middle chair of three placed strategically in front of the computer interface, the communication controls, and the gunnery controls.

"Hello, Riley," the captain said, without turning.

"Your add-ons could get annoying," Riley said.

"I like to unnerve people."

"Particularly old friends."

"Old maybe. Hardly friends."

"We'd better get friendlier if we hope to survive," Riley said. "This ship is a piece of junk that should have been scrapped. And the crew isn't much better."

The captain swung around. "We'll have time to whip them into shape. This will be a long voyage."

"We?"

"You're going to have to help, Riley. And maybe Tordor, too, and the woman, Asha? You've all had ship-time experience, and the crew hasn't."

Riley was taken aback. "Asha, too?"

"So Tordor told me."

"She didn't tell me."

"Maybe she had her reasons. You're the X factor in this equation. Nobody knows why you're here and what your intentions are—"

"Is that any different from anyone else?"

"—and I'm sure you're not going to tell me," the captain concluded. "You're not like the rest of these pilgrims, or even like me. You aren't a starry-eyed dreamer, longing for a grander state. You're a pragmatist, and you're a warrior. I'd say you were an assassin except I don't know anybody aboard whose death would benefit anybody. We're probably all on a one-way trip."

That long outburst seemed to have exhausted the captain's store of conversation. Riley stood in front of his old crewmate wondering if he should say something, if there was any way to address the captain's accusations. There wasn't. Not without revealing more than was wise or perhaps, considering his pedia, possible.

"For someone who couldn't get along," Riley said, "you and Tordor seemed to have shared a lot of confidences."

"It was a charade, you know. Tordor knew that you were the natural choice but also that his fellow galactics wouldn't accept you—or any human, for that matter—unless your choice became inevitable. We agreed on that."

"I'm touched by your faith in me," Riley said.

"Faith? No. Belief. Necessity. Tordor felt that way, too."

"You struck it off."

"He was the first galactic I've met who didn't exhibit contempt for humans."

"Or who concealed it best."

"Maybe."

"Where does the ship stand now?"

The captain waved a hand and a holographic display took shape above the control panel. At first, the absence of light made the representation seem like a black hole, and then Riley began to pick out a few dim points of light.

"That's even more disturbing than the display in the passenger lounge," Riley said.

"We don't want to upset the passengers more than they already are. The display there isn't doctored. It's just a couple of Jumps delayed."

"I'll have to share this with them," Riley said.

"I thought you would. It will help solidify your position with them."

"Can I assure them that you know what you're doing and where we're going?"

"Only if you want to lie. How you handle the passengers is your problem now. You know my situation. I'm waiting for the next Jump coordinates, and there doesn't seem like there's much galaxy left."

"And you want me to handle that?" Riley asked. When the captain swung back to the control panel without answering, Riley turned and went back the way he had come.

As he opened the hatchway door, his pedia said, "Duck."

He ducked his head as he entered the passengers' quarters and looked back at the hatchway. At neck level, he could now see, a nearly invisible line had been stretched across the entrance, at the right height to have decapitated him as he entered.

No one was around. Apparently everyone had retired to his or her or its quarters or cubicle. Riley got a pair of impervium gloves from his cubicle, carefully removed the death line, coiled it, secured it with an impervium tie, inserted it into an impervium pouch, and stowed it away in his pack for possible later use.

"Someone thinks you are the Prophet," his pedia said, "and wants to kill you."

"Or the Prophet thinks I'm a threat."

"Your task becomes more imperative: identify the Prophet."

"You identify him for me," Riley said.

Someone didn't like him. Or feared him. Or distrusted him. He needed to find out why, and remembered Ham's comment that no one knew why he was on the ship or what his intentions were. That was, of course, true. And it would be better for him, and for what he had to do, or decided not to do, if it remained true.

He retired to his cubicle, inspecting all the possible traps his would-be assassin might have planted for him, and went to sleep thinking about why he was there.

CHAPTER FIVE

Riley remembered how his personal pilgrimage began:

The room's absence of light oppressed him. Not just dark. The light seemed to have been swallowed, consumed. He had the feeling that if he had a light stick with him, it would have cast a cone of black.

He thought he knew what was doing this to him: a phased transmitter that canceled light waves. It also canceled sound better than a room designed as an anechoic chamber. And he knew its purpose: to soften him up, to make him agree to anything in order to regain the real world of sight and sound. But what did they want—and who were "they"? He tried to feel his way around, ignoring the possibility that he could run into something dangerous or even fatal, or that he might be standing at the edge of a bottomless pit, but there was nothing to touch, not even a sensation of touch or even the feeling of weight on his body or the connectedness of muscle, nerve, and bone. Even if he had a light stick, he wouldn't have been able to feel it, much less turn it on.

Whatever they were trying to do wouldn't work. They couldn't make him scream and beg no matter how long they left him in this place. Whoever they were.

He would keep himself sane by going back over the events that had brought him here.

For more days than he could remember, he had lost himself in the sim section of the pleasure-world habitat of Dante off Rigel. Sharn had left him twenty days before, saying that he didn't need a friend or even a companion, he needed a nurse and a chiatrist. He knew what he needed: a job, a feeling of worth, a confirmation that life was better than death. Governments and corporations recruited industrial and interspecies spies, they hired assassins and mass murderers, but no one seemed interested in the services of an unspecialized soldier of fortune.

He could remember bits and pieces of what followed: ceutically induced euphoria followed by depression eased by more ceuticals; encounters in the dark with what he took to be sims but might have been real women; similar encounters in the glare of midday and the exposure of the marketplace; massages that blended into nerve stimulation that blended into sensory overload and free-associating drift; battles that maimed and slaughtered thousands, and one-on-one barroom fights with their satisfying impact of fist on flesh, given and received; and all sim, including himself. Or so he thought.

He had tired of excess, wearied of indulgence, sickened of depravity, and had pressed the panic button next to his right hand, roused himself from his tank, and checked out, determined to seek Sharn and build a new life, maybe together. But multiple assailants had waited for him in a corridor almost as dark as this place. He had disposed of several of them, one fatally he thought, before they had taken him out with a blow to his head. Of course they might have been handicapped by instructions to capture him alive.

Or maybe it all was part of his sim-experience, and he had been removed from his tank already anesthetized. Or maybe what he was experiencing now was a sim that someone else had programmed for him.

If he could feel anything, he would feel bruises and aches, he thought, but even those might be sim. The back of his head had hurt, he remembered. An injury of some kind at the base of his skull. If it was real.

It was a hell of a universe: a galaxy divided uneasily between alien species that once had sworn war to the death now trying to find a way to coexist; technology beyond humanity's dreams, some the product of human ingenuity, some modified from alien sources; and all of it used to distract, to divert, to suppress, to maintain. Riley had joined many expeditions into the unknown; he had met dozens of adventurers like himself, most of them now dead, and dozens of creatures with innovative ideas about how to do better, be better, improve conditions and possibilities for everybody . . . and all of them defeated, if they were still alive.

He had been one of them, early. He had worked his way through the Institute as assistant to a succession of brilliant scientists. He had studied mathematics and computer science and physics and astronomy; he had immersed himself in comparative cultures and alien art, and, most of all, in space-time engineering. He had imagined himself a diplomat or an inventor, making peace or a better future, but he had been recruited as a mercenary, trained in a dozen different ways to kill a creature silently and a half-dozen ways, undetectably, equipped with extrasensory apparatus. He was sent to scout alien intentions on alien worlds until, on his fifth assignment, he was captured and tortured. Eventually he was ransomed and restored to what the doctors called a state of health. After that his employers lost faith in him, or maybe in his luck. They told him he would be taken care of, but as soon as he was able to walk they let him go, to find his own way in the universe. He was always going to be damaged. The way to a better future seemed now permanently closed.

Humanity had ventured out into the galaxy to claim new worlds and discovered the galaxy already occupied. Dozens of alien species, many of them older and more advanced than humanity, though none of them more deadly, traversed interstellar space as if they owned it. They tolerated one another because anything else was suicidal. But humanity tipped the balance. Was it humanity's fault? Was it humanity's aggression or humanity's disappointed dreams? Or was humanity simply the unknown factor that ended the status quo, a development with an outcome no other species could calculate or risk? The interstellar wars began.

Education had delayed his service, but now he was called up, good for nothing more. He fought in a dozen battles on as many worlds, each of them brutal, each of them vital to the welfare of humanity, each of them inconclusive, each of them meaningless. He had lost an arm in one, a leg in another, an eye in a third—each replaced after hospitalization. He was no worse for all his experience except for wounds inside; the surgeons could not reach them; the chiatrists could not ease them. His only remedy was to drown them in one illusion or another. Maybe that was what Sharn had seen in him and despaired.

Was there a lightening of the darkness? Did he hear movement? Was feeling returning?

Sharn had been his surgeon in one of his restorations. He forgot which of them it had been, there had been so many. But he could not forget her deft fingers in the surgical console or her dark eyes focused on the images magnified on her scope or occasionally raised to meet his own. Within them was all the hope and promise that he had thought forever lost.

They had reminded him of his first love, the tomboy named Tes, who had raced him through the streets of Clarkeville on terraformed Mars, and up the slopes of the towering mountains whose summits they could never hope to reach or along the shores of the new seas. Her eyes had been dark, too, and they had teased him and taunted him, and looked up at him, widened by passion and squeezed tightly in fulfillment, and he had loved her and known then that he was destined for great things.

He had grown up on Mars, terraformed over the centuries by bombardment with fragments from the asteroid belt and by water-laden comets and pieces of Saturn's rings. His father had emigrated there with his new bride and his dreams of a better life. Jef Riley had built a hydroponic farm with his own hands, and prospered for a time, selling vegetables to new arrivals before he decided, in a fit of hubris, to try dry-land farming and lost everything. In desperation, he volunteered for the Interstellar Guard. He drilled for a month a year and for two days every month. He was promised that the Guard would never be used except for defense of Mars.

Riley had worked inside the greenhouses and on the shifting red Martian soil, and before and after work his mother schooled him with computer programs and televised lessons. He loved the freedom, loved the new world, loved his mother, who was strong and beautiful, but hated the labor and his father's folly, not realizing until much later that his father had cherished the same dream as his son—to get free, to be better than he was, to surpass his own limitations. All Riley could see then was the need to get away from the farm, from Mars even, and to take Tes with him.

But Tes had been the first to volunteer as soon as she was sixteen and had been killed, like his father, in the first battles of the interstellar war. Riley had already been accepted to the Solar Institute of Applied Science, and his mother insisted he go. There had been enough death, she said; it was time to build, not to destroy. He had gone, not unwillingly but saddened, trying to make sense out of catastrophic change, trying to hate the aliens who had killed his father, his sweetheart, and his dreams. He was tortured by unanswerable questions: Why had the wars occurred? Why had the aliens attacked? Who were they? What did they want? How could humanity resist? Would humanity survive?

It was difficult to focus on studies when the war raged through outer space, when media reports depicted attacks and victories and strategic withdrawals, complete with explosions and gouts of flame and the terrible faces of aliens looming out of the melee, brandishing weapons, or scattered across a barren battlefield like harvested grain. But Riley persisted, transferring to the classroom and laboratory the anxieties of wartime.

Sharn had visited him in the recovery room, checking on his arm. Yes, it had been his arm she replaced, and in demonstrating its strength he had pulled her, unresisting, into his hospital bed. She came to him often after that, and he found that her fingers were good for more than working a surgical machine. Her body was trained and supple and responsive, and her mind was quick and perceptive. They talked more than they made love.

They talked about humanity's dreams of reaching the stars and the great ache in the heart of all humanity at the discovery that the stars belonged to someone else. That was what the wars were all about, Sharn thought: the battle for real estate. That was what all human wars had been about, she said, and the interstellar wars were no different. Good land was always scarce, and planets of the right size and the right distance from their suns were even scarcer. If humanity wanted any, if they wanted a future, they would have to take it from those who had it.

Riley didn't agree. "A classical humorist once said, 'Buy land. They ain't making any more of it.' But they are. Every system I ever visited had habitats. Mined-out asteroids, most of them. People living there, being born there, growing up there. Soon that's all they'll know. Lot of advantages to habitats. People don't need planets. They can make their own living space—sometimes better."

"But it's not land," Sharn insisted. "It's artificial, and sooner or later the people, or creatures, who live in them are going to become just as artificial."

Riley pointed out that she was living and working in a habitat, and she replied that she hated it. And anyway, she said, if it wasn't land, what were the wars about?

Fear, Riley said, and misunderstanding. The aliens had been co-existing for a long time—many long-cycles—before humanity came out. The basic fear was of difference. How can you trust someone or some thing totally different, truly alien? You don't know what they think or what they feel, or even if they think or feel the way we understand those terms. Then there was the fear of inferiority. Was some other species smarter, more inventive, more powerful, more aggressive? The aliens—the various galactics—had learned to live with that. But humanity was the joker. It could be anything from potential slaves to potential workers to potential rulers, and the cycles-long truce broke down. Now the truce has been reinstated.

After how many millions dead? Sharn asked. After how many worlds ruined?

But will it last? Riley said. He flexed his new arm, and they made love again.

That was the last good time they had. It wasn't the disagreement about interstellar policy or even war—he hated that more than she did—it was her growing fascination with transcendentalism and his release from the recovery ward and his growing realization that he was finished. There was no role for an adventurer in a galaxy organized to minimize adventure, or a role for a warrior in a galaxy bent on peace at all costs. And no role for a diplomat who had killed too many aliens and bore their wounds on the shell of his body, and inside.

If he had grown moody and combative, if he had tried to ease his pain with ceuticals smuggled out of the pharmacy, if he had quarreled with Sharn too often and resisted her pleas to become the person she had first known, that she knew he once had been, the person who dreamed of something better—then her leaving him would have been understandable. But the way it happened—with no explanation, no apparent reason—leaving him was not.

Did the darkness brighten? Did sound and feeling return?

The disembodied voice was everywhere and nowhere. "We have a job for you."

"Who is 'we'?" Riley asked but he could not hear his own voice.

"That information is unnecessary; receiving it is unwise."

Riley could not tell if the voice belonged to a man or a woman, or a machine. It was devoid of emotion, uninflected. "How can you hear my voice, and I cannot?"

"Unimportant."

"Where am I?"

"Meaningless."

"All right, then, what is the job?"

"You will join a pilgrimage starting from Terminal in some thirty days."

"A pilgrimage to where?"

"That is what you are hired to find out."

"A pilgrimage has to be headed somewhere."

"It is seeking the shrine of the transcendentals."

"But no one knows where that is."

"Until you find out."

"And how will I do that?"

"You will accompany the pilgrimage until it reaches its destination."

"And how will the pilgrimage know where to go?"

"Most on the ship will not, but we have information that the Prophet will be among the pilgrims."

"And who is that?"

"We do not know. That, too, you will discover."

"Maybe the Prophet doesn't know where to go. Maybe the whole thing is as illusory as all other religions. Maybe it's all supernatural."

"That, too, you will discover."

"How do you prove a negative? If the pilgrimage gets nowhere, does that mean there is no shrine? That the Prophet was not aboard? That the Prophet was aboard but has forgotten where the shrine is? That the Prophet was aboard but discovered my presence or the presence of others and decided not to head for the shrine . . . ?"

"Your assignment is to see that the pilgrimage reaches the shrine, if it exists."

"You don't ask much for your money!" Riley said as dryly as he could. "And, speaking of money, how much is this job worth?"

"Money is irrelevant."

"Not to you, maybe."

"You will be handsomely rewarded."

"Easy for you."

"Funds have been deposited to your account. They will pay for your expenses with a sizable sum left over. If you are successful, you will have your choice of a habitat, a habitable moon, or an estate on a favorable planet."

"You seem sure I will accept."

"You have no choice. Your family is gone. . . ."

"Except my mother," Riley said.

"She, too. You have not heard yet, but she was killed in the last alien attack on Mars before the battle fleet was destroyed."

"You bastard!"

"These are facts. Sharn has left you. . . ."

"What do you know about that?"

"Everything. We had to be sure you were the right person for the job."

Resentment filled Riley's mind. He would have tasted bile if he had been capable of tasting anything. "Why do you expect me to accept?"

"Because of the kind of person you are."

"You have abducted me. You have raped my past. You plan to control me. Why should I want to work for you?"

"Because of the kind of person you are."

"You think you know me."

"Yes. You, too, were once in love with transcendence, but life has wounded you and disillusioned you, and now you want to immerse yourself in a task that will consume you. What better task than this? Adventure, violence, romance, adversaries, little chance of success, even of surviving. . . . This is what you were looking for on Dante. And this is a search for transcendence—the goal that you have abandoned."

"Maybe you do know me," Riley said. "But what makes you think I have any chance at all?"

"We have given you an edge."

"What?"

"First of all, you will know more about the pilgrimage than any of the others. Second, you have a new pedia."

"A new pedia?" He remembered that the back of his head hurt, when he could still feel.

"An advanced model. Perhaps one of a kind. It is many times as powerful as any predecessor."

"In what way?" Riley said skeptically.

"It has a massive storage capacity stuffed with information and sensory extensions that make other senses seem pallid by comparison."

"And you have implanted this without my permission, without my agreement to take this job?"

"We had no time for fine distinctions."

"And why shouldn't I have this thing yanked when I turn you down?"

"That would be fatal."

After a silence that stretched into a gulf, Riley said, "Fatal?"

"The new pedia is a biological computer that establishes its own network throughout the brain. Therefore it not only is difficult to remove, the attempt leaves the brain damaged beyond repair. On the other hand, you will find the pedia so powerful you would feel only half a person without it."

"Yeah?" Riley replied, contemplating the thing in his head like a metastasizing cancer—if it existed. "If this is so great, why doesn't everybody have one?"

"Something like this, if it became generally available, has the potential to upset the balance of power in the galaxy, and if more than one were implanted the technology could spread beyond a few chosen users to many, and then beyond humanity to aliens, or, if aliens discovered that it exists, they might join to eliminate humanity before it achieves a unique advantage."

"All that is"—a word appeared in his mind—"Machiavellian."

"Machiavelli's advice to his prince was aimed at giving his masters an advantage. Our goal is to maintain the status quo."

"And that is why you want me to sabotage the pilgrimage."

"Not sabotage. First of all, discover if there is any truth to the rumors. If a practical method of transcendence exists, humanity must have equal access, or it must be destroyed. Destruction may be safer."

"If it exists, how do you propose I destroy it—whatever it is?"

"You are an ingenious man. You will think of something."

"And if it is only another religious myth?"

"Even myths can be powerful. Maybe more powerful than the reality. If you discover who the Prophet is, you will kill him."

"It's a person?"

"It may be an alien."

"Death is pretty final."

"Millions have died already. Better one should die than many millions more. Think how many died in the name of the ancient prophet Christ."

"As I recall," he did recall, "he *was* killed."

"That is a chance we are prepared to take."

"And who is 'we'?"

"As we said before, that is unimportant, and it would be unwise for you to know."

"Well then, what gives you the right to make these decisions for humanity?"

"All of that is irrelevant. We have the right; we have the knowledge; we have the means. You have your instructions and the resources to accomplish them."

"One last question: who else knows about the pilgrimage and the Prophet?"

"The pilgrimage: many. The Prophet: perhaps one, perhaps several."

"And who else knows about my assignment?"

"Only us."

"The royal 'us'?"

"Only us."

"And how will I contact you if I need help?"

"If you need help, the mission has failed; it will do no good to contact anyone. Good luck and good-bye."

The darkness faded to a neutral gray. Riley felt again: his bruised body, his aching head. He opened his eyes and sat up, rubbing the slime from his face and eyes. He was back in the sim tank. Maybe he had never left. Maybe the whole experience had been a sim. He felt the back of his head. A surgical incision had been neatly sealed with glue.

Where am I? he thought.

"You are in a simulated experience tank in Sim City on Dante off Rigel," a voice replied. It sounded very much like the voice that had spoken to him in the darkness.

Who was just talking to me?

"I was activated only one thousand nanoseconds ago," the voice said.

Who activated you?

"The information is not available in my data bank."

As Riley rinsed the slime from his body and got dressed, he considered his options. They were few. He had this thing in his head that he could not remove, or he could try to have it removed but if the voice was correct it would be his last action. The thing in his head might be the voice that had given him his instructions. That made his flesh prickle: the possibility that he might be carrying his employer around with him, and what would determine the fate of humanity, what was acting in the name of humanity but perhaps not in its best interests, was a biological computer in his head. Or maybe the voice had simply used the computer to converse with him.

Who had spoken to him? Who had known all these things about him and about the pilgrimage? Were they what they said? Were they acting for humanity? For all he knew, they might be a renegade group of humans with a crazed agenda, or some devious plan to seize power, or to start another war. On the other hand, they could even be aliens, with their own alien plans.

He shrugged. There was no way to know. He had to depend upon his own judgment, his own ingenuity, and the pedia inside his head.

He bought passage to Terminal.

CHAPTER SIX

Riley woke with the feeling that Martian sand spiders had been running over his body all through the sleep period. What made his skin crawl? The memory of the treachery that had put him here? The realization that someone hated him or feared him enough to want him dead? Or simply wanted to be rid of him, which was maybe more disturbing. To be killed for a reason is understandable. But the thought that someone might want him to be killed because he was an inconvenience made him feel as inconsequential as a sand spider someone might step on. No place was safe anymore; he could never relax.

He didn't feel good, either, about the half-sentient thing that lived in his head, warning him of dangers while propelling him into their midst. And making all those comments about his thoughts and behavior, like a wife who now recognizes the flaws that the blinders of the courting process had led her to overlook—or to believe she could change.

Outside or inside—there was nowhere to hide.

No use contemplating extinction, he thought. Death had been a companion for too long to treat like a stranger.

" 'A coward dies a thousand deaths—' " said his pedia.

"Oh, shut up!" Riley said aloud. The words reverberated in the compartment and spurred Riley into motion.

Climbing down the ladder, he saw Tordor at the entrance to the passengers' lounge and Asha beyond, talking to the Alpha Centauran near the food dispensers. Tordor had been watching Asha, Riley thought, but looked up as Riley approached.

"Greetings, Representative," he grunted. Now there was almost no delay between his utterance and the pedia's translation.

"Greetings," Riley said. He hesitated and then continued, "In my last excursion I noticed the disrepair of the ship and the lack of discipline in the crew. At the first crisis, everything may fall apart. The captain is competent enough, but he has been given a shoddy vessel and a surly crew."

"So I saw."

"We must do something."

"What?"

"The passengers have more experience and skills than the crew. You commanded a ship, true?"

"A fleet."

"Anyway," Riley said. He considered Tordor. "Apparently the process of joining this pilgrimage is more selective than the assignment to crew it."

"Are you suggesting—mutiny?" Riley's pedia hesitated at "mutiny." Perhaps the Dorian language had no word for "mutiny," maybe no concept.

"More like reformation. I suggest we combine our efforts, improve the ship, and retrain the crew."

"And what will the captain be doing?"

"Nothing," Riley said. "There are about thirty of us and a few more than that in the crew. They have weapons, it is true, and we have none—that we know of. But the captain cannot kill us or imprison us. Not simply because he can't return with dead passengers and has no means of controlling us alive—he gets his navigation instructions from someone on board."

"You?" Tordor asked bluntly.

"He doesn't know who, and neither do I."

"That's what you would say if it were you," Tordor said.

Riley shrugged. "It could be you or any one of us. Or one of the crew. Whoever it is conceals his identity for a reason, and the reason is that if he were known the rest would turn on him."

"At least they would keep him alive," Tordor said

"Or beat him to death trying to get information out of him. Not just our destination but what awaits us there—if he knows. Why should he take the chance?"

"Then the captain cannot act without risking the voyage. But is he committed to the voyage even if the difficulties are such that anyone else would turn back?"

"As much as you or me," Riley said.

"As much as me? You I am not certain about."

Riley recalled the captain's remarks. "Nor I you," he said. "Nor can we be sure of anyone's commitment. Maybe we should find a way to peer into each other's souls."

"Souls?" Tordor said.

"Our inner selves," Riley said. "The part that is peculiarly us. The part we keep separate from the world."

"More Terran mysticism," Tordor said.

"Maybe Dorians have no identity problems," Riley said, "or any other galactic. But I doubt it. I think you've just stopped talking about it. And we've got to start talking about it if we're going to organize ourselves into a group that has any hopes of survival."

"How do you propose to do that?"

"That's your problem," Riley said. "They'll listen to you. My problem is dealing with the captain."

Tordor turned his ponderous body to look at the lounge, and grunted for attention. "We must organize ourselves to help the crew," he said. Two dozen aliens turned toward him. "The ship needs our assistance if we are to achieve our ends. To do that we must accept roles, each according to the ability of each."

The galactics turned once more to their council of consensus.

The galactics filed after Riley through the passenger compartment hatch. He led them toward the control room, crew members watching with expressions that ranged from surprise and alarm to disgust, He stopped at the captain's quarters. The second-in-command was at the helm in the control room; the hatch to the captain's quarters was closed.

Riley held the grab bar beside the hatch and pounded on the door. It slid open. The captain stood in the hatchway, fully dressed. Surprise competed with another emotion for control of his face. Concern? Frustration?

"What's this?" the captain asked.

"We've come," Riley said, "to give you some help."

The captain looked down the hallway at the odd assortment of galactics and the crew members beyond. He waved dismissal at the crew. They slowly dispersed. "You know why that is not only illegal but unwise," he said to Riley but loud enough for Tordor and Asha to hear, and perhaps others beyond.

"Illegal maybe," Riley said. "Unwise, no. Tordor and I agree—the ship is in poor condition and the crew isn't much better."

"I agree," Tordor said.

"We make do with what we have," the captain said.

"That isn't good enough for a venture as fraught with peril and the unexpected as this one," Riley said.

The captain studied Riley and then looked at Tordor and Asha. He shrugged. "When I agreed to a representative from the passengers," he said, "I thought we had solved a problem. I see now that we have created a bigger one."

"Whether we like it or not," Riley said, "we're in this together. You'd like to reach our destination safely—and return—and so would we. Tordor and I—and maybe others if they had had our chance to observe—don't think the ship will make it as it is. The ship needs work and maybe the operating systems, too, if the rest of the ship is any indication, and the crew needs training and discipline."

"That is true," Tordor said.

"It is not a reflection on your command," Asha said. "You were given a ship that should have gone to salvage and a crew that had no other choices."

"Possibly this voyage was never meant to succeed," Riley said. "It may have served as a convenient way to dispose of potential troublemakers."

The captain looked at them with an air of superior wisdom. "It may be true, but is it workable?"

"We will make it work," Tordor said. He waved his hand at the galactics behind him. "They have agreed to do it, and we have many skills represented here."

"The crew may be the scrapings of the spaceports," the captain said, "but they're not stupid."

"Neither are they suicidal," Riley said. "They may not have our motivations—unless they have been selected by a process we don't suspect—but they'd like to survive. Right now I'd say their best choice is—mutiny." He said the last word softly so that only the captain and Tordor could hear. And maybe Asha.

"And your galactics are going to solve that?" the captain said. Riley noticed that the captain hadn't rejected the possibility.

"Your passengers want the mission to succeed," Riley said. "No matter what the risks."

The captain addressed Tordor. "You still haven't said how this is going to work."

"We'll assign a galactic to every crew member," Tordor said. "Each according to its ability and experience. The galactic will work as the assistant or apprentice to the crew member, becoming familiar with duties and the ship, repairing and upgrading equipment, encouraging better performance."

"And you think the crew will stand for that?"

"We galactics were sailing these skies for long-cycles before you humans ventured off your little planet," Tordor said. "Any sensible creature would recognize that."

"As you may have discovered," the captain said glumly, "humans and other humanoids are not always sensible."

"We will need to increase rewards," Tordor said, as unperturbed as ever, "and we will schedule daily meetings to instill discipline and increase group solidarity. That is the part," he said, "that I will be in charge of."

"Agreed?" Riley said.

"Do I have a choice?" said the captain.

Riley shook his head. "But the plan is better for you as well. You know the weaknesses of the ship and its crew. This will increase your chances, too."

The captain shrugged.

"We know that this seems like a threat to your command and an insult to your captaincy," Asha said. "But it seems like the only way this mission can succeed."

"You may be right," the captain said, "because I've just received the latest Jump instructions, and the next one takes the ship into the Great Gulf!"

The image on the view screen in the passenger quarters was epic. The giant pinwheel of the galaxy was reduced to a size that could be covered by a bedsheet, but nothing could minimize the psychological impact of its ponderous immensity: the center blazing with light, spiral arms trailing off into nothingness. Beyond that the deep, dark void between the galaxies.

But that wasn't what drew the gaze of the watchers. They looked at a spot far down one arm where, they thought, they could imagine the *Geoffrey* and, adjacent, the emptiness between spiral arms that the captain had called "the Great Gulf."

"But that isn't our galaxy," Asha said.

"So it might seem," Tordor said, speaking with the authority of a million years of galactic history. "But, in fact, this is an image processed from signals sent by creatures of the galaxy you call Andromeda."

"What?" Riley asked.

"True," his pedia said. "Or not."

"That's incredible!" Riley said.

Tordor made a motion that humans might have interpreted as a shrug.

"Sometimes," Riley said, "I don't know whether you're telling the truth or making a joke. Do Dorians make jokes?"

"That would mean," Asha said, "that this picture is millions of cycles out of date."

"The stars move slowly," Tordor said.

"Why would they send it?" Riley asked. "Whoever sent it."

"Maybe as a gesture of fellowship; maybe as a trap. It all happened thousands of galactic cycles before humans emerged from their system, even perhaps before they emerged from their caves. It was discussed for years in galactic circles, but finally, after grave deliberation, the decision was made not to reply. In any case, the reply would take two million years to arrive, and it was unlikely that the senders would still be around to receive it."

"Did you receive any other messages?" Asha asked.

"None."

"None of that makes any sense," Riley said. "Why should this human ship have a galactic image in its computer?"

"When peace was declared," Tordor said, "humans were allowed to download galactic data of all kinds. Histories, art, culture, maps . . . How else do you think this ship can navigate from nexus to nexus?"

Riley did not reveal that capturing—and translating—the galactic navigation maps had been a turning point in the war. Instead he returned his gaze to the display. "Whether all that is true or not is irrelevant. Right now we must consider what lies in front of us. Those galactic maps don't cover it."

"The Great Gulf," Asha said. She contemplated the dark space without emotion.

"It isn't empty space, you know," Tordor said. "There are stars in the Gulf, just faint and few."

"But the distance is still immense," Asha said.

"And it isn't certain we can get back if we miss a nexus or if one has evaporated," Riley said. "We may run out of fuel with no chance of getting any more."

"And even then the next spiral arm is unknown," Tordor said.

"What?" Riley said. The surprises were piling up.

"True," his pedia said.

"We think of the galaxy as being a single entity," Tordor said. "But it is a series of spiral arms, and our civilization occupies only one of them. Getting to the next one is a perilous enterprise. Close to the galactic center, where the stars are neighbors and the next spiral arm is not so distant, radiation is high, and living creatures do not survive long. In the historical past, five expeditions, each manned by a different species, set out, but only one returned. The crew was dead or dying and the dying were insane; even the ship's records were indecipherable."

"Well," Riley said, "are we going to go along with this gamble?"

"It isn't our decision," Asha said.

Tordor turned to the galactics who had been milling uneasily behind the triumvirate of Riley, Asha, and Tordor himself. "The captain has informed us that the next Jump is into the Great Gulf. You all know what that means. Should we consent? Resist?"

What followed would have been described among humans as a hubbub. Among galactics it was a cacophony of hoots, whistles, grunts, whispers, and limb and torso motions. Finally Tordor turned back to Asha and Riley. "They agree that we should go forward into the unknown," he said, "but only after the ship has been thoroughly inspected and repaired."

Fifteen cycles later Tordor reported to the assembled passengers that they were passengers no more but could accurately describe themselves as adjuncts to the crew. Together they had overhauled the ship, and in the process had restored the discipline and morale of the human and humanoid crew. They had become, Tordor said in a burst of eloquence, "our own Transcendental Machine."

"He's laying it on a bit thick, isn't he?" Riley muttered to Asha. They were standing well to the side of the group and detached from it, near the entrance to the sleeping compartments.

"He has his own transcendental motives," Asha said.

"I wish I knew what they were," Riley said. "In fact, I wish there were some way to get to know all of these galactics better. But they won't open up to me, an uncivilized barbarian."

"Let me see if I can think of something," Asha said.

"Let it come from her," his pedia said.

"And so," Tordor concluded, "let us venture into the unknown, certain that we are as prepared as any ship and crew can be. The engines have been disassembled and rebuilt; the navigation system has been recalibrated; the star charts have been checked and re-checked; the communication equipment has been vetted; weapons have been tested. Let us proceed."

Tordor gestured toward Riley with his proboscis, a movement with which Riley had become familiar. Riley nodded and slipped back through the hatch that no longer was locked and guarded. The corridor walls had been cleaned and refinished, and the crew members he passed were dressed uniformly in one-piece yellow suits. They saluted as he passed.

He located the captain in the control room. "The galactics have given you the go-ahead."

The captain grimaced sourly. "Nothing good will come of this usurpation of my authority."

"You could have said that about this trip from the beginning."

"Then, at least, we had a chain of command. Now, you can count on it, when a crisis arrives, as it must, no one will know who is in charge. Chaos will follow. And then catastrophe."

"Or transcendence," Riley said. "Hasn't that always been the choice?"

The captain looked at Riley once more. "Did we ever get along?" He turned to the communicator. "The Jump will begin in ten ticks," he announced.

Riley sat down in the navigator's chair, no longer so confident of his ability to handle a Jump standing up. "We never got along; we endured," he said.

And then the Jump began, the bulkheads shimmered, and the ship lights faded into the blackness of another reality. Riley felt his breathing stop and his heart beat strangely, even stranger because it was outside his body and he could see it, contracting and expanding, sustaining the natal emergence of one universe into another.

And then his heart returned to his chest and he breathed again, and in breathing brought back the ship and his own reality. "That was different," he said, trying not to gasp.

"It's always different," the captain said. "This time the Jump was longer and the nexus was fragile. It may not have been used for millions of years. It may not have been there at all."

"But it was," Riley said. "And somebody on this ship knew it was there."

"Yes," the captain said.

They brooded about it until Riley returned to the passengers' quarters. There he found the passengers focused on the view screen. It revealed a darkness relieved, if at all, by one faint glimmer of light in the upper left quadrant.

"So," he said to Tordor and Asha, "we are launched into this—"

" 'Sea of troubles,' " his pedia said

" '—sea of vast eternity,' " Riley finished defiantly.

"Without a shore in sight," Asha said. "Tordor has an idea about how we can sustain our morale and gain insights into our companions. He suggests that each of us tell the others how we came to be on this voyage to elsewhere."

"We might be able to open a window into each other's souls," Tordor said.

CHAPTER SEVEN

Tordor's Story

Tordor said:

I was born on an ideal world of great sweeping plains and flowing rivers of sweet water and oases of trees where we could doze in the heat of the day. The sun was yellow, the pull of the world was solid, the days were long, and I was happy to eat and sleep and play mock battles with my tribe-mates. I had two good friends: a male my age named Samdor, who was my constant companion, and a pleasingly muscled female named Alidor that I secretly admired and allowed to beat me in our games. And then I turned five and the recruiters came from the distant cities and my parents said I must go with them. I was bewildered and afraid. Why should my parents send me away? What had I done wrong?

The recruiters were thinner than us grass-eaters but tall, strong, and distant. They came in a big, gas-filled aeronef, and they spoke to the recruits only to give orders and said nothing to each other. Some fifty of us had been collected from the plains tribes, most of them my age, a few younger and a couple a year older and meaner. They bullied the younger ones, stole their food, and made them fight each other until they rebelled, and then the older recruits beat them. The recruiters did not seem to care. Later I learned that letting the recruits fight among themselves and establish their hierarchy was the custom, that children had to learn how to survive under difficult circumstances, in strange lands, and without friends. We were being transformed into good Dorians.

Only two of us died on the long trip to the northern highlands. One of them was Alidor.

I had never seen a city before. My parents had told me stories about powerful Dorians who flew through the sky and traversed the great void between the stars, but I thought they were fairy tales, like the fanciful stories my tribe-mates spun during the long evenings. But the city of Grandor, the great city of Doria, grew out of the northern mountain range like a forest of fairy palaces, glittering with crystalline reflections in the evening sun and, as the sun dropped behind the mountains, glowing with light. The spires of the city seemed to rise above even the peaks that surrounded it.

It was as marvelous as my parents had described it, and I would have exclaimed at its beauty, and the people who had built it, if I had not been bruised and afraid. We were herded off the ship and prodded into crude quarters, little more than stalls for sleeping, without privacy. Drink was available at a central trough; to eat we had a poor quality of grass, without grains or fruit. Later I learned that this treatment was intended to toughen us against future hardship, and, anyway, quality food was expensive to bring from the plains and was reserved for the citizens who governed the city and the world and the worlds beyond.

We got used to it, as young people will, and to the morning run up and down the mountainsides, to the mock combat in the afternoon, with and without weapons, and to the classrooms where we were taught mathematics and engineering and spacecraft, the military history of Doria, and the minor skills of computers and accounting. The classrooms were the good times when it was possible to doze off if one had a classmate willing to nudge one awake when the instructor looked one's way. Otherwise, a club was likely to come crashing down upon one's skull, and more than one young Dorian met his end that way. I was lucky. I got only a lump or two, but I had a thicker skin and a thicker skull than most. My classmate died. Sometimes I envied him.

In the evenings Dorian heroes would tell us stirring tales of combat, and I wondered if I would ever be like them: strong, confident, swaggering, deadly, full of honors, mating at will. I could not imagine it. None of us dozed then. Sometimes they showed us patriotic films or films of space combat. The ones we could follow seem staged for the cameras. In the real ones we could observe nothing except for moments when battles were too confused to distinguish friend from enemy. We were always tired. If we napped then, nobody cared.

So it went, year after year, as I grew to be even taller than the recruiters and my plains fat was converted into muscle. I was the one who triumphed in the mock battles, even when I faced our instructors, and I gloried in my new-found strength and skill. One by one my fellow students, those that survived, recognized my preeminence. Of my cohort of fifty, only twenty reached the age of decision. I personally killed the two older ones who had bullied us on the way to Grandor.

The age of decision was ten. I no longer wept for my parents and my siblings. I had given up ever seeing them again. I knew that if I returned they would be required to put me to death as a disgrace to the family and the tribe, and I would have to kill them instead. So I only dreamed about the flowing plains of grass and the sweet streams and the clear blue sky, and about running, running endlessly and untiringly under that yellow sun, knowing that it could never be anything but a dream.

We lined up at graduation to learn our fates, and heard our records read aloud and our destinations announced. Some fulfilled my worst nightmare: they were rejects, to be returned to their families and certain death, or to wander the plains as rogue males, ostracized by everyone they met and subject to termination by anyone. Some became factory supervisors. Some became engineers or scientists. Some were assigned to bureaucratic posts within Grandor or one of the lesser cities scattered along the coasts to the far southernmost tip of land, while others received postings to other planets under Dorian rule, or became recruiters, like those that came for us five years before.

And a few were appointed to the military academy.

I was one of those.

The military academy was situated in a valley among tall mountains that divided the southern continent from the north, and near the spaceport at the equator, with its space elevator that we were told had been invented by a Dorian scientist but I later learned was the product of technology that had been acquired from humans—perhaps the only thing we learned from them besides ferocity. We had our own taste of ferocity, among ourselves and among the savage Dorians who occupied the southern continent, separated for long ages by the mountain range. With the superior technologies of the north, they could have been subdued centuries before, I learned from a wise master, but our rulers had decided they were of greater utility as anvils on which to hammer out the blades of our soldiers.

We fought the savages with their own weapons, not with ours, and we prevailed, not because we were stronger or more blood-thirsty but because we were disciplined. That was our first lesson—discipline or death. Fight as a group or die as an individual.

Sometimes, as if by pre-arrangement, the savages attacked the academy, and we were roused from our stalls to grab our weapons and repel them from our walls. More often we ventured forth in hunting groups and fell upon them in their villages, killing them all, males, females, and children; we did not venture too far south lest we reduce their numbers beyond replenishment. Sometimes they ambushed our groups, and we had to fight for our lives. Often groups returned with their numbers depleted. Those who returned without their fellows were beaten and those who returned without their fellows' bodies were expelled—south of the mountains. Sometimes groups did not return at all.

In my first five years at the academy I had learned survival. The cadets among whom we were thrown would have treated us in the same way as the bullies in the aeronef, but I had prepared the dozen of appointees sent with me. We would present a united front. We would not fight among ourselves, but we would fight anyone else as a group. And we would fight before we would submit.

I fought the cadet leader on the day we arrived. He was older and more experienced than I, but he was overconfident, and I was determined not to surrender to his official sadism. His cohort carried him off the field, unable to intervene because my cohort stood solidly behind me. After that no one touched us, no one taunted us. Another leader was chosen, but unofficially I was the leader, and consulted about plans and procedures affecting my group. My group was not sent on missions without strategic goals and training. We operated as a unit with advance scouts and side scouts and rear scouts, and we knew the terrain and its ambush points as well as we knew our own plains. None of my group died.

Even the academy instructors began to notice. Ordinarily they let the cadets create their own culture, but now they understood that the culture had been taken over by a newcomer who was flouting tradition and its custodians. They feared novelty, since their standard practices had worked for so long. They tried to break my will and my power over the group. They separated me from the others, but I had warned my team of this possibility and deputized Samdor to serve in my absence. They imprisoned me for a time on imaginary charges and sent me out to do battle alone. I survived and returned with grisly proof of my success.

Finally they recognized my leadership and the success of my organization, and let me install my program for the entire academy, forming the cadets into cohesive units and letting each choose a commander—with my approval—and preparing for battle with the same kind of strategic planning. Casualties dropped. Successes mounted.

Life at the academy was not all skirmishes with the savages or combat training within the yard. We were being prepared to be the new Dorian military leaders. We studied military strategies, combat maneuvers, enough space navigation to understand—and sometimes check upon—the navigators, weapons and weapon repair, chemistry and physics and mathematics, but no literature or art. That we had to acquire—if we had the taste for it—in our leisure hours, such as they were, and secretly, for they were considered suspicious if not, perhaps, subversive.

We had only limited exposure to current events and politics. We knew about alien civilizations—their citizens were considered lesser creatures who had ventured, almost by accident, into space and could serve, at best, as suppliers to Doria, and, at worst, as servants and their lands potential Dorian dominions. Alien languages were not part of the curriculum. "Let them learn Dorian" was the official attitude. Although I did not understand why this was so, I sensed that this was a mistake. We could not depend upon translators, particularly alien translators, nor even upon mechanical translators. Within each language, I came to believe, was the heart and soul of

the people who spoke it. So, as I did with literature and art, I studied alien languages, beginning with the language of the savages to
the south. It was then I learned what moved them and how to work
with them in ways other than combat.

In our fourth year we learned of humans—these pretentious inter-
lopers who emerged from their single system as if they were the
equals of the long-established Dorians and the others, who, though
unequal, had been part of the galactic scene for long-cycles. Our
instructors let us know, not by word but by intonation, that humans
were inconsequential, that they were nothing to be concerned about
except as they disturbed the aliens whom we allowed to coexist.

This, perhaps, was a Dorian error that was almost fatal, not simply to us but to the entire galactic civilization that had existed for
so many long-cycles in equilibrium—an uneasy equilibrium like
supercooled water but equilibrium all the same.

And then it was time for graduation, deliverance from the petty
tyranny of the academy and into the great tyranny of military service. But our instructors had one more graduation barrier for us to
hurdle—one final hand-to-hand combat to the death for a pair of
matched champions—and I learned that the academy may yield but
it does not forget. It matched me against my old tribe-mate and
second-in-command, my best friend, Samdor.

I would have refused, but it would have meant death to us both.
Samdor did refuse, but I persuaded him that it was better to kill or
be killed in combat than to be executed as a coward. I knew he was
no coward. He loved me, as he, and I, had loved Alidor. I wanted
him to kill me, to end this misery we Dorians called living, but in
the end, in front of the jeering instructors and the quiet cadets,
something in me deflected his blows and parried his thrusts. I had
practiced survival too long.

I killed Samdor and with that blow became a true Dorian.

*   *   *

Our superiors assigned us to military posts by lot, they said. Only later did I learn that the system was manipulated to place the new officers where they thought we should go, just as the combat by lots was fixed to pit friend against friend. I went to my post as the gunnery officer on a Dorian light-cruiser off the farthest Dorian outpost, where our empire met the humans. They were always encroaching with their inexhaustible numbers and appetites for land and conquest. I went with an empty heart, always seeing the eyes of Samdor as he accepted my fatal blow, seeing the light behind those eyes fade and go out. I tried to accept that, but what I could not accept was the expression of gratitude that flashed over his face at the moment of his death.

Was death so welcome? Or was his love so much greater than mine that he wished to buy my life with his death?

The journey to the outpost was long. They did not waste wormhole technology on newly commissioned officers, and we were jammed into the hold of a cargo ship like bales of hay. But we had little hay. We were on short rations from the start of the journey, and many would have died along the way had we been left on our own. Like in the military academy, the fittest were intended to survive. But I organized a small group of natural leaders to see that the rations were divided equally, and that we all lived in a state of semi-starvation. Only one died.

When we reached the fleet, I reported to the commanding officer. His name was Bildor. He was the biggest Dorian I had ever met, and his body was crisscrossed with the scars of battle—Dorian battle, I learned later. He looked at me as if he saw me as a potential rival, but I was clearly his inferior in everything but promise. He would gain nothing by challenging me, but he challenged my ideas instead. "So, you are the newly commissioned officer who thinks he has a better way of doing things?"

"There is always a better way," I replied with proper deference.

"Tradition has brought us to this mighty empire," he said.

"New challenges arrive daily," I said, "for which tradition has no responses."

"You will perform your duties as a proper Dorian," Bildor said.

I bowed my head and was dismissed. But I knew that Bildor was watching through his senior officers.

We skirmished with human ships whenever we came across them. But between skirmishes we socialized. I met them, and other aliens, in bars or theaters. I learned a bit of human speech and what passed for humor between us both. We told jokes. I learned something of human history and the history of other species in the galaxy and compared them to our own. That was my education in xenology. I learned what made them drunk and broke down their limited reserves, and tried to hide from them what made Dorians drunk. Not that it would have mattered. Dorians become sullen and withdrawn when drunk on—shall I reveal it?—fermented hay.

I even grew to like the humans, perhaps even more than I liked my superiors. My superiors were determined to make us hate the humans as much as we hated one another. They pitted us against one another for promotions, in what they called "fight days" that were carryovers from the military-school survival programs. I was clearly the best at personal combat, but after Samdor I refused to fight to the death. Instead, I defeated my opponents and spared their lives. Only one of my superiors dared to challenge me, and in his case I made an exception and killed him. That gained me a promotion to his position as second navigator, and freedom from challenges from below or above. Even Bildor seemed to relax his vigilance.

So I made my way up in the Dorian service, from lowly officer to second-in-command, and then, when Bildor got killed in a personal duel with the commander of another ship, I got my own ship. I changed the discipline, did away with fight days, encouraged my subordinates to come to me with their problems, to make suggestions, and generally to work toward a harmonious crew.

Change did not come easy. Dorians are herd creatures, as are most grazers, elevated to sentience long-cycles before by hard times. Some historians have traced the transformation to a tumultuous period of volcanic activity that contaminated the Dorian atmosphere with smoke and ash, causing the death of grass almost everywhere and the near-extermination of the Dorian people. Other scientists point to deep pits in the Dorian soil caused, they say, by meteoric bombardment raising clouds of dust and smoke that caused similar death and near-starvation. Whichever is correct—and perhaps both are—Dorians were forced to change. They had to learn. They had to invent. Most of all, they had to survive, often at the expense of another group or another individual. The most successful of these founded Grandor, so remote from Dorian experience and nature, and then the other cities of the northern hemisphere, and, more recently, the southern.

When, over long-cycles, the crisis passed, those who had founded the cities under the pressure of necessity saw Dorians relapsing into their former indolence and herd mentality, and began a regime of recruitment and training such as I had experienced, with a system that set out to replicate the conditions that had produced the Grandorians. If nature could not be trusted to provide harsh necessity, the system would supply something similar.

Humans, I learned, were more fortunate, if that is how it might be termed: Earth was not as benign as Doria, and humans had competitors against which they had to struggle, along with more frequent moments of cosmic catastrophe and mutating radiation. Humans' view of their environment was not the gentle Doria but, as one human poet described it, "Nature, red in tooth and claw." Fortunate, I say, because humans evolved through struggle and their social systems evolved to ameliorate the pain of survival, not to replicate it. Their aggressive attitudes toward the universe are innate rather than nurtured. Dorians, on the other hand, have to be brutalized before they adopt the more aggressive attitude of humans.

I thought it was time to change. Perhaps the Grandor system was needed at one time, but Dorians had passed that point. Curiosity, learning, the need to achieve, could be instilled at an early age through programs of education. Battle skills and obedience to command could be developed through programs that emulated real conditions rather than replicated them. Dorians, I thought, could be more like humans.

I had two short-cycles to retrain my crew. The lower-ranking crew members were as resistant as the officers. Like them, they had survived the Dorian survival-of-the-fittest system, and they would surrender their attitudes, and their positions of privilege, reluctantly if at all. The process was like retraining an abused animal: repeated kindnesses and frequent strokings are required to reverse a lifetime of avoiding predators and the blows of masters.

I was succeeding, I thought. Morale was higher. The crew seemed once more like my childhood herd, happy, responding better to requests than to orders, coming forward with suggestions, developing into a team rather than a group of individuals. There were throwbacks, to be sure, quarrels, batterings, surly responses, but they were growing progressively less frequent.

And then the war broke out.

* * *

We never knew what started the war, or what was at stake. For long-cycles, after the legendary Galactic War, which probably was a series of wars initiated by a new emerging species, the star empires had worked at keeping the peace. And the uneasy truce that followed the human emergence had seemed a recognition of earlier folly. But it was a truce easily destroyed by a careless action, a misunderstood intrusion, a failure of communication. And then every empire turned upon every other.

Wars are mass confusion; no one knows who is winning until one side turns and runs or loses its will to continue and sues for peace. Only the historians are able to decide who came out ahead and on what terms, and they are often wrong. Interstellar wars are far more difficult to evaluate. News of battles comes only after many cycles, and even then the information is unreliable. How many of the enemy ships were destroyed? How were they identified? What had their mission been? How many ships did the Dorians lose? What were our casualties? How many colonies were destroyed on each side, how many planets laid waste? How many replacement ships have been built? How many crews have been trained? Do we have sufficient resources to withstand the terrible drain of conflict?

Many cycles will be required before any of this becomes clear. The historians are still computing.

At first our enemy was the humans. They were the newcomers, the troublemakers. We fell upon them near the Sirian frontier, and massacred their ships. I tried to stop it, but I had no time after the orders came. And then the humans retaliated, their ships appearing in our midst out of wormholes that we did not suspect, or detect, and wreaked havoc on our fleet. Only the superior organization of my crew allowed the Ardor to survive, damaged as it was. We were the only ship in the fleet to emerge without a casualty, despite being in the midst of the action.

At first the high command accused us of cowardice, but visual records proved the opposite. And then I was given command of a fleet and told to attack the humans in return. I disobeyed. I contacted the human fleet commander and spoke to her in my broken Glish and arranged a meeting. Face-to-face we worked out our differences and I returned to my superiors with the offer of peace. Again I was placed on trial for treason. I almost resorted to a personal challenge of the court, once more, but refrained and argued my case with all the urgency and eloquence I could command.

Reluctantly the high command accepted the terms, and we allied ourselves with the humans against the Sirians and then with the humans and the Sirians against the Aldebarans, and with the humans, the Sirians, and the Aldebarans against the Alpha Centaurans. Finally, exhausted with battle, the galaxy strewn with broken ships, broken worlds, and broken creatures, we made a peace. Ten years of war, a thousand broken planets, and a thousand million casualties, and nothing more. Never again, we vowed, would we go to war. Anyone who broke the peace would be turned upon by all the others. Boundaries were established, spheres of influence were agreed upon, mechanisms for settling disputes were created. We would study war no more.

I returned to Doria a hero, commander of a battle group that had won every engagement, the inventor of new strategies of command and tactics, but most of all, the crafter of peace. I thought I could challenge the high command. I thought my innovations in training and organization would provide a strategy for change. I thought I might even compete to be the successor to the High Dorian. But instead I was once more placed on trial for disobedience and treason, and escaped punishment only through the basic right of personal combat. The high command had succeeded once more. Doria had won but not in the Dorian way, and the high command,

and Doria itself, was not ready to accept victory on any terms but those that emerged from its own traditions. It had used me and now was prepared to throw me away.

I did not blame the high command or Doria. I wasn't good enough. I realized my failings as a Dorian, as a sentient creature. Perhaps no one was good enough. Not on Doria, nor on any world. At least we had peace, and I decided to retire to a world at peace, to a galaxy at peace.

But peace was not so simple. The galactic powers had to set up an interspecies board to evaluate new inventions and their potential for creating change and conferring superiority on one species or another. All such developments, like the human space elevator, had to be shared by all.

And then came transcendentalism with all its mystery and promise. Now, perhaps, I could be good enough, and here I am.

The group dispersed with the silence that in galactic culture represented acceptance or, sometimes, approval, and sought sleep or rest or contemplation, as individual needs and species behavior patterns determined.

CHAPTER EIGHT

Riley awoke with the memory of Tordor's story still winding through his head. He wondered if his pedia was responsible, but for once it was blessedly silent.

When he emerged from his cubicle he found a group of galactics gathered in front of the view screen. He extracted a scanty first meal from the dispensers on the opposite wall: an ambiguous citrus drink in a sealed container with a built-in sipping tube and a bag of unidentifiable synthetic grain. He began sipping the drink as he moved to a spot just behind the group staring at the screen. A stranger would have wondered whether the equipment had been activated. The screen was almost completely dark, with only a flicker of light in the upper right-hand corner that could have been mistaken for static.

"A goodly number of our fellow pilgrims have risen early," Riley said to Asha, who was standing behind the flower child.

"Some do not sleep," Asha said.

"Like you."

"I rest."

"I don't see Tordor."

"Perhaps his storytelling tired him," Asha said.

"Or maybe it was the artfulness," Riley replied, and squeezed a bit of cereal into his mouth.

"But it was a fine story," Asha said. "What do you suppose he meant by 'soul'?"

Riley motioned to Asha that they should move away from the galactics gathered in front of them. He did not know how well they could hear—if they could hear; the flower child had no apparent auditory organs . . . but some conversations should be limited. "He was referring to a remark I made to him earlier—that we needed to understand each other better, to peer into one another's souls. He dismissed it then as 'human mysticism.' We should note the Dorian capacity for irony."

Asha joined him in his strategic withdrawal, although she seemed impatient with his precautions. "The Dorians look plodding and passive, but they have a reputation for subtlety. Grazing leaves time for long, slow thoughts."

"A boy's will is the wind's will," Riley's pedia said, "and the thoughts of youth are long, long thoughts."

That doesn't make sense, Riley thought.

"Rumination and ruminant come from the same root," Asha continued. "Don't underestimate Tordor."

"And don't believe his stories," Riley said, finishing his breakfast. "I understand. What about our situation?" he continued, nodding toward the view screen.

"The captain has announced that the nexus ahead is some days' journey from here and that we should expect no change until further notice."

"And how are our fellow pilgrims reacting?" Riley said. "Sometimes it's hard to tell. But now . . ." He gestured at the galactics clustered like statues in front of the view screen.

"Even galactics have moments of uncertainty," Asha said. "They have a long history of encountering the unknown and somehow making it galactic—"

"They weren't that good with humans," Riley said.

"They thought they knew us, and what they knew they didn't like—the aggression, the arrogance—the kind of behavior galactics have forgotten they themselves ever exhibited. Now they think only about the good of all. Or so they believe."

"We should have been happy with the crumbs they were willing to let fall our way," Riley said.

Asha dismissed his sarcasm with a wave of her hand. "But none of them has ever been this far into the unknown, with no way back. Their galactic confidence doesn't work well out here. They may turn catatonic."

"And yet they continue."

"That's the contradiction. The pull of the transcendental on the other side balanced against the fear of the unknown."

"Why do they do it?" Riley asked.

"Why do you do it?"

Riley shrugged. "I'm not like them. Someday I'll tell you why I'm here."

"I can't wait," Asha said. "I have long suspected that you don't believe in transcendence."

"I'm a hardheaded ex-soldier," Riley said. "I believe in what I can see and touch."

"And maybe you think you can't be improved," Asha said.

"Rather that there's no practical method for making improvements outside of self-discipline and learning from one's failures. A man is what a man is; he recognizes his deficiencies and tries to conquer them or plans around them."

"So—why are you here?"

"Because you're all here," Riley said, "You and the others—you believe in spite of everything you know, in spite of everything life has taught you. Maybe you're right."

"These galactics," Asha said. "Their experience teaches them that there is always something new, something better. But they don't equate that with good; for them change is dangerous. But they have to go find it because to leave it undiscovered is even more dangerous."

"That isn't too much different from most humans," Riley said. "But there are always a few humans, among the rest, who don't believe in the status quo, who look to the future for something better, who believe that in change there is hope. Maybe these galactics belong to that group."

"Or maybe they're sent to make sure that the kind of creatures you're describing don't return to endanger the status quo."

Riley would have replied but he was interrupted by the entrance of Tordor from the corridor outside the passengers' quarters. The weasel followed him.

Tordor said, "Xi reports that he has found the bodies of Jon and Jan in the cold-storage locker."

"This person was checking food stores when the human equivalent withdrew because of cold," Xi said. Even in translation, the "cold" reference seemed scornful. "Xifora are raised to ignore personal suffering."

"Xifora have the evolutionary advantage of being able to re-grow lost appendages," Riley said. "Humans have only one set that must last their entire existences. What happened in the storage locker?"

"This person seized the opportunity to explore two remote cabinets that the human equivalent had avoided. The frozen bodies of the two missing humans were in them."

"Does the human equiv—the crew member—know that the bodies have been discovered?"

"The human equivalent has no knowledge."

Riley looked at Asha. Her expression didn't change. He looked at Tordor, but Tordor's alien face was always unreadable. He looked back at the weasel named "Xi." He must remember that.

"I never forget," his pedia said.

"This person—I thank you for this important information," Riley said. And then to Asha and Tordor, "What do you think this means?"

Asha shrugged.

Tordor said, "The captain told us otherwise. Only he knows why, or why the bodies are in cold storage."

"And what are we to do about them?" Riley said, gesturing at the galactics some meters away staring silently at the display of their celestial isolation.

Tordor flicked his proboscis. "They will adjust."

"For masters of the galaxy," Riley said, "they seem remarkably fragile." Their enraptured positions were beginning to concern him. Many of them hadn't moved since he entered the lounge.

"Masters are only masters in their own domains," Tordor said. "Remove them and they are even less confident than those who have never known security. Galactics have known vastnesses, but these are not the vastnesses they know."

"And if they don't adjust?" Riley insisted.

Tordor flicked his proboscis again. "They will die."

"And you think Asha and I are not affected because we've never been secure in our positions?"

Tordor blew through his long nose. "The polite answer is that the Big Gulf is no more intimidating to humans than the galaxy itself. You have emerged too recently to be affected by the unknown."

"The impolite answer," Asha said, "is that humans are too stupid to realize the peril of the unexplored."

"So much for the pursuit of the transcendental," Riley said. He glanced again at the group in front of the view screen, who represented the best, perhaps, of the ancient species that discovered space-flight long before humanity discovered fire and took dominion over their spiral arm of the galaxy.

"It propels us all," Tordor said, "from the earliest cluster of cells surrendering their comfortable individual existences in order to sample the untested potential of cooperation."

"Evolution equals transcendence?" Riley asked.

"Except evolution has become too slow," Asha said. "Technology has accelerated everything. The environmental change that once took long-cycles now takes only short-cycles and sometimes even days. Such time-spans magnify dangers, and change transforms conditions as we watch." Tordor waved his proboscis in what appeared to be agreement. "For a time sapient creatures such as ourselves substituted social evolution, an attempt to direct natural transcendental forces into safe channels. But we were fools.

"We didn't understand that technology is the new evolution," Asha said, "Like robots, like computers, technology reaches a point where it grows and changes and evolves into something new and strange and unimaginable."

"And so," Tordor said, "the Transcendental Machine was inevitable. We may be fortunate that technology has produced the Transcendental Machine and not the transcendent machine; that technology has offered us the opportunity to perfect ourselves rather than technology itself."

"If, indeed, we are perfectible," Riley said. He turned toward Asha. "You seem to know a lot about galactic matters."

"I spent a good deal of my life among galactics," Asha said, "while you were fighting them. Someday I may tell you about it." She smiled as if to indicate that she knew she was repeating Riley's own nebulous promise. "But galactics are only humanity writ large. They evolved as we did, and from a beginning that none of them understand any more than we do ours. The only difference is that they have had thousands upon thousands of years to get accustomed to difference and how to coexist with it. Now they must face it again. Whether they can adjust again is the question they must answer."

Riley turned to Xi. "What about it? Can you adjust?"

"As easily as growing a new limb," Xi said, exhibiting its new arm.

Riley shrugged and went to see the captain.

The captain was not apologetic. "Where did you get this information?" he demanded. The two of them in his compact quarters were almost nose to nose.

"Does it matter?" Riley asked.

"This is what concerned me when you forced upon me the crazy scheme of passengers mingling with the crew."

"That the truth would emerge?"

"That my authority would be challenged. You can't run a ship like a democracy and certainly not like a galactic consensus council."

"You can't run a ship on lies, either, Ham, and you aren't going to run this ship at all unless you bring the passengers along with you," Riley said. "Right now they're petrified in front of the passenger lounge view screen."

"Our glorious galactics?"

"Yes, and we humans, including your crew, are too dumb to be afraid of the Great Gulf. I've been through all that already with Asha and Tordor. The fact is that the galactics are terrified, like agoraphobics, because they're outside their limits."

As the captain sat down, the stool swung out from the wall to support him before he could reach the floor. He didn't notice. "Then maybe they have ceased to be a factor."

"They'll either be a burden and worthless when they are needed, or they will emerge from their psychological paralysis angry and prepared to lash out at anybody who put them here."

"But they agreed to venture into the Great Gulf!"

Riley leaned back against the bulkhead and folded his arms across his chest. "How many times have you agreed to something under duress and detested the authority that made you choose?"

Ham shrugged. "What makes you think we'll need them?"

"Wherever we're going," Riley said, "we're going to need every body we can call upon. You know what happened when we humans blundered out into a galaxy already owned by older civilizations. The next spiral arm is going to be even more dangerous because it's going to be even more alien."

"What do you expect me to do?"

"The first thing: show me the bodies."

The captain shrugged in resignation and led the way down progressively narrower passageways to the storage compartment at the rear of the ship, next to the engine room. Antique automated equipment chugged away turning refuse into plastic containers and filling them with reconstituted foodstuffs recovered from sources Riley had never wanted to think about. His breakfast turned sour in his stomach and threatened to rise into his throat. At the back of the storage compartment was an insulated hatchway. When the captain activated the lock, the hatch swung open and cold air gushed over Riley.

The captain silently led Riley past upright and horizontal lockers filled with natural and irreplaceable eatables, Riley hoped—though he feared they were empty—until they reached a row of horizontal lockers in a far corner. They were depressingly similar to the cabinets in which the passengers spent their sleep periods.

The captain pulled open the closest of the cabinets. Inside, snuggled in insulating foam, was the body of Jan, eyes closed, face peaceful as if in sleep. The captain motioned to the cabinet just beyond. "Jon is there."

"Why?" Riley asked.

"Jan fell victim to his own assassination plan—or staged event intended to be discovered for reasons not apparent. His death seems to have been an accident."

"How do you know assassination was intended?"

"He arrived on the ship with information about how to activate disabled long-sleep processes, and once aboard he must have obtained information on how to enter the passenger quarters and which cabinet you occupied."

"Presuming I was the intended target and not someone else, or anybody else."

The captain nodded. "Jon told us that much before he froze up—literally. He didn't know about Jan's condition until my first mate let it slip during interrogation, and then Jon turned on some internal apparatus and turned to ice before we could act."

Riley remembered the half-sentient creature in his head and wondered whether it had that capability. "Let's wake them and ask."

The captain shook his head. "Our chances are less than fifty percent. Even at its best, the long-sleep process killed one out of five, as you know. And I don't want assassins wandering around."

Riley didn't tell the captain that at least one other assassin besides himself was wandering around nor that he had instructions to assassinate the Prophet if that became necessary. Instead he said, "Let me see what skills we have among the galactics."

Riley nodded at Asha and Tordor as he returned to the passenger quarters and immediately wondered if Tordor knew what a nod meant. "The bodies are there all right," he told them. He motioned to Xi, who was sucking nourishment from a tube at a different location on the food dispensing wall. "I have seen the bodies that you described," he said. "Where you said they were. How they were."

The galactic's face, as usual, was impossible for Riley to read. He whined. "So," Riley's pedia translated.

"So," Riley said, "they are not dead but frozen, and unless we can think of a reason to thaw them and a way to do it that isn't likely to leave them truly dead they are likely to remain so. Like your fellow galactics." He gestured at the group around the view screen.

"Frozen but not dead?" Tordor said.

"And about as much use," Riley said, and, as if on impulse, spun and made his way through the immobile galactics to the far wall. He reached up into the holographic display and flipped the hidden switch.

The display went dead. The difference was scarcely perceptible, but after a moment the audience reacted, each of the galactics in its characteristic equivalent to a human blinking its eyes and focusing on what was in front. But then, they all moved as one in a surge toward Riley.

"Hold on!" Riley said, as alien noises made talking difficult. "We're fellow pilgrims." Most of the mob didn't stop, but the flower child and the Sirian hesitated.

Then Tordor was beside Riley, speaking basic Galactic. "Stop! Let the human speak."

The mass movement slowed and then stopped, but Riley could not discern any reduction in galactic fury.

"I am here as your representative to report on two matters." The mob tension eased. "The first is that the two human crew members, Jon and Jan, have been found by Xi, and I have observed them in cold storage, frozen but perhaps not dead. They represented a threat to one or more of the passengers, the captain has said, and perhaps to the voyage itself. Whether they will be thawed depends on the captain's assessment of risk and the availability of methods to thaw them successfully. We, too, must consider what information they might provide that is worth the risk to us."

The galactics moved apart and began to look at one another as if questioning their earlier surrender to mob emotion.

"Second," Riley continued, "I ask that you allow the view screen to be turned off until we have something better to observe."

The easing tension seemed to build again, and Tordor gave Riley a sideward glance, which involved a turning of his massive head, as if warning against pursuing this line of discussion.

Riley pressed on. "We're all on board this battered old ship heading into the unexplored in pursuit of the unknown." He paused to let the various pedia do their job. "We humans have been told that we have emerged too recently from the prison of our solar system to appreciate the terrors of the Great Gulf." He paused again. "Maybe so. But we humans know that we would never have emerged if we had allowed ourselves to fear the unexplored, and the experience of your species must have been the same."

He looked over the diverse group assembled in front of him, like a microcosm of the sentient galaxy itself. "To make it through to the other side of the unknown we will need everybody to contribute whatever skills and wisdom they have developed. For that reason we have started telling each other about ourselves so that we can become a successful team. Tordor started, and—" looking up, Riley saw the weasel speaking to Asha "—and Xi will follow."

Xi moved in a way that might have been interpreted in a human as a start of surprise or even of alarm.

The barrel-like Sirian moved forward. Its voice, too, sounded like echoes from the bottom of a barrel. "A nice deference," Riley's pedia translated. "The human is right. We have become feeble of will and weak of action. We should not need the humans to remind us of our responsibilities. We should admit them to our consensus."

The galactics did not seem to confer or move toward one another but a muted cacophony reached Riley and Tordor. "So be it," Tordor said.

He led the way through the throng to the other side of the compartment. "You are members of the community," Tordor said to Riley and Asha. "Not exactly full members, but you will not be excluded from our consensus."

"That's good news," Riley said.

"I am learning the subtleties of human irony," Tordor said.

Riley raised his eyebrows in Asha's direction. "Now," he said, turning to Xi, "we will be looking forward to hearing your story."

"I do not understand the term 'irony,'" Xi said.

CHAPTER NINE

Xi's Story

Xi said:

Xifor is a cruel world of rocky continents and cold seas whose misery is relieved by a few fertile valleys near the equator. According to Xifora scientists, Xifor life began and civilization emerged in those valleys. Xifor's sun is old and dim. Xifora scientists speculate that Xifor was a rocky wanderer from outer space that strayed into the Xifor system late in its evolution and was captured and dropped into orbit by the competing tyranny of its gas giants. Certainly Xifor is unique among the other planets of the system, which are all gas giants, although some have Xifor-size satellites. Some scientists insist that Xifor is one of those satellites torn free by the attraction of a massive passing body and condemned to an obscure orbit among the giants.

No matter. Xifora have always felt that Xifora must fight to stay alive in a universe that does not love these persons. The geology of Xifor means that most Xifora are born and raised in the unforgiving mountains. Many creatures love their planet of origin, but Xifora do not love Xifor. Xifor is respected, like the whip that transforms a weakling into a creature of strength and endurance, but not loved.

Today's Xifora are the descendants of ancestors driven from the fertile valleys by the privileged few, the hereditary nobility that were strong when the land was weak, and seized possession when, for many generations, the land was held by all. When population grew too great, the nobility cast out the persons who tilled the fields and harvested the grain. The exiled Xifora's only food became what these persons could steal from the valley-dwellers or hunt down upon the crags among creatures as hungry as these persons. But these persons scratched terraces out of mountain slopes, domesticated animals for food and clothing and used their dung to fertilize their terraces, stared at the stars, dug deep in the land, and, after many more gemerations, built machines.

Out of deprivation came strength. Out of suffering came a people for whom suffering was a familiar companion. Out of these persons' pain-filled past came these persons' glorious future. Being cast out of paradise made mountain Xifora strong and proud. These persons prospered and the valley-dwellers decayed until these persons prevailed and created a new world—still harsh and beautiful in its harshness, but fair. When the mountain Xifora were strong enough these persons took back the valleys from those persons who had grown soft and weak from lack of struggle.

The mountain Xifora cast out the valley-dwellers to live or die, as the mountain Xifora were forced to do in long-cycles past. From the history of mountain Xifora the Xifora learned the essential lesson the universe has to offer: suffering is good, the easy life is the way to racial ruin, Xifora cannot depend upon the kindness of others, that the only resource Xifora have is these persons' own strength and resolve, even when soaring hatchling rates caused these persons to resort to the same solution as that of the hereditary nobility.

To cope with the ugly reality of their circumstances, Xifora turned to technology. The machines Xifora had developed to make these persons' existence possible and to take back the valleys from the decadent valley-Xifora, these persons now adapted to fly above

the mountains rather than to crawl upon those cold and cruel ex-
crescences of these persons' world. And then these persons looked at
the gas giants that oppressed Xifor and Xifora, and saw those worlds,
like the valley-Xifora, hoarding resources that Xifora could use and
the satellites that could provide a home for more Xifora, perhaps
more hospitable than the Xifor mountains.

Xifora dug ore out of the Xifor mountains and smelted the ore
into metal and worked the metal into ships that conquered empty
space, mined the atmospheres of the gas giants for precious fuel and
materials, and took the satellites as these persons' own. Within a few
centuries the Xifora had turned this oppressive system into new and
better Xifors. The pygmy interloper became the master of the entire
system. The Xifor will conquered the giants' power.

Life went too well. Some of the satellites were more favored by
geology and climate than rocky Xifor, and their Xifora became as
soft and decadent as the valley-dwellers. The governors responded,
acting with stern kindness to transport children to the remote areas
of the home planet to harden or die. Many died, but many survived,
prepared now to suffer as a way of life and to act as needed without
direction.

But with machines to protect these persons from the cruelties of
nature, even Xifor became too soft, and the Xifora turned these
persons' eyes to the stars, knowing that the stars were cold and distant and uncaring, and that space itself, like the remote regions of
Xifor, was the ultimate test of Xifora will and strength. Xifora ventured forth and discovered that the galaxy was not as empty as the
giants' satellites; like the valleys, it was already owned. Once more the
Xifora were thwarted, deprived of the Xifora birthright. Here, again,
the Xifor past informed the Xifor present: Xifora would be better
and tougher, more determined to succeed and more willing to persist
over long-cycles, over failures, than other galactics.

So events have gone, these long-cycles past. Gradually, through faith and perseverance, the Xifora have become one of the co-equal members of the galactic ruling council, recognized for Xifora determination to succeed over obstacles, Xifora willingness to sacrifice for Xifora beliefs, Xifora inventiveness in solving great problems, and Xifora—but Xifora must not be boastful. It suits Xifora temperament best to suffer in silence and revenge at length.

All this account is one reason for Xifora sympathy for humans, who emerged into the galaxy to find it already populated and settled and governed by others, just as Xifora discovered, in long-cycles past. But Xifora find impatience and complaint offensive, and for these barbarisms Xifora do not like humans.

All this is prologue to this person's story. Xifora are hatchlings, and like all hatchlings, dangerous companions. Xifora know that in the mountains Xifora live or die alone. So life was for this person. This person was the smallest of a brood of a dozen hatchlings, of which five died and were eaten in the nest. This person would have been eaten as well had not this person's cleverness and will led to survival in this person's first days out of the shell. This is the way of the nest: hatchlings eat or are eaten. Those that the stronger hatchlings could not fall upon and eat they delighted in tormenting, depriving them of food, tearing away limbs in sport, or so the stronger hatchlings call it. Those persons called it part of the Xifor way, to make sure the fittest survive, but the game was actually survival itself. The fewer that survived the more food and more status for those who lived.

This person survived the loss of numerous limbs, usually one and never more than two at a time. Others, in this nest and neighboring nests, were less fortunate: if three limbs were lost, the game is lost. The fourth limb would be doomed, and the hatchling consumed before the limbs could grow back. This person understood that consequence early, concealed food in a corner of the home nest where a rock could be rolled into place, and retreated there furtively and in haste as soon as a limb was lost. Many periods were spent growing new limbs.

The only safe time was during school hours when hatchlings were taught the history of oppression and the language and tools of justice. Science explained the unloved place of Xifora in the universe, and technology provided the means by which Xifora could liberate Xifora from the cruel Xifor environment. School was good, not least because it provided a period when survival was not at stake and wits could be turned to the larger issues that lay ahead. And the best part was that the worst hatchling tormentors were the poorest students; those persons who depend upon size and power discovered that strength alone was not enough, that the mind had powers beside which the greatest physical endowments dwindled to insignificance.

Where were these persons' parents while these cruel games continued, the listener to this story may ask. Such a question would never have occurred before Xifora encountered the Galactic Federation, where mercy is considered a virtue. Xifora parents were like Xifor itself: hard, demanding, unsentimental. Like Xifor, parents bred offspring hardy and self-reliant. Those persons survived who should survive because those persons were strong of body or will; the weak failed and were eaten; and thus Xifora grew stronger and more capable with each generation.

Before this person left the nest, this person found a piece of unusually hard wood that this person sharpened to a point by rubbing it hour after hour against a rock, and this stick became a defense against this person's nestlings. After a few accidents to other hatchlings, this person lost no limbs from personal teasing. Instead this person took vengeance against this person's chief tormentor, Vi, the largest and most promising of the nestlings. When attacked once more, rather than losing a limb this person raised his pointed stick and Vi ran upon it, in that person's vulnerable eating sack. After the accident, this person stood aside while the tormentor was consumed by the other nestlings. Vi was gone and would torment no more; this person did not need to consume any of the remains to be strong.

As soon as the feast was over, this person left the nest and began existence in the mountains of northern Xifor. The nights were cold and the days only slightly warmer, but this person soon trapped a furry creature and fashioned warm garments from its hide. This person stole fire, cooked meat, and fashioned weapons, first a sling for propelling rocks, then a mechanism for projecting small, pointed spears, and finally, when a dump of discarded materials was stumbled upon, weapons shaped from metal scraps, and then tools that this person used to build smelters for ore, and finally to construct machines.

When this person was nearly adult, this person encountered this person's parents once more. This person recognized them by their resemblance to Vi and by their family pheromones, and for a moment ancient fears and hatreds flared. The natural attempt to kill this person was anticipated and foiled, with only the loss of a single limb by the female parent. Then this person convinced the parents that this person was indeed a member of the parents' brood, that the killing of the largest and most promising of the brood was justified, and that this person's survival should be celebrated and not condemned. This person demonstrated the machines this person had built. Suitably impressed, the parents accepted this person as a member of their family and enrolled this person in a scientific academy situated near the equator.

There, not far from the valleys where the Xifora had developed from clumsy beasts crawling out of the sea onto the land, this person learned Xifor history, art, science, and technology. This person also learned that the machines in which this person had placed so much pride had been invented before, and better. The discovery was a lesson in humility that this person carries to this moment. With that insight, this person's career as an inventor and a scientist came to an abrupt end. Instead, this person became a philosopher and a politician. On Xifor the callings are almost identical.

Then, fatefully, this person was discovered. Not by the most able leader of Xifora history, Xidan, but by that person's chief assistant, Xibil, who had been the philosopher behind Xidan's resplendent political career. In this person Xibil saw a promise that no other person had observed: the ability to produce new solutions to old problems. This person's real life began.

Xidan had not been responsible for the invention and production of spaceships that occupied the satellites of the gas giants, nor the interstellar flight that made contact with the Galactic Federation, nor, indeed, with the negotiations that resulted in the acceptance of Xifor as a junior member of the federation. All these events happened many long-cycles earlier. Xidan's great accomplishment was to bring all the colonies of Xifor under the absolute control of the native world and with the loss of only a few million Xifora lives and only a single satellite. Under Xidan, Xifor finally gained full membership on the Galactic Council.

All was good; Xifor was beginning to reap the benefits of galactic goodwill and the full range of galactic science and invention. Xifora basked in the illusion that the universe had changed and the stare of hatred had become the smile of love. And then humans emerged into the galaxy. Unlike the Xifora, humans were unwilling to accept a proper role as apprentice galactics. Humans insisted on full membership immediately. Old allegiances were threatened. Ancient agreements were broken. War happened.

War, Xifora understand, was the natural condition of the universe. Xifora were born with this knowledge. Xifora must kill or be killed, eat or be eaten. But, as Xibil has eloquently explained, sublimation of this instinct to survive by all and any means, and the sublimation of the instinct to defend these persons' territory and these persons' honor to the death, was the price of civilization. To honor that hard-won principle Xifor produced warships for the federation and manned them and thrust them into battle. No longer were hatchlings killed, but instead sent forth in geometric numbers to Xifora the battleships. Xifora pride themselves that Xifora numbers and Xifora production were a major component of galactic strategy.

Humans would have been defeated within hours and forced back into the nothingness from which they came if other galactics, less committed than Xifora to the consensus principles of the federation or sensing an opportunity for political advantage, had not protected the humans from the righteous rebuke of the Galactic Federation.

This person volunteered to be among the warriors, but Xibul insisted that this person's best place was in Xifor councils, to help plan the tactics of battle and the strategies of the peace that, sooner or later, would follow. The end of war, Xibul counseled, was the time when scales were rebalanced and adjustments were made, when the ready had the chance to seize power and to hold it, just as the Xifora nobility had seized the valleys long-cycles before. Xifor could become one of the major powers, perhaps the major power, in the council rather than a junior member, seldom heard and often ignored. Xifora were small but Xifora would not be overlooked.

One of the tactics this person proposed, which became standard battle procedure, was the sacrifice of a part—a ship, a fleet, or a world—to gain an overall advantage. The peculiar advantage of this tactic is that it is rooted in Xifora physiology and evolution: in personal strife, clever Xifora emerged victorious by offering an arm while the other appendage wielded a deadly weapon.

Envious rivals spread the rumor that the tactic originated with a subordinate and not with this person. Every administration was ripe with such knife wielders; the secret to survival was not to offer a back to colleagues. Such an accusation was easy to dismiss: Xifor tradition and law prescribed that all products of labor or thought were the rightful property of the superior; the unfortunate subordinate died by accident before the subordinate could confirm this person's primacy, but after that no question was raised.

Before the subordinate's body was cold, the tactic was directly communicated to Xidan. Xibil was involved in discussions concerning the next envoy to the Galactic Council, the previous envoy having been killed when the envoy's ship was attacked by a human vessel.

Only after the war did this person discover that the tactic of sacrifice had been discovered independently by humans. Even though humans were too soft to accept sacrifice willingly, humans had a strange custom in which those persons modeled human behavior in something called "games," which those persons then applied to everyday behavior, including war. Thus the tactic was not as successful as this person or Xidan had hoped, nor Xibil had feared.

Xibil, to be sure, had accepted this person's strategy as proper Xifora behavior, recognizing the fate of ingenious subordinates. Then as quickly as the war had begun the war ended in a truce. Xifor opposed the end of hostilities, but the envoy's death left it with little influence, and even the passionate words of the assistant envoy, who fortunately had survived the attack that killed the envoy, went unheeded. Less hardened galactics had tired of sacrifice and traded honor for peace.

Now was the time for Xifor to act. While other galactics were fatigued by war and eager for peace at any price, Xifor determination and willingness to sacrifice would give Xifor the opportunity to seize the Galactic Council and shape the federation's future. Xidan turned to Xibil and asked Xibil to accept the position of envoy to the council. Xibil accepted on the condition that Xifor sacrifice its ambitions on behalf of federation harmony and civilization.

Then Xibil met with an unfortunate accident.

In the tradition of Xifor, Xidan turned to Xibil's assistant, and this person was named envoy but without the unnatural conditions for sublimating Xifora behavior that Xibil had urged. Many time periods elapsed before this person joined the council and came to an understanding of the council's operation and secret levers of power. The council was a large and deliberative body that, like a glacier, moved slowly but inexorably downhill, seeking consensus. The council was hard to stop and impossible to steer; the council could only be shattered into maneuverable segments.

The council was a devastating disappointment. This person had expected opposition but found turgid indifference. Other council members were older and, let this be admitted in all humility, wiser. This person tried to move the inertia of the council into action, with Xifor at its head. This person was listened to and agreed with but nothing happened. No opposition could be identified; no other person stood in the way; an accident to any person or group of persons would change nothing.

This person learned patience.

Patience brought with it an acceptance of the way things are, and a hope that change would emerge through a slow accumulation of minor alterations. That was not the Xifor way; it was the Galactic Federation's way. The galaxy turned slowly, and the spiral arms were distant. The federation was old, and it had gotten old by minimizing change and its accompanying potential for conflict. The emergence of humans had disturbed the galactic balance; change had occurred, and the federation didn't like change. Now, with the Great Truce established, the federation was ready to return to the ancient ways that had worked so well for so many eons, keeping aliens from the breathing tubes of other aliens.

And then word came of a new Prophet emerging. Without a name, without an origin or place, without a species identification or description, a creature was rumored to have announced the possibility of transcendence—not the long Xifora way of deprivation and inner strength but an instantaneous mechanical ascension. This person cannot describe the state of chaos in the Federation Council that followed this unsubstantiated rumor. The old and wise councilors became frantic and frightened. Evolution was understood by all, but evolution was slow and the massive federation could adjust. Physical transcendence could happen instantly. A person or a species could, it was feared, gain superiority. The current balance—some have called the condition "stasis"—was threatened. All sentient life might be terminated.

Councilors dispersed across the galaxy, fleeing home for consultation or consolation. This person did not, knowing that the change this person had sought had become change of another sort, but change nevertheless, and in change is the possibility of something better. Xifora share that with humans.

Xifora also share with humans a passion for transcendence. Not in the human way, for humans already believe they are a favored species, chosen for greatness, deserving of good fortune; while Xifora

knew that all life was a cosmic accident, an improbable joke, and
that Xifora had been badly treated from Xifora's earliest existence
and must fight for everything. Somewhere, somehow, the universe
owed Xifora transcendence.

Then came an intervention. This person was summoned to a
meeting of soft-spoken aliens. What kind of aliens, this person
could not identify, for the aliens used distortion fields and translation devices to conceal their species. But the aliens made clear what
this person had not yet suspected, that the members of the Galactic
Council were not the supreme legislators of the galaxy, or perhaps
not the only supreme legislators, that other, unknown forces operated at a distance though perhaps even more effectively.

Whether economic, political, or religious, these forces acted with
great decision and foresight. The aliens informed this person that
the new religious fervor sweeping the galaxy could be a blessing or
a threat. If true, transcendentalism could cause the start of a new war
that would destroy the galaxy, when one species achieved transcendence and tried to exert its superiority; or it could be the beginning
of a new and greater federation in which every species would achieve
its own perfection and the galaxy would blossom with wealth, art,
and goodwill. If untrue, transcendentalism could send the galaxy
into a depression of disappointed expectations from which it might
not emerge for long-cycles; or the concept of the new religion could
be adopted by the proper authorities to set the galaxy on a path toward individual species betterment that would launch a new era of
mutual aspiration and tolerance.

What transcendentalism is, the aliens said, must be discovered,
and this person was ordered to find out, to join the pilgrimage, to
determine if the Prophet was on board the ship, and to learn whether
the Transcendental Machine was real and how it worked and to
bring it back, or if this person could not do one of those things, to

destroy the Prophet or the machine before the Prophet or the machine could be misused by the wrong persons or species.

This person reveals these truths now because the facts have become apparent: the Prophet is aboard the *Geoffrey*, although not revealed; and the machine, therefore, may well be real; and other creatures aboard also have been commissioned by unknown powers—Jon and Jan, no doubt, and perhaps others. This person's revelation may be doubted. Why should this person reveal this person's mission? Reasons are many; the time for revelation is at hand. If this pilgrimage is to succeed, all must work for all.

And so, in full knowledge that this person was betraying Xidan's trust and this person's opportunity to seize greatness for this person and for Xifor, this person abandoned this person's post without informing Xidan, found resources unexpectedly in this person's accounts, and took passage for Terminal.

This person chose Terminal because of the direction of the secret power, but why did the many persons gathered here choose Terminal? This person will not recount the many difficulties this person had to overcome to reach the place from which this ship departed. All persons gathered here survived similar obstacles, and many others surely misread the signs and flocked elsewhere to wait for a ship that never came.

That would have been a proper fate for a Xifora.

CHAPTER TEN

Xi's story kept replaying in Riley's mind as he went about his preparations for another wake period. Or maybe his pedia was the one mulling Xi's narrative as Riley waited in line for the shower. Many of the aliens never bathed; others had special needs met, no doubt, as unsatisfactorily as his. The chemical sprays besieged him from all sides for mere seconds, then were sucked back into multiple outlets and followed by gusts of drying air. He emerged into the stark dressing cubicle feeling scarcely cleaner than when he entered.

Why had Xi confessed to a meeting with unknown and unseen powers, so much like, and yet so much unlike, his own? Did it know of Riley's encounter and was it trying to elicit a similar confession from Riley? Or did it want to tell Riley, subtly, that it knew all about Riley and his situation and that they were linked together by unseen threads? Or that they acted for potential adversaries and to warn him against carrying out his orders? Or that they might need to join forces at some point to achieve mutual ends?

Was Xi overcome by the spirit of the tale-telling moment to reveal information it otherwise would have kept hidden? Or was its motive the one it had related? How could one know these things about an alien, particularly one hatched from an egg and who could grow new limbs?

"I'm not sure these stories are working out the way you planned," Asha said. "They're raising more questions than they answer."

Riley looked at her. She never lined up for the shower—or maybe, since she never seemed to sleep, she used the shower in the depths of the sleep period. She never seemed to need it. She was always clean, always neatly dressed in worn space coveralls, always attractive—not beautiful but with a pleasing shape that suggested itself under unrevealing clothing, and an appearance that said, "This is a healthy woman with a quick and independent mind, who is close to realizing whatever her potential might be—and someone it would be dangerous to take lightly."

"She is the only woman within light years," his pedia said. "You shouldn't let that fact cloud your judgment. She may be your most dangerous adversary."

Riley wasn't sure she wanted to be appreciated as a woman. He had no hint that she did. But why was she on this pilgrimage?

"I never thought they would unmask anyone," Riley said. "But I think we are getting to know ourselves a bit better—the lies we tell about ourselves may be more revealing than the truths we incautiously reveal."

"You're subtler than I thought."

"I'm not just an unlettered ex-soldier."

"I never thought you were. No one ventures on a pilgrimage like this without some stirrings of intellect."

"Or imagination," Riley said. "Intellect alone would instruct us to stay home where there is some small chance of success."

Asha nodded. "We need both—the imagination to perceive where the pilgrimage will lead us and the intellect to get us there despite great difficulties."

"At least we learned from Xi that powerful agencies are at work in the galaxy—"

"That was not news to me," Asha said, "and, I'm sure, not to you."

"And that they have their hand in what happens on this pilgrimage—"

"That, too."

"And in what happens on this ship."

"We all have agendas," Asha said, "including Tordor and me—and you."

"And what is your agenda?" Riley asked.

"I'll show you mine if you'll show me yours," she said.

But before either of them could reveal anything, Tordor arrived. Riley looked at him as if he thought that, in answer to Asha's accusation, Tordor was about to confess to secret agendas. When he looked at Asha, he thought she was looking at Tordor the same way. Tordor looked at them, first one and then the other, as if he understood that he had interrupted something important, and that, maybe, they were expecting something of him. The Dorian said, "The situation has changed. The captain has locked us in."

He led them to the hatch, saying, "Kom told me that when it went to begin its duty tour with the crew the door would not open."

"And who is Kom?" Riley asked.

"The Sirian," Tordor said, as if surprised that Riley didn't know the Sirian's name.

Kom was waiting for them by the hatch, its hooded eyes open wide but inscrutable in the relative darkness. It stood, impassive, its fins pressed flat, more like a statue than a living being. In spite of the creature's effort to contain its internal heat, Riley could feel it radiating from the high-temperature alien.

Riley squatted down to examine the lock. He tried the combination that had released it earlier, then punched combinations randomly, hoping that his pedia would find one that worked. But his pedia did not respond and the hatch remained stubbornly shut.

Riley ran his fingers around the edge of the hatch.

"What are you doing?" Tordor asked.

"The edges are still warm," Riley said.

"What does that mean?"

"The captain has welded the door shut," Asha said. "He's locked us in."

Riley looked at the others. "Let's keep it among ourselves until we've figured out what to do. No use starting a riot."

Kom uttered a series of sounds that Riley's pedia translated as, "Galactics do not riot."

"They gave a good imitation last wake period," Riley said.

"I could break through the hatch," Tordor said.

Riley eyed Tordor's bulky body. "No doubt. But surely the captain is prepared for that."

"I could melt my way through the weld," Kom said, extending a digit. "Sirians possess extremely efficient means to control and direct their body heat mechanisms."

"That we can always do," Riley said. He looked at Kom's body, shaped with ribs and fins like a radiator. Once more he marveled at the adaptability of life in the universe. "But I suggest we analyze the situation before we react."

Tordor said, "You are not offended?"

Kom's sounds, like the bubbling of a pot, were translated as, "A human should not interfere with the actions of a galactic."

Riley looked at Kom as if he could read something into the Sirian's leathery features. For all he knew Sirians expressed emotions by a fluttering of fins or a release of pheromones. "To be offended is to lose control of the situation," he said. "First we might decide what the captain has to gain, or what we stand to lose."

"The only thing that has changed is the discovery of the bodies of Jan and Jon," Asha said.

"That we know of," Riley said.

"Possibly the captain doesn't want them revived," Tordor contributed. "They might reveal information that would endanger this journey."

"Or the captain's intentions for it," Riley said.

"Do you think those are different from ours?" Asha asked.

"Aren't all of ours different?" Riley replied.

"We have agreed about that," Asha said. "And yet, how different are the captain's?"

"But why has the captain locked us in now?" Tordor asked. "What has happened other than the discovery of the frozen crew members?"

"The captain may have heard Xi's story," Riley said, "and learned of other forces at work."

"Surely that should have come as no surprise," Asha said.

"And how would he hear?" Tordor asked.

"Perhaps these quarters have been wired," Riley said. "That would be a prudent action. Or he may have an informant in our midst. That, too, would be prudent."

Tordor and Asha looked around the cramped quarters and the odd collection of aliens, each with its own history, each with its own biology and environmental challenges, each with its own evolutionary path toward sentience and galactic union. No one could be trusted to act on behalf of a common goal. Their motives were as different as the odors they emitted, some inadvertently, some as pheromones or even vehicles of communication.

"On the other hand," Riley said, "the captain is not necessarily a prudent man."

"You know him," Asha said.

It was not a question, but Riley answered anyway. "We have a history in the Terran fleet."

"What are the chances of that?"

"Slim and none," Riley said. "Clearly events are being steered by unknown—and unseen—forces."

Without warning, the ship plunged into a Jump. The walls wavered around them. Riley grabbed for Asha and then for the solidity of Tordor. Kom stood there solidly, ready for anything and surprised by nothing. Rather than the disappearance of the surrounding ship and the illusion of floating in no-space, reality spun around them, alternating between ship and no-space in a mad frenzy of sensory chaos. The ship shuddered, and they almost lost their balance in spite of Tordor's tripod. Riley reached out to touch the wall, apprehensive that his fingers might sink deep or pass through entirely. Over the years, he had been through countless Jumps, but this one was unlike any other.

Finally—it must have been no longer than a few seconds—the universe settled back into its normal solidity, and the ship's walls stabilized. Riley released his grasp on Tordor and then, more reluctantly, on Asha. Tordor stood impassively, as if untouched by the experience. Asha rubbed her upper arm where Riley's fingers had tightened.

Riley finally spoke. "That was as bad a Jump as I've ever experienced."

"Perhaps we have overestimated the captain's skill," Tordor said.

"Or perhaps the captain's coordinates are off," Asha said.

"Or perhaps," Riley said, his words coming slowly, "the captain has been given the wrong coordinates."

The three of them considered the matter while Kom stood impassively, two paces away, next to the frozen hatch.

"Which means," Riley went on, "that we may not be able to find our way back."

"What do you mean?" Tordor asked.

"If the coordinates are slightly off," Riley said, "they will be off even more on the return trip. And that may be what the creature who has been providing the captain with guidance wants."

"Either success or death," Asha said, as if amused by the thought.

"Or total dependence on the unknown navigator," Riley said.

The three of them considered the implications of what had just happened—the welded hatch and then the ragged Jump.

"What did you mean, 'the unknown navigator'?" Asha asked.

"The captain is getting his coordinates in periodic transmissions from someone within the ship," Riley said. "Someone he doesn't know. Or so he says."

"Do you believe him?"

"Clearly he had to get them from somewhere," Riley said. "The Great Gulf is uncharted."

"That can't be true," Tordor said.

"Why not?" Riley asked.

"The ship has Jumped through three nexus points already."

"Using coordinates transmitted to the captain's pedia," Riley said.

"But where did the coordinates come from?" Tordor insisted.

Riley shrugged.

"Tordor has a point," Asha said. "Someone went this way before, or there would be no nexus points to transmit, and no report of a Transcendental Machine."

"If the reports are not fabricated, or distortions of all myths," Riley said.

"The fact that the nexus points have worked so far—even though the last coordinates may have been off-center—indicates that somewhere a chart exists," Tordor said.

"How could it?" Riley asked.

"The same way all the other charts were created—by some galactic ship coming upon a spatial anomaly and risking everything to explore it. All sorts of nexus charts float out there in the cybersphere," Tordor said, "some of them thousands, even hundreds of thousands of years old, some legitimate, some spurious, all of them suspect. No respectable galactic would risk his life or his ship to one of them."

"But a human might," Asha said.

"Yes," Tordor agreed, "a human might."

"Because they have so little to lose?" Riley asked.

"That," Tordor said, "and they are so young a species that their risk-taking gene has not yet been hobbled by their wisdom gene."

Riley thought about the matter for a moment before he shrugged. "You may be right. But it doesn't get us to the issue of who is supplying the coordinates to the captain."

"Not one of the crew," Tordor said. "Surely the captain would be able to identify a plant."

"Not if those who assigned him to this ship wanted another agent to control the journey," Asha said. "Unknown forces are at work within our midst. There is nothing that proves they are not at work within the crew as well."

How much does Asha know? Riley wondered. *How much does she suspect?*

"Your suspicions are not only appropriate," his pedia said, "but should be extended to everyone else on board this vessel."

"The captain thinks the only being who would have the coordinates is the Prophet itself," Riley said. "The Prophet could be among the crew, but is more likely to have shipped aboard as passenger."

"If the Prophet exists," Tordor said, "and is not merely a convenient myth."

"Maybe we should search everybody's pedia for the charts," Asha said.

"We all know that isn't going to happen," Riley said.

Tordor didn't have to answer. No galactic would allow its near-symbiotic relationship with its pedia to be violated.

"So," Riley said, "it is likely that the Prophet sent off-center coordinates for a purpose."

"Unless," Asha said, "the coordinates simply get increasingly inaccurate as the ship gets further into the Great Gulf."

"Or unless the captain himself wanted to eliminate the possibility of return," Tordor said. "He could have cut the bridge to the other spiral arm himself."

"Or made us all dependent on his coordinates to get us back," Riley said.

"And you still think we should wait for the captain to make a move before we break out of our confinement?" Asha said.

Riley shrugged. "I have the feeling the captain will act before we do."

"Kom is able, still, to melt the welds," Kom said.

Riley had forgotten the Sirian was nearby, and hearing everything. "Not yet. I have the feeling that it's better for the captain to recognize his own mistake."

As if in response, the edges of the hatch began to glow, and, moments later, the hatch opened. The captain was on the other side, looking in at them with an expression of glowering intensity. "All right," he said. "What are the right coordinates?"

Riley stepped forward to take the captain's arm in his right hand. The captain looked down at it coldly, but Riley didn't remove it.

"This isn't the place to discuss coordinates," Riley said. He nodded at Kom. "Maybe it isn't the place to discuss why you welded us in."

"Where then?" the captain said.

"We have no privacy here," Riley said. He turned to look at the multipurpose lounge filled with aliens, who were still unaware that they had been imprisoned but still milling around uncertainly, talking about the ragged Jump.

The captain turned to crew territory. "Come with me."

Riley motioned to Tordor and Asha to accompany him and they followed the captain through the passageway, no longer as redolent, no longer shabby. When the small group reached the captain's quarters, the captain turned and looked angrily at those who had followed. Riley turned. Behind him were not only Tordor and Asha but Kom as well. Riley should have recognized the heat source earlier.

"We can't all squeeze into my office," the captain said.

"The crew's lounge won't work for reasons that may be obvious," Riley said. "How about the control room?"

Sourly the captain agreed, turned and put his hand against the reader of the hatch nearby, and entered when it cycled open. He dismissed the two crewmen on duty there and then waited while the four passengers entered. Even the control room was crowded, hot from the Sirian's radiations, and destined to get even hotter.

The displays above the control panel were black—not because

they were turned off but because the ship had been swallowed by the Great Gulf.

"All this," the captain said, "to answer my question about the correct coordinates?"

"All this," Riley said, "to get an answer to why you shut us in."

"Nothing else seemed to work."

"That wouldn't have worked, either, if we had decided to defy your efforts and break out," Riley said.

"Is not proper," Kom said in Galactic Standard, "to confine galactics."

The captain seemed to restrain resentment at the contempt displayed by the Sirian. "Put it down to a moment of pique," he said finally. "As captain of this ship, I had had enough of my supercargo's infuriating interference."

"Nothing more?" Tordor asked.

"Nothing more that I'm going to discuss with this ad hoc group," the captain said defiantly.

"Nothing to do with the proposal to thaw Jan and Jon?" Asha asked.

"I've said all I'm going to say about the matter. Now I want to know who is transmitting coordinates," the captain said. "I'm sure Riley has told you that I am getting my coordinates transmitted by someone within the ship, certainly a passenger, and probably the Prophet. The last Jump was almost a catastrophe that could have destroyed the ship and everyone aboard . . . galactics as well as humans," he added after a hesitation.

"But apparently carefully calculated," Riley said.

"Off just enough to eliminate any possibility of returning but close enough to complete the Jump," Asha said. "That takes a lot of computing power. And maybe experience. The sort of computing power and experience available to a ship's captain."

"Nonsense," the captain said.

Riley studied his former shipmate. "I, for one, believe you," he said.

"Thanks," the captain said.

Riley understood the irony that the galactics probably missed. "But the fact is, we're committed to going on, and our only hope of getting back is if whoever is sending the coordinates decides to send you the right ones—and you trust them. Or we find the Transcendental Machine and it allows us to do whatever transcendental thing is required."

"Or we find whoever—or whatever—is sending the coordinates and get the complete set, or the charts that generate them," the captain said.

"You know how unlikely that is," Riley said.

"No galactic, coordinate sender or not, would allow his pedia to be searched," Tordor said.

"Then we're at an impasse," the captain said.

"No," Asha said. "We can go forward. Now that the passenger hatch has been unsealed, the coordinate sender may well send the next coordinates."

The captain looked surprised. "I've just received new coordinates," he said.

"Which means," Riley said, "that none of us is the sender."

"Return to your quarters so that I can input the new coordinates," the captain said. After seeing the looks he got from all four of them, he added, "No more sealing of hatches. I promise."

"And the revival of Jon and Jan," Kom said unexpectedly. "I have experience in such matters."

The captain looked uncomfortable, but nodded.

When they returned to the passengers' quarters, Riley turned to Kom. "You have experience in thawing humans?"

"I will tell you all my story," Kom said.

CHAPTER ELEVEN

Kom's Story

Kom said:

The life of Sirians is dominated by their suns. Sirius is a hot, bluish-white star with a white-dwarf companion, and its planets are all gas giants except for a few rocky quasiplanets beyond the farthest giant's orbit. The habitable worlds in the system are all satellites, some of them larger than the planets of less dominant suns, and Komran is one of them. It revolves around the gas giant Sirians call Kilran.

Komran is the second-largest satellite of the fourth gas giant from the sun. As a satellite, it bakes in Sirius's glare half a day and freezes in Kilran's shadow for the other half, while Komran rotates a half-turn to bring each of its hemispheres alternately into light and shadow. Komran, then, is enslaved to Kilran but tyrannized by Sirius. Sirians must adjust to this complex climatic state.

Earth, I have learned, has a hot period of half a year over most of its surface followed by a cold period that lasts the other half. Komran has a summer and winter every day, a cycle moderated only by Kilran's gravitational attraction, which Komran translates into internal warmth, and by planet-shine.

Life struggled to come into existence on Komran. Not only was life inhibited by temperature extremes, but the incessant movement of the world's crust caused by Kilran's constant push and pull trapped life-forms under falls of rock and surging seas, and the creatures that finally emerged were hardy and temperature-sensitive. They thrived for half a day in the warmth and shut down for half a day in the cold until, finally, they evolved more efficient mechanisms for controlling internal temperature in the form of their present beautiful radiating fins. It is this triumph of matter over energy that makes Sirians fierce competitors and even fiercer friends, and it is their unique planetary situation that makes Sirians special in the galaxy.

Sirians are live-born but immature, like larvae. They develop inside their fathers' bodies for a period as long as they gestate inside their mothers. The maturing process, consuming special food stored for their nurturing during the mother's gestation, is idyllic, and remembered by adults as the happy time when food was always available, when temperature was constant, and when there was no competition. It is this time that Sirians long to regain, that controls their lives and shapes their dreams.

For reasons that are beyond rational analysis, Sirians associate that dream with Sirius's companion star. That white-dwarf sun is always assumed, never named. Although Sirius gave us birth, the companion gives us aspirations. To live in the feeble glow of its blessed rays is every Sirian's consuming passion. But the companion star has no planets. Creation myths tell Sirians that our companion sun is the source of our existence, that it once was even larger than Sirius but was diminished by the nurturing of a group of worlds that were stolen away by his mate and given as satellites to the gas giants. In sorrow and dismay at the inevitable end of love, the companion sun at first became angry and red with rage, but weakened by the nurturing process and by the betrayal of its mate it collapsed into its present shrunken state, all life gone but for a feeble glow.

Some astronomers confirm these myths with speculation that the satellites of the gas giants such as Kilran were indeed the offspring of the white dwarf who shall not be named. Others, less mystical, believe that they were once independent worlds of Sirius captured by the gas giants, or worlds drawn into the system from the great disk of planetary matter beyond the farthest giant.

Our astronomers tell us that beliefs about the dwarf companion who shall not be named are ancestral memories of the Sirian system, that the companion went through a normal cycle of expansion and collapse, that its planets, if it had any, were consumed in its red, expansion stage, or expelled into the great darkness. But Sirians have nightmares of being stolen from heaven, never to return, by a powerful blue-white goddess.

Sirians imagine that if they were more powerful, if they could only perfect themselves, they could build a new world around the companion and protect it from the tyranny of their hot blue sun, or liberate Komran itself from the grasp of Sirius as well as Kilran, and rejoin their father. There, on this paradisiacal dream world, they would shed their fins and live as beings that choose their own fates rather than having them chosen by their solar goddess.

All that is mythology, of course. Sirians know this, but they are dominated by it anyway. I tell you this because these facts control who we are and why we think and behave the way we do, and, ultimately, why I am here, with you, on this ship.

After we have eaten our way out of the father's body, changed, fully developed but still small, often the father dies, having not stored sufficient food for the brood or having a larger brood than customary, or not being strong enough to sustain his own vitality while nurturing the brood. For these reasons families are carefully planned in these days of scientific understanding, and Sirian females choose mates with care. Today only one father out of ten dies, and the death of the father is considered the fault of the female, a crime that is often punished, sometimes up to and including execution. But some fates are worse than death.

Becoming a father, however it turns out, is a life-changing experience entered into only by the brave and the strong. Even if a father survives, he often is damaged by the experience so that he lives a life shortened by physical debility and an uncertain ability to control internal temperature, which itself can be fatal. No male is a father more than once, and used-up males litter the nursing homes and retirement villas. Some philosophers advocate voluntary suicide or euthanasia to clear the scene for greater Sirian accomplishment.

The continual flexing of Komran's surface is a second fact of life. Sirians are born knowing that the stability of the land itself is undependable. This understanding gives Sirians an advantage over many species that have an unreasonable confidence in their physical circumstances. Sirians know that the unexpected can happen at any moment, that they cannot trust their environment, and that they must be ready to adjust to any emergency. This realization made them daring sailors on Komran's tumultuous seas, and, once spaceflight began, sure space voyagers and confident warriors.

And, to say truth, it is safer to be a sailor or a space voyager or a warrior than a nurturing male.

I do not remember when I ate my way through the belly of my father after the food he had stored was consumed by his greedy offspring, but my father told me stories about it and I saw it happen to others. I dreamed about it often. My father was a great male. After separating myself from my siblings, my father told me about treating his nurturing pouch with antibiotics and then sewing up the holes we unthinking creatures had chewed. Out of all the others, he picked me as the repository of his wisdom, and we spent many happy hours together as he prepared me to assume the position and power that would have been his if he had not chosen to sacrifice everything for love.

I wish I could say the same for my mother, who ate my father when I was still young and our little piece of Komran was torn apart by quakes. "Do not worry," he told me. "Komran will provide, and the hungry times will pass. Your mother does what she must to keep herself and her children alive, and she will see that you gain the advancement you deserve." But she never did.

I did not eat, having already consumed too much of his substance in my unthinking larval state.

But my father was right. The hungry times passed, and our family grew sound again feasting on my father's memory as we had feasted on his body, and the wise counsel that I passed along in his stead. I became the wise male who served as the head of the family, and part of my wisdom was to reflect that my father did not grow old and feeble like so many males of his generation, sacrifices on the altar of love.

I left home as soon as I could, escaping my mother's ravenous regard and refusal to shield her children from her heat, and gave myself over to the state, whose concerns, and even its punishments, were blessedly impersonal. Because of my father's once-promising career and the wisdom that he had communicated to me I was appointed to the academy for pre-spacers, where I was educated in the mathematics and the physics of space, astronomy and cosmology, history and practices of spaceflight, galactic culture, and the pre-eminence of Sirians among galactics.

My apologies to fellow galactics for Sirian parochial attitudes. We teach greatness so that our offspring can rise above the treachery of their biology and so that they will never encounter a galactic or a situation except on terms of equality. We teach greatness so that we can imagine it, and, having imagined it, achieve it.

I studied hard, though with the skepticism that lies behind every thoughtful Sirian's consciousness of place. We know that the universe is unrelenting and unstable, and so we seek the truth that is unspoken, the reality behind the deception of appearance. And I studied to make my father proud and his sacrifice meaningful. I was passed on to the space college as the most promising academy student of my class.

College was far more demanding, requiring not only the discipline of the mind but also the discipline of the body that lies at the heart of the Sirian experience. We must perform not only the exercises that enable Sirians to achieve and to endure but also the rigorous protocols we must learn to control our inner states. Komran provides its offspring with such physical extremes of temperature and Komranology that we must divorce our inner states from our outer existence. Our happiness is dependent not upon events but upon our determination. We will our happiness just as we will our internal temperatures.

In the third cycle of college Sirians are introduced to space, first on a ship manned by experienced crews and then on ships operated by senior cadets. On my first trip I discovered my natural habitat. While my fellow students were panicking, floundering in weightlessness, puking in corners, and pink with shame, swinging a cloth in an attempt to blot the evidence, I felt as if I had come home, as if I resided once more in my father's belly. It was for this, I knew, that my father had nourished me and shared not only his body but his wisdom. I was a natural spacer.

Among brighter students now, I was not as successful as I had been before. My classwork had grown more difficult and my academic efforts frantic. Even calmed by the remembered voice of my father, I could not excel as I had been able to do before. But my space-faring skills made up for everything. Where other students had to think before they acted, every decision came to me as if a product of body, not mind. I rose to a position of eminence, what humans would call the captain of cadets, on skill—and the attitude of leadership that accompanied it.

By the time my class had reached its final year, I had already been assured of the first place to open on the premier ship of the Sirian fleet. In response, my performance in intellectual pursuits improved, and once more I began to succeed, sometimes more than my peers, in Sirian history, in political science, and, preeminently, in space navigation, engineering, gunnery, and command.

Then I met Romi. She was a first-year student from Komran's other hemisphere. In the ordinary course of life we would never have met. Not only distance but status separated us. I was a commoner, who had survived the hungry times only by reason of my mother's moral turpitude. But here, in the space college, I was the superior, and as captain of cadets able to give orders to first-year students and expect them to be obeyed instantly. Even unreasonable orders—in fact, as tradition and common sense dictate, the more unreasonable the better, for crews must obey without thinking, without considering whether an order is reasonable.

But I could not command Romi. She was the most beautiful

Sirian I had ever met, and she was in love with me. I felt stirrings within me, thoughts of storing food within my belly, thoughts of ingesting larval children. And then I remembered my father.

I understand that love takes many forms across the galaxy, and that some are powerful and enduring while some are fleeting and casual. I do not know what love is like for a Sirian female—I think it involves the predatory—but for a Sirian male, love is a great passion that prepares him for what may be the ultimate sacrifice.

I endured the situation for the rest of the academic cycle, trying to limit my contacts with Romi, but every time she was near I felt the primal urges that I knew my father had felt, the urges that betrayed him. I even went out of my way to make sure our paths did not cross. But I met her in my dreams.

I understand that some galactics do not dream; some do not even sleep. The dream life of Sirians, however, is as real as—no, more real than—the waking life. We discuss our dreams as if we have lived them. We analyze them. We write them down. We manage them so that they end satisfactorily, giving us strength or wisdom, or reinforcing our self-image.

But I could not manage my dreams of Romi. They always ended with small Sirians eating their way through my belly while I stared down, helpless to control them or my temperature, leaving me helpless and weak, doomed to a lifetime as an invalid. And I told no one.

Finally my ordeal ended. My class completed its classwork and we were assigned to ships. Somehow I had managed to retain my status during my inner turmoil, and I joined the *Kilsat* as junior pilot-in-training. I left Romi behind as a second-cycle cadet and put her out of my mind.

I was happy. Space was my environment; Romi no longer haunted my thoughts or controlled my dreams. I was a natural pilot, responding intuitively to subconscious cues, as if my dear father were guiding my actions from his place of honor near the star that shall not be named. I made friends with my fellow spacers and filled my off-duty moments with good male fellowship. We bonded as Sirian crew members do in the unifying environment of space. We talked of challenges and accomplishments, of ambitions and achievement, and never of family or sacrifice.

The *Kilsat* made its first Jump during my maiden voyage. That took us beyond the narrow confines of our Sirian system. The experience shook many of my crewmates, but I found it exhilarating, not only space but the realization that the hidden universes within space were my real home. During the second Jump I was at the controls and gloried in the power of transcending time and space. All the universe was mine, I felt, and I dedicated my joy to my father's memory.

By the time we made our third Jump we were in galactic space, surveying the magnificence of the Galactic Center. Xi told us about meeting with the Galactic Council. What he did not describe was the center itself—not the center of the galaxy but Galactic Center, where the representatives of the great peoples meet and the galaxy is governed. Galactic Center is an insignificant system of rocky planets orbiting an insignificant sun. No one would think of it as a place of greatness, as a place of any importance at all. And that, no doubt, is why it was chosen, along with the fact that it was uninhabited, at least by any member species. And although representatives to the Galactic Council and innumerable bureaucrats inhabit those planets, some for their entire lives, the destruction of the Galactic Center would mean little except to those personally involved.

To look at that impoverished system and realize its importance makes even the most robust Sirian realize the value of inner strength and the pitfalls of appearance. We had learned that principle from the shiftings of Komran beneath our extremities, but here it was brought home to us again.

We looked, we admired from afar, and we departed, learning nothing of the workings inside the capitol of the galaxy beyond what we had learned in the academy. But it was enough for simple spacers, and we pondered its meaning as we returned to Sirius and our lives there, now a crew in the true meaning of the word, functioning as the brain and central nervous system of the ship, working as a single entity. For the first time in my life I felt as I had when I was part of my father, at peace with my world, content in my way of life. The *Kilsat* had become my father, or, perhaps more accurately, now the *Kilsat* and my father were one.

But when we returned to Sirius, Romi came back into my life. It was time for the cadet cruises, and, by the evil goddess, she was assigned to the *Kilsat*. When I saw her, I knew my time of greatest temptation had arrived. Without a word to anyone, I went to the nearest two-person fighter craft, crawled through the tunnel that linked it to the ship, detached it from its mooring bolts, turned off the communications gear, and drifted away before I started the propulsion system.

I knew where I was going. I was headed for the nexus point that everyone knows and nobody dares use, the Jump that ends in orbit around the white dwarf without a name.

To speak truth, my reaction was not the awe and reverence that I expected. During the lengthy trip I had managed to neutralize the panic that had driven me from Romi, but I anticipated a psychic fulfillment that never came. The Companion was an ordinary white dwarf, shining wanly on a ruined desert of orbital space while Sirius burned brighter than any star above the Companion's shawl of night. The Companion had not been stripped of planets, as mythology had told us. Instead, while I watched as if from a height, cinder after cinder swam into view. If they had once been gas giants, the gases had been blown away, leaving only a few charred fragments behind. If they had been habitable worlds like Komran, their atmospheres and seas had been stripped from them, along with all the living things that had evolved there. The Companion had consumed its own children long before life came to sentience on Komran.

My father was not there, nor was any other spirit. The desolation before me was matched by the desolation within.

What was there, as I discovered when my black mood eventually lifted, was a lonely beacon, like the sign of intelligent life in a lonely universe. I tracked it to a location near the Companion. There was no planet, no satellite, no ship, nothing within the discernment of my sensors that could send a signal.

The passage from the outer reaches to near-solar space took many periods during which I saw much closer the devastation caused by the Companion's expansion phase. Finally I came upon the source of the signal: a battered escape capsule of an unfamiliar design turning slowly in the Companion's wan radiance, getting just enough energy from its rays to sustain its limited operation.

I connected the capsule to my small ship. I could not decipher the instructions beside the capsule's hatch—they were incised in a cryptic series of lines—but I finally found a button that set off explosive bolts. I sampled the atmosphere, which was within tolerable limits and without apparent toxins. Inside the capsule was a still functioning deep-freeze chamber, and inside the chamber was the ugliest creature I had ever seen—a creature with four weak extremities emerging at awkward angles from a shrunken and fragile central torso and topped by a strange growth dotted with openings and covered in places with threadlike tendrils.

Only later—my apologies to present company—did I discover that this was a human. This was the first human I had ever seen, certainly the first human any Sirian had ever seen except, perhaps, at the highest level of galactic leadership where, I learned later, human emissaries already were making their demands that soon would result in war.

But all of this was yet to come. Here, now, was this alien creature, and it was dead—or so nearly dead that the difference was imperceptible. If any other galactic had discovered this castaway, the end would have been certain, but Sirians have such fine control of their temperatures that freezing is not necessarily fatal. Indeed, Sirians have been discovered in hidden glaciers and been revived after being frozen for many hundreds, even thousands, of cycles.

I opened the chamber and set about reviving its occupant, elevating its temperature fraction by fraction, easing the transition from cell to cell, from external to internal, over a period of almost a cycle. Finally the occupant made a sound and shortly thereafter opened what I later learned were its viewing organs.

It made organized sounds that I later learned was something like, "What in the hell are you!"

But we got on and within a cycle, we were able to converse with the aid of my pedia. This human, a male, was part of an expedition to decipher a nexus chart that had been bought from galactic traders or sold by traitors—he never knew which—and all had gone well until flaws in the coordinates destroyed the ship and all his shipmates, and launched his escape module through the nexus into the Companion's system. That I should have discovered the module was a chance beyond calculation, depending as it did upon my fleeing Romi and setting my course for the Companion.

The human told me his designation was "Sam." He told me many things about Earth and about humans and their history and literature and art. We had nothing to do but communicate, and Sam loved to talk. He was, he said, making up for his long, silent, frozen cycles. He never realized that his stories about Earth horrified me: the struggles, the competition, the battles, the wars. Even in literature and art these bloody activities were celebrated. I realized that I had to get this information to our leaders, and he— unaware that he had revealed humanity's blood thirst and its inability to live in a civilized fashion with others—wanted to get back to his leaders with the information gathered about our precious navigation maps.

Of course he had no chance to get back. I did not tell him that when we left the Companion we would return to Sirius and Komran where he would be interrogated at far greater length and in far less pleasant conditions than on my vessel, cramped as it was. I could not let him return with his information, and I had to return with mine. And then, when he was well enough to travel and we were on our way to the nexus point, he sickened and died. The last words he spoke were, "You are an ugly son-of-a-bitch, Kom, but you've been a good friend way out here next to nowhere. It's been great knowing you."

I felt much the same way as when my mother ate my father.

When I got back to Sirian space, I discovered that my information had arrived too late. I had been gone for a dozen cycles, and the war was over. But the rumors of the Transcendental Machine were traveling fast. My leaders were concerned. Because I had spent so many cycles with an alien, and especially because that alien was a human, I was urged to volunteer for this pilgrimage.

I agreed, of course. My experience with the Companion had changed me forever. I was no longer a simple Sirian, bound by myths

and biological imperatives. I had experienced both the reality and
the unreality of others. I was prepared. And, more important, Romi
had chosen another, who already had nurtured her larvae to maturity and suffered the consequences.

Why, you may wonder, did I spend such time and thought with
Sam? I wondered myself. And then I began to see that when I
reached the Companion I lost the reality of my father's spirit and
found Sam. I had begun to think of Sam as my father, and his loss
affected me as much.

And he told me, during our long conversations, about the human
family and its process of procreation. What if Sirians could procre-
ate as partners, like humans? Could we transcend our biology?

CHAPTER TWELVE

Riley woke feeling relaxed and pleased with himself, the way he had felt when the world was new and he had not yet been wounded by its indifference, the way he felt after he had been with a woman. The cubicle even seemed to hint of passion and pheromones.

But that was all illusion. He knew now that the universe offered nothing for rational existence but heartache and pain, and he had not been with a woman for more than a year. The cubicle did not smell of a woman, it smelled of sweat and dirt and stale emissions, human and alien. And he had no reason to feel relaxed, here halfway between the known and the unknown, confined with enigmatic aliens in a tin can traveling toward holes in space at one-tenth light speed, protected from the universe's hungry void by a fragile metal shell. And his pedia was silent. Not that this was unusual. It was often silent when he needed it the most, as if it were programmed not to comfort.

He slipped into his simple space coveralls, opened the cubicle door, slid himself out feetfirst, and climbed down the ladder. Asha and Kom were waiting for him.

"Kom wants to thaw Jon and Jan," Asha said.

Riley turned to Kom. "Why?"

Riley's pedia translated Kom's rumble, "I thought you understood."

"I understood your story," Riley said. "You lost the human you had tried to save, and now you want another chance."

"That's only part of it," Asha said.

"I understand the other part, too," Riley said. Kom's relationship with his dead father, if it had been anything like the one between Riley and his father, was not something he would have wanted to discuss. That is, presuming Kom's story was true and not simply a convenient half-truth hiding a deeper, darker truth. "But the captain isn't going to like it."

"The captain," Kom rumbled, "can't refuse."

That was true. When Riley and Kom confronted the captain, he waved his hand and said, "Do what you want," as if it didn't matter anymore. But it did matter, Riley knew, though why it mattered he wasn't sure.

The captain had other worries.

"What's wrong?" Riley asked. They were in the control room, but a control room more disordered than Riley had ever seen it. Crumpled paper nearly obscured the air-return vent and handheld pedias adorned several of the flat navigator panels, as if the captain was checking every calculation to find one in which he had confidence. And half the readouts were blank, as if the captain had erased them as Riley and Kom approached. "A disordered control room," his pedia said, "is evidence of a disordered command."

The captain looked at him as if it was a question too obvious to answer, and as if the answer was too intimately related to the responsibilities of decision for Riley to appreciate. "We have another Jump coming up," he said.

Riley shrugged. Space travel was one Jump after another.

"The last one was off."

Riley shrugged again.

"The next one may be off as well."

"And it may not," Riley said. "Whoever is sending you coordinates wants to get to his destination as much as you do, and probably doesn't want to die, either, or spend eternity somewhere outside of space and time."

"But he may not be as competent as we have been led to think."

"After so many accurate nexus points in the uncharted space between spiral arms, it suggests a certain degree of reliability."

The captain ran his hand through the untrimmed gray-flecked stubble on his head. "Even if he knows where he's going and knows how to get us there, he may be cutting off our avenue of retreat."

"Do you want to retreat?" Riley asked.

"I don't know. Yes. No. No, I don't want to go back," the captain said. "But I don't want to go forward blindly or to have my decisions preempted."

Kom spoke up, surprising them both by his existence. "The passengers would rebel if you tried to turn back."

The captain turned on him. "Fuck the passengers!" And then changed his tone: "No, wait. I don't mean that. The passengers are important. But they were willing to turn back a couple of Jumps ago."

"Fear, yes," Kom rumbled. "Decision, no."

"In any case," the captain said, "you can tell the passengers that the coordinates come only to my pedia, and without me they could be stranded out here."

Kom might have shrugged if he had shoulders. "Whoever is sending the coordinates would not like to be stranded out here, either."

Riley did shrug. "So, you see?" he said to the captain. "Like everything else, your decision may be only an after-the-fact rationalization."

The captain looked unappeased. "I don't have to like it."

"We're past the point where likes and dislikes matter."

"Go!" the captain said to them both. "You're no help."

Riley turned and led Kom to the storage room near the rear of the ship.

The crewman in charge of the storage room took one look at Riley and Kom and stood aside. "We have the captain's permission to move the bodies," Riley said.

The frozen bodies looked like replicas of the real Jon and Jan carved from ice and colored by hand. Kom lifted them gently from their cabinets, first Jan, then Jon, and lowered them onto a motorized gurney. They trundled it through corridors, careful not to brush brittle limbs against passageways or compartment hatches, until they had the gurney back to the passenger quarters.

Kom had an alien cubicle already chosen—bigger even than the one he had occupied. This one allowed him to position himself between the bodies of Jon and Jan. He closed the cubicle door.

It was, Riley thought, like a cocoon from which might emerge, eventually, three butterflies. The idea of Kom as a butterfly brought a smile to his face.

"You're smiling!" Asha said. "You should smile more often. It lights up the room."

"You, too," Riley said.

She smiled and the passenger quarters did seem to brighten. In fact, it transformed her face from ordinarily attractive to something special, even beautiful. He felt as if he had never seen her before. He turned his gaze away before he revealed his reaction.

The Jump hit them then, without warning, as if the captain was punishing them for questioning his authority. Riley staggered and almost fell, but Asha absorbed the shock without apparent effort. Squeals and cries from the commons room provided evidence that the Jump was a surprise there as well.

This was a Jump as off-center as the previous one. The real world splintered around them like a mirror shattering from within. The hand Riley had placed behind him sank into the gelatinous substance the metal wall had become. Asha sprouted tendrils like a rotting potato and then split into pieces that recombined into grotesque new shapes. He fell through the floor into a stinking pit of writhing entrails that hissed and turned into serpentine aliens. One of them had the captain's head. It sneered at him before it bared its teeth and struck. He felt its fangs sink into his belly. The pain of its entry turned into a fiery stream that surged through his veins until it reached his brain before everything disappeared and he found himself floating in a universe filled with diamonds against a background of impenetrable darkness, the diamonds connected by almost invisible traceries like a gigantic spiderweb.

He floated in their midst for a moment before he realized that he was the universe, or rather that he had expanded to fill the universe, and that the diamonds were the neurons in his head, each one filled with pain like exploding stars, and the web that connected them burned its intricate connections into his mind, and he was being torn apart by tides of gravity, by some internal black energy that scattered him everywhere and he could no longer keep himself together. And then a voice, like the voice of some ancient god, said, "Hang in there. This will be over soon."

And it was. He found himself back in the ship, outside the stack of alien sleeping cubicles, facing Asha. "That was a bad one," he said, as if it had been some fleeting gas pain.

"As bad as they get," Asha said. "I wonder how the others are taking it."

In the commons room Tordor was solid and unmoved, as usual; Xi was jittering around the room alarming most of the others, who were already in various states of panic. The coffin-shaped creature, though, remained motionless in a corner, and the flower child stood among the terrified aliens like the central pillar of a crazed merry-go-round.

The flower child spoke. It sounded like the whispering of a breeze through a field of grain. "She says that she has felt worse," Tordor said.

"Actually," Riley's pedia said, "she said that the universe had far worse fates for thinking creatures."

"Why do you use the female pronoun?" Riley asked.

"Pronouns are an artifact of your language," Tordor said, "but it is true that, like most evolved creatures, the flower children of Mur reproduce bisexually, and this flower child, known as Four one zero seven, produces seeds when fertilized by the male through the intermediary of a small flying creature."

"That's more than I needed to know," Riley said.

"But not me," Asha said. "Go on."

"She suffers from separation trauma," Tordor said. "Murans live surrounded by others, like their ancient ancestors, and she has never been far from her native bed."

"Will we ever get back to civilization?" 4107 whispered.

"The question is: will we ever get to the other spiral arm?" Riley said.

"The real question is," Tordor said, "will the captain allow us to get there?"

"The captain is as uncertain as we are," Riley said. "When Kom and I confronted him about Jon and Jan, he was trying to decide what to do about the next Jump."

"Then the captain isn't behind these faulty coordinates?" Tordor said.

"I hope it isn't the navigation computer," Riley said. "If it fails we'll never get back."

"There are always two backups," Tordor said.

"But who knows what condition they're in," Riley said. "They may be as poorly maintained as the ship itself was, before we up-graded. Or, if the navigation computer is infected, the others may be as well."

"We will drift out here," 4107 whispered, "for eternity, far from our native soil."

At that moment Xi pointed to the screen that for a long time now had been nothing but black with remotely scattered spots of light, like tiny imperfections in a solid field. "Hai!" he said.

Riley saw a faint line of brightness in the far corner of the screen. If he looked at it with his peripheral vision he could see the sugges-tion of what might become a river of light. "The other spiral arm!" he shouted.

Most of the aliens turned to look at Riley and then at the corner of the screen toward which Xi pointed with his new arm. A satisfied murmur rose from among them, punctuated here and there by dis-cordant sounds that might have involved apprehension.

"It looks as if we may get to the other arm after all," Tordor said.

"And what will we find there?" Riley asked.

"A happy, moist, and warm place without predators," 4107 whis-pered.

Tordor turned his massive head so that only Riley and Asha could hear. "She means where there are no grazers like my species."

"She means the Alpha Centaurans," his pedia said.

Xi had come up to the group unnoticed. "We will find a place where every being can fulfill its most ambitious dreams, where ev-eryone can be king and need never watch for knives."

Tordor looked at Xi and 4107 with what in a human would have seemed like condescension. "More practically," he said, "we might consider what this spiral arm contains: aliens who know nothing of our confederation, who may have evolved in a wholly different fashion, whose culture and technology may be long-cycles in advance of ours, whose very matter may be poison to galactics from our spiral arm."

"As newcomers," Riley said drily, "we humans may have a lot in common with them."

"If these aliens have created a Transcendental Machine," Tordor said, "they have had an opportunity to surpass anything we might consider common."

"And the likelihood," Asha said, "that they may have millions of cycles of advantage over us."

"Neither of those are necessarily so," Riley said. "We don't know that the Transcendental Machine exists, or if it does, what it actually accomplishes. And any such device might arrive out of the blue, some alien genius's inspiration rather than the crowning achievement of a technological pyramid."

"How do you think the nexus points between the spiral arms were charted?" Asha asked.

"They could as easily have been identified by explorers from our spiral arm," Riley insisted.

Asha turned to Tordor. "Galactics protect their charts like treasure maps, so I've never asked. But let me ask now: how did they get created?"

"All that is lost in ancient history," Tordor said.

"They know but will not tell," Riley's pedia said.

"At least," Riley said, "someone from this spiral arm made the journey or we would not be getting the coordinates now, much less the stories about the Transcendental Machine."

"Maybe stories," Tordor said. "Maybe reports."

"My theory," Asha said, "is that creatures from the other spiral arm evolved first, or developed technology first, moved outward to ours, and maybe the others, leaving behind evidence of their passing in the form of ruins found on many worlds, and charts of nexus points inherited by the galactics."

"If that is so," Tordor said, "where are they?"

"How do we know," Asha asked, "that they are not still among us?"

Riley studied Asha's impassive face, as if to judge if she were joking, and noticed that Tordor was looking at her, too, though it was difficult to imagine how he would be able to interpret a human expression.

"That is a conspiracy theory to top all conspiracy theories," Riley said.

"We would have no way to identify such an alien," Tordor said.

"For that matter," Riley said, "where did any of us come from?"

"Every culture has an origins story," Tordor said.

"Most attribute their origins to the supernatural," Riley said, "and then elevate their discourse to the natural."

"If they were here," Asha said, "they wouldn't necessarily know their origins, either."

"Millions of years is a long time to remain civilized," Riley said.

"They could have degenerated," Tordor said. "They could be any of us." He swept his proboscis in a wide arc. "Any of us."

"Or none," Riley said. "If we're speculating, they could have planted life adapted to our planetary conditions throughout this spiral arm, and then retreated to their own arm, leaving each of us to develop along lines they laid out, like gods, until they came again to fulfill their own ambitions—whatever they are."

"That *is* ridiculous," Asha said.

"No more than any of the other theories, or any other creation myth."

"Then why have they not returned?" Tordor said. He seemed to be taking Riley's jest seriously.

"Maybe they have," Riley said, "and found us wanting. Or maybe the aliens from still another spiral arm planted them to realize their ambitions."

"Or maybe they just forgot," Asha said.

"We'll soon find out," Tordor said.

Riley found his gaze returning to the screen with its faint line of stars like the promise of a distant shore.

The line had grown no brighter by the time that most of the passengers used for their sleep period. Nothing had happened to change the atmosphere of uncertainty in the passengers' lounge. Kom had not emerged from his cocoon. Passengers had wandered aimlessly through the lounge and through the ship itself, working, eating, conversing, contemplating, or playing what seemed to be games of skill or chance. Anything to make time pass while that distant line edged closer.

Riley climbed back into his cubicle. He had not been asleep for more than a few minutes when he heard the cubicle door open. He prepared for an attack before he sensed, by touch and odor, the presence of another human, a female. "Asha!" he said.

"Shh," she said.

"How did you get in here?" he asked.

"You always ask that," she said. "You have your skills; I have mine."

"What do you mean 'I always ask that'?"

"I'll explain later," she said.

The cubicle was scarcely big enough for one person, but Asha made it seem larger. She was out of her garment effortlessly and he had nothing to remove. He wanted to ask again why she said it was a question he always asked, but his hands were busy in the darkness and soon his mouth was as well.

Even in the dark Asha's body was wondrous: full where it should be full, slim where it should be slim, firm where it should be firm, soft where it should be soft. She was strong and supple and as sensually aggressive as he, sure of what she wanted and as determined seeking it out.

Their lovemaking lasted for more than an hour before, satiated, they lay side by side in each other's arms. That would have been romantic if there had been any choice, but suddenly the cubicle that had seemed so large now seemed tiny again.

"That was good," he said.

"Yes."

"But why?"

"It seems perfectly natural to me," she said, resting her head against his shoulder.

"True," he agreed, finding a convenient place to place his free hand. "We're the only humans—among the passengers, anyway."

"Not only that," she said, "and not because the captain and his human crew are inconvenient, and relationships unwise."

"I didn't appreciate how beautiful you were until you smiled."

"I knew the first time I saw you."

"Women are smarter about these things."

"Not just that you were the only man available," she said. "I knew that I could love you."

"Love is a big word."

"We've got a big job," Asha said, "and we need all the help we can get. You and me against the universe."

"The way it has always been, from the beginning of time." He gave her a squeeze, feeling an expansiveness of spirit and a warmth that he had not felt for many cycles, perhaps not since he had left Mars. "But why now?"

"What makes you think this was the first time?"

He remembered the unanswered question and the pheromones in the cubicle. "And why did you say 'You always ask that'?"

"You won't remember any of this," she said.

"You think I could ever forget?"

"Oh, you have. Many times."

"How—?"

"You will remember everything," he told his pedia.

"You should have told me that before," his pedia said. "This woman has abilities that you cannot imagine."

"I have other abilities besides opening locked doors," she said.

"I believe you," he said. "But let me make a case for not using them."

"Go on."

"Perhaps you can make me forget," he said, adjusting his body to fit better with hers, "and depend upon my general feeling of affection and appreciation."

"Yes?"

"But I think it is time to join forces in full awareness of who we are and what we mean to each other. We can help each other far better then."

She thought for a moment. "Yes. Who are you?"

"There are things I can't tell you, not because I won't but because I can't."

"Because of the thing in your head," she said.

He stiffened and then relaxed. "You know about that?"

"I know many things."

"I am not a pilgrim."

"Careful," his pedia said. "I might have to kill you. And if you die, I die."

"I am—. I can't say."

"I know who you are," Asha said. "It's something you will have to fight out on your own, but it's a fight you can win."

"She knows too much," his pedia said. "Kill her."

"And your job is to kill me," she said.

"Who *are* you?"

"I am the Prophet," she said, "a reluctant Prophet. And it is time you knew my story."

CHAPTER THIRTEEN

Asha's Story

Asha said:

The generation ship *Adastra* was halfway to Alpha Centauri when we were intercepted by a galactic patrol ship. I say "we," but I had just been born. The crew and passengers did not resist. They had no weapons, and the alien ship, clearly armed, had appeared, magically, out of nowhere. All this I heard from my father, who would repeat it to me, on my birthday, like a tribal history that I should never be allowed to forget. Then he told me about my mother.

A galactic crew boarded our ship and navigated, in a few Jumps, to the Galactic Council system. I do not remember the process, but my father tells me that I cried every time the ship passed through un-space. He held me tight, trying to be brave but as frightened as I was. The experience of the Jump is terrifying the first time and many times later before it becomes routine, but my father knew what I did not: that our ship had been taken over by monsters with knowledge and powers and hungers we did not understand. For all he knew they were hungry for human flesh and were taking us to a celebratory feast in which we would be the main course.

The Galactic Council system is small, remote, and impoverished. No one would ever travel to the system by choice, or suspect that it was the center of power in our spiral arm. Its sun is small and dim, and its planets are barren and cold. It was an ideal location for the council, whose energy resources made their worlds livable but hidden from everyone except those who needed to know. That knowledge replaced our fear of being eaten—we were as poisonous to them as much of their food was to us—with the realization that they intended we would never leave.

Our ship was taken to the moon of one of the system's meanest planets, where we were removed to housing that was little better than a prison. Another human crew was already there. Its ship, the *Vanguard,* had set out from Sol twenty years after ours but had been intercepted first. Half its crew and a fourth of its passengers died in a futile resistance. A computer technician named Ren was its highest surviving officer.

We were schooled every day. My father, who was a xenologist, taught human history, psychology, and languages. Ren taught mathematics, science, and technology. Syl, a junior officer from the *Vanguard,* taught composition, communication, and group relations. Instruction was a break from our chief occupation, which was survival—everything alien was poisonous or deficient in human nutrients or trace elements. My mother was the first victim of alien food. After the second and third deaths we were allowed to return to the *Adastra* and its gardens and yeast cultures. The galactics, with their mastery of nexus Jumps, knew we had no chance of escape.

There I grew up, orbiting the moon we humans named Hell, of the planet we named Hades. Half a dozen other children were one or two years older, half a dozen were much older, and two were younger. The imperative to multiply almost vanished when we became prisoners.

Most of our captors remained on Hell, with only a handful of aliens within the *Adastra* itself, rotating frequently as if to avoid contamination. The *Adastra* was as dangerous to them as Hell was to us. Most of them were Xifora, famous for their paranoia and treachery—ideal jailors, the galactics thought. A few were Sirians, solid pillars around which revolved the volatile Xifora. A Dorian was in charge.

My father devoted himself to studying them and their language. He was ready to give up when some of my classmates pointed out that each group had its own language, but they also had a common language that they used to communicate between different species, a language we later learned to call Galactic Standard. We taught my father the concepts we had begun to associate with sounds and gestures, and he began to piece together a grammar until he had mastered the language, as nearly as a human can be said to master any alien language, and spoke to our captors.

All were shocked, as if the apes in a zoo had opened conversation with their keepers.

All this time, we learned, some of the Xifora that we thought were guards were really scientists who had been studying us. They came to the conclusion that we were only clever animals who had been sent on ships built by our owners to test experimental devices before they trusted them with their own lives.

We children had become skillful in recognizing reactions among the Xifora, and even spying on the conversations they thought we were incapable of understanding. We even learned to understand Sirian grunts but never Sirians. Some of us had begun to distinguish among members of the same group, some by markings, some by behavior. We even made jokes about them and gave them names. Now we saw consternation among them, even what we interpreted as alarm.

My father had been teaching us Galactic Standard grammar and then, as we began to pick up proficiency, the rudiments of Xifora and Sirian grammar as he was constructing them. I can't tell you how liberating those abilities were; we had been able to understand isolated fragments, but now that we could understand our captors' conversations, we began to understand how they thought. Our minds expanded until I was afraid they would explode. That was the first time I became aware of human limitations.

Meanwhile my father attempted to convince the Sirians that we needed to talk to their superiors—it was no use talking to the Xifora, whose suspicions would not let them consider us as anything but threats. After lengthy delays, my father finally was taken to Hell and allowed to meet the Dorian in charge. His name was Noldor, and he listened to my father's explanation that humans were a technologically advanced, peace-loving species that deserved to be treated like all other civilized intelligent creatures.

Noldor listened patiently and said, "No."

My father returned to our ship and continued his studies and his teaching and his efforts to communicate with our guards. He made friends with one of the Sirians—if the concept of friendship is applicable to Sirians—and persuaded him to take to Noldor a message he had recorded in Galactic Standard. The message contained music, poetry, art, and performances of dance and drama, all from our shipboard library, as well as my father's commentary on human history, philosophy, and civilization.

He waited. Nothing happened for a cycle, while we children grew older, bigger, and wiser in the ways of the galactics. And then Noldor gave my father a second audience and said that humans would be allowed to petition the council.

That period we celebrated.

The next period we returned to our customary condition of despair when Noldor selected our human ambassador: my thirteen-year-old brother, Pip. Pip was taken away, casting imploring glances over his shoulder at me and the other children and my father, who was protesting in broken Galactic that Pip was only a child and not a proper ambassador. Nobody listened.

Many periods later Pip returned. He had not been harmed but was often sickened by *Adastra* food that had become contaminated by alien carelessness. He was always frightened. He had been questioned by aliens of many different kinds about Earth and humans and our history and literature and folk tales—particularly folk tales. He told them, he said, that he had been born aboard a generation ship and knew only what he had been told and that he did not speak or understand their language well, but they kept pestering him with the same questions. When his answers differed they would pounce, and ask him to explain. Some of the aliens seemed gentle and understanding; some of them, brusque and contemptuous. He learned to suspect the gentle and understanding ones.

"They don't like us," Pip said. "I did the best I could."

We all assured him that he had done well, though my father told me privately that he was afraid the council was preparing a case against humanity. He renewed his request that he be allowed to represent our group—and, perhaps, all humanity—before the council. "It is a terrible responsibility to represent all humanity," he said to me, "but someone must do it, and circumstances have chosen me. You'll understand that someday."

A cycle later his request was finally granted. He would be allowed to petition in person for an audience. He boarded the next alien supply ship headed back to the Galactic Council planet. We did not see him again for three full cycles. Meanwhile I grew into womanhood, and boys and a few grown men began to look at me differently. Ren continued our instruction but was increasingly involved in research of his own, which he kept concealed from our guards and even from his students. But he could not hide it from me.

Finally my father returned, looking older and tireder. The Galactic Council world, he told us, was a rabbit warren of officials whose sole function was to maintain their positions by making as few decisions as possible. His time there had been one bureaucratic frustration after another. He had been passed from office to office, repeating in virtually identical phrases his need to address the council, or, if that was impossible, someone in authority. Some of the bureaucrats pretended not to understand his attempts at Galactic. Others simply offered the equivalent of a shrug and sent him to another office. Each encounter left him further from his goal than before. He might, he thought, spend the rest of his life being shunted here and there.

His only comfort was the company of other aliens of many different species and origins who were in the same situation, petitioning for acceptance into the galactic community, and suffering the same indignities.

Then Ren came to my father and disclosed that he had been able to break into council computer files. "What does that mean?" my father asked.

"I have downloaded their navigation charts," Ren said. "We can use their nexus points to open up the galaxy for humanity. Humans need no longer be primitive plodders. We can be the equal of any galactic."

"Only if we can get the charts back home," my father said, his face resuming the dejection that had become its constant expression. "And we are prisoners."

Ren, too, looked dejected.

A cycle later my father was summoned before the council.

*   *   *

Our classes continued. Other instructors picked up my father's classes, though none of us were in the mood for study. Ren continued his secretive research, looking more frantic and more haggard every period. When, finally, my father returned, they both seemed like old men, though my father was only middle-aged and Ren was ten years younger.

By this time I was mature—or thought I was—and I was allowed to overhear their conversation in the most secret of human locations, that is, in the midst of a babble of childish chatter. We did not think our captors had learned any human languages, but my father wanted to take no chances.

Ren was in love with me, and I thought I was in love with him, although it may have been only sympathy for his plight and admiration for his dedication, and the influence of his position as my teacher. He had taught me well, including skills as a navigator that I had no reason to believe I would ever be able to use.

"You've got to escape," my father said.

"What happened?" Ren asked.

"The council is preparing for war with humanity. They're using our own revelations against us."

"Pip?" I asked.

"He was only a child," my father said. "But I should have known better."

"What did you tell them?" I asked.

"I told them nothing. It was the documentary I foolishly prepared for them, particularly our poetry, our art, our drama, even my own commentary on history and civilization—all based on conflicts resolved by conciliation or rationality or love or recognition of common humanity, but often by force. They picked out the violent parts and said humanity was not only unfit for galactic membership but a danger to galactic civilization."

"We'll have to prepare," Ren said, looking even more haggard.

"No time," my father said.

"The Xifora are beginning to act more paranoid," I said. "I've heard them talk about the best way to kill a human. Most of them prefer knives, but a few talk of poison."

Ren suddenly looked decisive. "We'll do it just before the next sleep period, when the current guards are leaving and the new ones haven't arrived. Asha," he said to me, "you get the children together. You," he said to my father, "organize the adults. I have developed a virus that will shut down their computers. The cells will open on Hell below. Everything will go dark. We will sneak away before they know we are gone."

"I'm staying," my father said.

"You won't have a chance when they find us gone," we said. "And even if they allow you to live, you won't have any food."

"There are the gardens on the *Vanguard*," he said.

We could not argue him out of his belief that a human had to remain behind to confront the council and to exhaust every possibility of making peace. He had a misplaced confidence in the power of rational persuasion. We knew the aliens better, but we also knew that our chances of a successful escape were nearly zero. Whether we stayed or went probably didn't matter.

But we succeeded. The galactics, as always, had underestimated human intelligence, ingenuity, and determination. As soon as the guards left and before the new shift arrived, Ren released his virus. Everything galactic stopped. We got the *Adastra*'s engines going again and drifted away before our departure was noticed, Hell awoke, our escape was discovered, and the race began.

Ren was masterful. He downloaded his stolen navigation charts into the computer, guided the ship to the nearest nexus, and initiated a Jump as skillfully as if he had been doing it forever.

We knew we would be pursued, and by our third Jump we saw a fleet of alien vessels emerge behind us. Ren packed half the crew and all of the children except me—I no longer considered myself a child and refused to go—into an escape vessel, programmed it to return to Earth by the quickest route, gave the senior officer a copy of the galactic navigation charts, and at the next Jump let it precede us by a fraction while we led our pursuers farther out onto the spiral arm. It wasn't until many cycles later that I learned about the war and then, much later, that the vessel had reached Earth with its precious cargo and its vital message. We kept only a single Jump ahead of the galactic fleet that was as intent on recovering the charts as it was on recovering us. The council had discovered Ren's theft.

It was then Ren made his fateful decision. We had reached the final nexus when he pointed us into the Great Gulf.

"Where are you going?" I asked. By this time I was checking Ren's calculations and performing the navigation when he was not on duty.

"Where they'll never follow us," he said.

"But that's no better than suicide," I said.

"I've found an ancient chart," he said.

"How do you know it's any good?"

"Why would it be hidden away like that—inside another chart that's older than the galactics' recorded history? It's like a treasure map." Ren's eyes were glowing, and I was suddenly afraid of him.

And we headed into the unknown.

You know how it went. You've experienced the same thing, including the nexus points that were off by a fraction. Ren said that the charts were so old that the white hole had drifted away from its co-ordinates. Those were not intentional inaccuracies. But the *Adastra* made it through as the *Geoffrey* will, and reached the other spiral arm.

We were almost out of fuel, and headed for a nearby solar system. We scooped up hydrogen from a gas giant. Ren led a landing party to an Earth-like planet to check our location and make contact with possible aliens. We found only ruins of what had once been an advanced technological civilization, probably older than that of any of the galactics and perhaps far older. But walls were still standing after hundreds of thousands, maybe millions, of cycles. Our scientists said they were made of virtually indestructible materials that they had never seen before, even among the galactics, but the ruins were overgrown with vegetation and overrun with curious alien insects and pests never seen in our spiral arm. Many of them, like the creepy depictions on some standing walls, were vaguely arachnoid.

And then, while we were studying the ruins of what seemed like the planet's largest city, we were attacked by larger spiderlike creatures. We lost half a dozen of our crew before the rest of us made it back to the lander and to the safety of the *Adastra*.

Most of the crew wanted to head back to our own spiral arm, but Ren said the galactics would be waiting for us. And, he said, he had found on the wall of what he took to be an official structure depictions of adjoining star systems, and one that seemed bigger and brighter than the others. That must be, he thought, the center of government of the local systems, and maybe of the entire spiral arm.

"Who knows what discoveries we might find there," he said, his eyes alive again and his figure once more upright and vigorous. "Intact civilizations. Technology. Maybe even allies against the galactics."

"And maybe dangers we can't even imagine," Syl said. "Maybe the arachnoids of this system, only larger and deadlier."

Ren prevailed, as he usually did, particularly when he announced that the nexus points we had followed to this point included coordinates for the next stage. Ren was right: the planet we reached was at least a regional center. But Syl was right, too. The arachnoids were larger and deadlier. I don't know what happened to the crew left on the *Adastra,* but the rest of our party was wiped out in savage battle. Only Ren and I fought our way into what seemed to be the major city still standing in relative splendor, pursued by creatures even bigger than those that had attacked shortly after our landing, and determined to kill us. We fought them until, finally, we reached an intact building that looked as if it might be a refuge. Ren held them off at the door while I escaped and found at the far end something like a shrine. I thought I could hide there until Ren joined me. But I must have activated something because I awoke in a remote room on a remote planet of our own spiral arm.

Everything that brought us to this time and place has happened as a consequence. I found myself as you find me now: healthier than I have ever been, stronger, smarter, more capable—it's as if all of my potential as a person has been released from bondage. I made my way to civilization. I picked up the alien language very quickly, but I was a bit slower about understanding the implications of my own experiences. I revealed more than I realized, and the stories about my appearance and my unguarded accounts of my experience before I learned better got garbled into the religious mythology called transcendentalism and rumors about a Transcendental Machine and a Prophet.

I'm the Prophet. The Transcendental Machine is real, as you will soon discover.

Trials and tribulations await us.

I told you on the climber that I could take care of myself. I can. But I can't take care of everybody else, and I can't get us to where we want to go without help.

CHAPTER FOURTEEN

Asha stirred in Riley's arms.

"What happened to Ren?" Riley asked.

"I don't know—probably dead."

"What happened to your father?"

"I don't know. I haven't been able to get back to the Galactic Council system. I can access its files, but there's no record of either one."

"And why are you going back?"

Riley felt her body tense and then relax. She had great control over her responses, but this was a question she had not yet answered for herself.

"I have many possible reasons," she said. "To find Ren, or what happened to him. To find the *Adastra* and the lifelong companions we left there, if they are still alive. To find the Transcendental Machine and try to figure out what it does and how it does it. And if I can do that, to create more transcendents like me and, with their help, to create a transcendent galaxy, a galaxy that releases all the potential of sapience. Which reason is the right one or the most important? I don't know."

Riley squeezed her upper arm. "Prophets are not always in control of their prophecies—nor of their motives."

"And you should kill me," she said. "I'm the Prophet everyone wants to destroy before I unsettle the fragile balance of the galaxy. As someone I discovered in an old book once said, 'I bring not peace but a sword.' Don't worry. I've blocked your pedia."

"You can do that?"

"Temporarily. While I keep my focus, it is cut off from your sensorium."

"Could you keep it blocked while it was cut from my head?" Riley waited for a twinge in his head or an explosion that would destroy his brain completely.

"Maybe," she said, "but there are no brain surgeons aboard."

"Unless one of the aliens is a surgeon."

"You would trust your head to one of them with a knife, even if they knew anything about the human brain?"

Riley thought about Xi and then about the carbon filament thread. "Now that I consider it, no. Won't my pedia be angry when you lift your control?"

"It will not be aware of the gap in its experience."

"Why not wipe out its entire memory?"

"Those connections are already permanent."

Riley held her a little tighter. "I'll help, if this thing in my head doesn't kill me first. But you already knew that." Even if he didn't like Asha and didn't admire her strength and decisiveness and intelligence and self-discipline, making love created bonds more solid than rationality. Asha knew that. And he didn't care.

"Yes. But we're going to need more allies."

"Can we get them without revealing who you are?"

"We have no choice," Asha said. "Letting them know the truth would turn everyone into potential assassins."

"Who else then?" Riley asked.

"The captain?"

"Ham? He has his own agenda."

"That's true of everybody, including you and me."

"Tordor?"

"Maybe. Dorians are hard to read. At least I understand Xifora."

"Xi? You think that little weasel can be trusted?"

"I didn't say I trusted him," Asha said. "I know where he stands. Not so about Sirians. I've never been able to understand them, or influence their behavior."

"What we have aboard this ship," Riley said, "is not only a group of outcasts but a group of overachievers longing for the ultimate overachievement."

"Unless they are agents of unidentified powers, as Xi has confessed to being."

"And I was trapped into being myself," Riley said. He told her his story, leaving out nothing, even the parts that made him look weak.

"I knew you had been co-opted, when I became aware of your implanted pedia."

"And how did you do that?"

"At first I didn't know how I knew. Then I realized that my potential for focus and analysis had been realized by the Transcendental Machine. Nothing magical. Just normal human abilities perfected. Like this."

She faded from his sight like the Cheshire cat in one of his boyhood books. If he concentrated, he could see a vague outline where her body had been and the whisper of her touch. As she slowly returned, he said, "What was that?"

"People see and feel and smell and hear what they expect. Their senses can be easily persuaded that they perceive what is behind me. An alternative can be as good as invisibility."

"Teach me."

"You're not equipped. Not yet."

"When?"

"After you pass through the Transcendental Machine. More important, who sent you on this mission?"

"Maybe the same agents who sent Xi," Riley said. "Maybe a different group working toward the same ends. Or different ends that only seem similar. The Transcendental Machine is the difference-maker. Every species in the galaxy would like to get control of it, or if they can't, destroy it. Current galactic powers would prefer that it be destroyed; those that don't have as much power as they would like, can go either way; the powerless want to change everything—unless it means another war—and that means there is a substantial portion of the powerless who would act to preserve stasis."

"What we must do," Asha said, "is survive until we reach the machine and then offer the powerless a different choice."

"We'd better get started then," Riley said, and began the disentangling of their bodies.

Riley emerged first before tapping on the cubicle door to let Asha know that the area was clear of observers, but discretion was unnecessary. The passengers' quarters was a turmoil of alien voices and flailing appendages. Only Tordor and the flower child were standing aloof.

"What's going on?" Riley said.

Tordor pointed to the holographic screen where the thin bright line across a far corner seemed even brighter. But that was illusion. The ship had not taken another Jump.

Underneath the display Xi and the Alpha Centauran were circling each other, looking for an advantage. Xi had a knife in this good hand, while his half-grown arm fended off the Centauran's quick jabs with its beak. On the far side of the room, two aliens were grappling with oddly shaped appendages in what seemed like a fight to the death.

"Why?" Asha asked.

"The possibility that our goal may be attainable has unleashed individual motivations and individual passions," Tordor said impassively.

"Aren't you going to do something?" Asha asked.

"These conflicts are better settled now than later, when they might involve the deaths of many."

Asha looked at Tordor in a way that Riley interpreted as disappointment in the alien's character, and moved with unexpected speed to separate Xi and the Centauran, knocking the knife from Xi's hand without detaching the alien's arm and pushing the Centauran back from its fighting stance. "Be civilized!" she said and turned to the aliens by the dispensary, grabbing each by an appendage and pulling them apart. "Be civilized," she said again, but this time she added, "Times will come when we will need to depend upon one another for survival."

The far hatch banged open, and the captain stepped into the passenger quarters followed by his first mate and two armed crew members. "Violence has been reported," he said, looking around suspiciously.

"All done," Riley said. "A misunderstanding."

"We can't have violence, you know," the captain said. Riley thought he detected a note of futility in his voice.

"We can't have a lot of things," Riley said, "including the intrusion of shipboard personnel into passenger business."

"Passenger turmoil is shipboard business," the captain said. "This voyage has been jinxed from the beginning—"

"And even before, as we are all becoming aware," Riley said.

"—and it threatens a worse outcome for us all if we can't control our passions or resist acting to further only our own selfish ends."

"We've already reached that conclusion," Riley said. "As we approach the far spiral arm our reasons for cooperation may be outweighed by our reasons for competing. That prospect may have precipitated the squabble you overheard."

"And the question," Asha said, "is how we will survive the breakdown of our mutual interest in getting this ship to its destination."

"And what do you suggest?" the captain asked.

"We are going to need new reasons for cooperating," Riley said.

"And what would those be?"

"Survival?" Riley ventured.

"We're approaching a portion of the galaxy that may—almost certainly does—offer unsuspected perils and unknown creatures," Asha said. "We're going to be like children venturing into adult territory. If we don't work together, we'll all die."

"All that's obvious," the captain said.

"What isn't obvious," Tordor said, "is that this obvious reason for working together may conflict with individual goals of reaching the Transcendental Machine first, or of keeping others from reaching it."

"And we have reasons to think that some aboard this vessel are acting under instruction," Riley said.

"From whom?" the captain said.

"That's the question, isn't it?" Riley said.

"Even granting the truth of what you all say," the captain said, "there doesn't seem much that can be done about it." He or his add-ons seemed impatient with all the analysis, as if they would rather deal with the violence that had brought them here.

"Except," Asha said, "to form bonds closer than being fellow pilgrims."

"We need to form associations within the larger group," Riley said, "like the protection groups we formed in the climber, only now we know each other better."

"I'm the captain of the entire vessel," the captain said. "I can't belong to any group smaller than that."

"That's understood," Riley said. "But we want your blessing on our efforts."

"You and Asha and Tordor?"

"And whoever we can persuade to join us, that we can trust, who will pledge to work on behalf of the group until we reach the Transcendental Machine itself," Riley said.

"I thought you didn't believe in the Transcendental Machine."

"My disbelief is beginning to waver," Riley said.

"But you still believe in your ability to judge whether creatures who don't have as close a relation to you as an amoeba are going to subordinate their individual goals to those of a group that includes humans," the captain said.

"What Riley and I believe in," Asha said, "is the ability of rational beings to recognize a superior strategy."

"And the ability of civilized galactics to recognize the virtues of civilized processes," Tordor said.

"My blessings on that," the captain said, and departed with his guards.

Tordor's gaze followed the captain to the hatch until it closed behind the captain's group and turned toward Riley and Asha. "We begin, then, with you two."

It seemed to Riley like a knowing glance and then he told himself that his reaction was the consequence of unexpected intimacy.

But then Tordor said, "Humans, like Dorians, need the companionship of the opposite sex. It is time you two got together."

"As I recall Dorian mating protocols," Asha said, unembarrassed at being discovered, "males have harems of females."

"True," Tordor said, "that is a common pattern for grazing species and one that our civilization must work hard to counteract. For us it is the totality of the female companionship that provides us with a full range of interactions at every level. But perhaps transcendence will raise us to the human level of monogamy and the resultant frustration that impels the human evolutionary drive."

Riley looked closely at Tordor but he could not detect any irony, if Dorians were capable of such subtlety, or if he were capable of interpreting Dorian subtleties.

"We must consider," Tordor said, "the effect on our small group of pilgrims of your partnership. As we approach the destination that looms closer with every Jump, any new social configurations are likely to change the group dynamics."

He did not say "group dynamics," of course, or "social configurations," either, and it was possible that neither concept was thinkable in Dorian, but that was as close a translation as Riley's pedia could provide.

"That is true," Asha said, "and it is why I joined with Riley here. Our little group was stable enough when we were far from our goal, but as it grows closer individual differences are going to emerge. It is time to form a mutual-defense group."

"You turned us down in the climber," Tordor said.

"I didn't need you then," Asha said. "Different situations require different approaches. Riley and I want you with us, each of us defending the rest from outside attacks."

"Until we reach the Transcendental Machine," Tordor said.

Now, perhaps, there was irony in Tordor's words, Riley thought. Or maybe only Dorian realism.

"I would hope we could help each other even there," Asha said. "I have the feeling that none of us could reach it alone. But at least until then."

Tordor gestured toward the holographic screen with its faintly shining streak across one corner. "What happens when we reach the other arm?"

Asha shrugged. Riley wondered, not for the first time, if Tordor understood shrugs. "We'll find out when we get there," she said. "It's as big as our spiral arm, with as many suns. It may not be easy discovering the one that contains the Transcendental Machine."

"But surely the Prophet knows," Tordor said. "Or whoever has been sending coordinates to the captain."

Riley's expression remained impassive, but he asked himself how much Tordor knew, or thought he knew. "What about Xi? Asha thinks she understands him."

"What is not to understand about the Xifora? Don't let them behind you. Watch their hands. Give them no reason to think your death will be to their advantage. You can trust them to choose whatever benefits them at the time."

"Xi, then."

"Kom?" Riley asked. "At least, like Xi, he was willing to reveal himself and his motivations."

"As I was," Tordor said, "and you can trust us all—to serve our best interests. No one can be certain about a Sirian, not even another Sirian, but it is better to have them with you than against."

"The flower child?" Riley asked.

"Four one zero seven?" Tordor said. "We have yet to hear a lot from it, and what it says is cloaked in obscurity. But I have no reason to doubt its ability to cooperate. Its evolutionary development has instilled a need for community."

"But not necessarily of community with meat creatures," Asha said.

"True," Tordor said. "But its record in the galactic community is clean, and no Aldebarani has been accused of eating sapients. They have their own protein supplies."

"What about the Centauran?" Riley asked with a slight nod at the birdlike alien.

"If we recruit Xi we may have difficulty with—"

But before Tordor could finish, the room began to dissolve around them.

"Damn it!" Riley said as his feet sank into the floor and the passenger quarters began to fade into the terrifying nonexistence of Jump space. First the walls and ceiling became transparent and disappeared and he stared into the awful emptiness of nothing. He reached for Asha. She was still solid, an anchor in a sea of antireality waves. The other aliens, though, were distorted into caricatures like drawings in a horror show. They seemed to be killing each other. He heard Tordor say something. "What?" he asked. It emerged as a giant interrogation mark before it fell and shattered on the floor, which suddenly had hardened, imprisoning his feet, and he could feel his outthrust arms imprisoned in walls that had suddenly pressed in upon him.

An exclamation mark materialized from the monster that Tordor had become. It soared toward the overhead where it broke into pieces like the question mark on the floor. And then it was over, as suddenly as it had begun, and Tordor said, "This should not have happened!"

Riley looked where Tordor pointed. The Centauran was on the

floor, or, more accurately, the parts that had once been the birdlike alien were on the floor—its beaked head detached from its body and lying a meter or so away, and blue-ish blood, or whatever fluid served as blood for the Centauran, pumping from its severed neck like the carcass of a chicken Riley's mother used to kill on Mars for special occasions.

Riley looked at Xi; the alien's knife was sheathed. "Now what?" he said. The words hung somewhere between Asha and Tordor, addressed to neither and to both.

Both Asha and Tordor were staring at the overhead display. The bright line had jumped toward them, and Riley thought he could almost distinguish individual stars. He turned to look behind him. The other pilgrims were standing immobile, gazing at the display and the evidence glowing upon it, not at the beheaded Centauran.

As he looked a tentacle lashed out and struck another alien, staggering it. The action might have been an accident, but it prompted retaliation and then general mayhem. Tordor moved quickly for his bulk and mowed his way through the battling aliens, using his strength and weight like a battering ram. The others scattered before him, some of them falling like game pins, and then Tordor returned, helping the fallen ones upright and slapping down arms and hands and tentacles.

When he returned to their side, he seemed just as placid and unmoved by the incident as he had been before. "Now this," he said, as if in answer to Riley's earlier question. "The time for cooperation is even closer than we thought."

Before they could answer, the hatch had opened again and the captain came through with his two armed guards. This time he was angry. "Now you've gone too far!" he shouted.

"And who is it that has gone too far?" Tordor asked.

"Look at that!" the captain said, pointing at the Centauran on the floor. "Now you're killing each other, and those who aren't killing each other are trying to do so."

"Isn't that our business?" Tordor asked.

"Well," the captain said. "Well—"

"Not well," Asha said, "but perhaps inevitable."

"As the captain, I can't accept limits on my authority aboard this ship. The result would be chaos and, ultimately, catastrophe for all."

"You have accepted limits, Ham," Riley said gently. "You have a passenger list of alpha beings, and they will not be ruled. You will have to let us solve our own problems and punish our own crimes, and we won't let anybody know."

"We can't have unannounced Jumps, either," Tordor said. "That is against the galactic code."

"The comm must have malfunctioned," the captain said. "The important thing is that the Jump was made without incident."

"Which means that we can go forward," Asha said, "but we go back at our peril."

"And yet we must go back."

"Unless we find the Transcendental Machine," Asha said, "and that will solve all our problems."

"In what way?" the captain said. "I don't recall anything about intergalactic travel."

"Consult your pedia, Captain," Asha said. "That's part of the legend. But I was being ironic."

"Irony is wasted on moments like this," the captain said. "Ah," he protested, "I can't do anything with you. Clean up that mess!" He pointed out the body on the deck. "And clean up your own situation here, or by the transcendental itself, I'll clean it up for you."

He turned angrily toward the hatch.

"Calmly, Ham," Riley said. "Calmly."

The captain moved more slowly and deliberately toward the hatch and closed it gently behind him.

"Now what?" Riley repeated.

"Now we must put into effect the mutual defense group about which we spoke before all this happened," Tordor said. "But first we must take care of this—" He indicated with his short trunk the body of the Centauran on the deck. Then he turned toward 4107. "Why?" he asked.

The flower child said something in the thin whispering of its species. Riley's pedia did not attempt a translation.

"Ah," Tordor said. He turned toward Riley and Asha. "It wants to tell us its story."

"The flower child killed the Centauran?" Riley said.

"No other creature could have done it," Tordor said.

CHAPTER FIFTEEN

4107's Story

4107 said (translated by Tordor):

We are called the People, just as species throughout the galaxy call themselves the People. Whatever language we use—the movement of air through passages that restrict its flow in various distinguishable ways, the rubbing of mandibles, the gestures of tentacles, the release of pheromones, or, in our case, the disturbance of air by the movement of fronds—the translation is always the same. We are the People.

Our world is called Earth, as every world is called Earth in its own language. You might call it Flora, because we were a flower people, and for uncounted generations we lived our simple lives of seedlings springing from the soil, growing into maturity and sprouting flowers, enjoying fertilization, dropping our petals and then our seeds upon the soil, and depositing our decaying bodies to nourish the next generation. The generations were uncounted because every day was the same, and every year: we were born, we lived, we reproduced, and we died. Flora was a big world, drawn by its massive gravity into great plains and placid seas, and we thrived in peace and plenty amid mindless warmth and fertile soil. That is the time the People look back upon as paradise before we were expelled.

True, Flora had grazers, herbivores who lived among us and

nourished themselves with our vegetable plenty, and predators who prevented the herbivores from destroying themselves by overgrazing and overpopulation, but the People responded with one of the great breakthroughs of Floran evolution: we made ourselves unpleasant fodder, and when the grazers evolved in response, we developed poisons. The grazers died off, and then the predators, and only weeds remained as competitors. We developed herbicides, and then we were truly supreme and supremely content in our mindless vegetable way. The process took many long cycles, but finally Flora was ours and we were Flora.

Then a passing astronomical body came into our ideal existence like divine punishment for our hubris, showering Flora with devastating radiation that nearly destroyed all life on the planet including the People, stirring Flora's inner fires and releasing continents from their loving embrace. The paradise that Flora had been became the hell that Flora was: eruptions poisoned the air and lava flows covered the plains; the continents crashed together and pushed upward great mountain ranges. The people perished.

Centuries passed and long-buried seeds poked their ways through cracking lava. Among them was a single great Floran, now known as One. Before One, Florans had no awareness of separate existence. All contemporary Florans trace their origin from One. Through a process instigated by the destruction caused by the invading astronomical body, perhaps, or more likely by the radiation that showered the planet from the passing cosmic missile or was released with magma from Flora's long-sheltered interior, One developed the ability to pull its roots from the soil, an ability it passed along to its descendants. With maneuverable roots, this great Floran no longer had to trust the uncertain breeze to distribute its seeds to suitable soils; it, and its descendants, moved meter by meter and year by year to sheltered valleys where Florans could deposit their seeds in soil prepared to receive them, with more than a hope that chance would allow them to grow and flower.

Each generation took as its designation an ascending number. I am the forty-one hundred and seventh generation since the great One. All the preceding generations have changed, generation by generation, to gain movement, intelligence, and understanding of the world that nurtured and then tried to destroy them, and the uncaring universe that destroys as blindly as it nurtures.

How can I describe the impact of intelligence? Every species represented here has experienced it, but none remembers. Florans remember. The history of our species is recorded in the seeds of their consciousness. At first it was only the memory of process, the irresistible bursting from the seed pod, the passionate thrusting upward toward the sun and downward toward moisture and food, the satisfying flow of nutrients through capillaries and their cellular transformation into substance, the delightful flowering, the ecstatic fertilizing, and the determined growth of seeds into which all past and future was poured, and the fading sere time that ends in death. But then awareness of environment entered, and from that all else flowed.

We learned that the universe was more than the sun, the soil, and water. The universe held many suns, the Earth held many soils, and the rivers, the lakes, and the seas held many waters, and some of these were nurturing and some were not. We learned that we could manipulate our environment, controlling the fertility of the soil and the rain that fell upon it, and then that we could manipulate ourselves, controlling the patterns of biological inheritance we passed along to our seeds. And we learned to limit our reproduction so as not to exhaust our resources and thus, having postponed our flowering and our going to seed, learned that we could postpone the dying that went with it.

Longevity beyond the season meant an acceleration of the learning process. We learned to develop special breeds, some for greater intelligence to provide more understanding of the universe, some for a new ability you call vision to perceive the world and the universe in new ways, some for manipulative skills to make us independent of our environment, and some for memory to store the wisdom gathered by the others. And finally we learned the terrible truth—that the passing cosmic body that had expelled us from paradise was not some chance interstellar visitor, not some cosmic joke by the cosmic jokester, but a relativistic missile flung across our path by uncaring aliens, envious of our world and eager to reap the benefits of a heavy planet and the mineral wealth that it might vomit from its depths.

We learned all this when the Alpha Centaurans landed in their sterile metal ships.

The shining vessels from a world far from Flora descended upon our world, glowing from their passage through an atmosphere thicker than any Centaurans had known but thinner for the passage of the invading missile many thousands of cycles before. They glowed with heat, these vessels, and slowly cooled before the Centaurans emerged like meat asserting its natural dominance over the vegetable world. They wasted no thought or pity on the Florans they had crushed or the paradise they had destroyed. Why should they? They were the gods of the universe.

So we also felt, at first. They had come from the sky like gods, and they came in machines unlike anything ever to touch the soil of Flora, or even imagined among those of us who dreamed of life beyond our Flora-bound reality. The vessels destroyed billions in their descents, and billions more as they sent machines to clear the plains, scything us down, trampling us beneath their treads, plowing us under, mindless of our screams and efforts to communicate, to worship their magnificence in our vegetable way. They put alien seeds in our sacred soil, dull, unresponsive cousins from other worlds. We tried to talk to them but they had nothing but primitive reactions to soil and sun; all awareness had been bred from them, if it ever existed. The Centaurans thought of us, if they thought of us at all, as alien vegetation to be adapted to their purposes or, if that was unsuccessful, eliminated. Finally we despaired and recalled old biological processes. Our herbicides almost succeeded in eliminating the alien vegetation, but the Centaurans responded with even greater destruction, clearing even the few Floran stragglers from their territories, protecting their seedlings with energy walls and developing herbicides of their own.

Finally we realized the terrible truth: they were not gods; they were invaders, and they would destroy the People if we did not find an effective way to resist. At first we developed sharp leaves stiffened with lignite to kill them when they came among us. You have seen them in action. They are dangerous even to ourselves in a gusty wind. But the Centaurans seldom came into the territories that yet were ours; they preferred to send their machines, against whose metallic hides our weapons slid harmlessly aside. So we developed missiles, poisoned darts that could be expelled by an explosion of stored gas. The Floran that launched such a missile died in the act, but went willingly, for we are all part of the whole. And yet that too failed when our enemies kept us at a distance. We could not use the poison that our ancestors developed to kill the herbivores, because the Centaurans did not eat us, being properly wary of alien evolution. We grew machines like theirs, only with rigid skins of vegetable matter, but they crumpled against the metal of our enemies.

Finally we realized that we could not defeat an enemy using the enemy's weapons, and we moved the battle to our field, the soil and the vegetation that grew from it. If their alien vegetation was moronic, we would elevate it; if it was alien, we would naturalize it. We put our specialized agronomists to work, and within a few generations they infected Centauran seeds with Floran genes subtly inserted to express themselves over the centuries. We took advantage of storms and high winds to scatter the seeds among the Centauran fields and waited while the Centaurans continued their campaign of genocide until only a few remote pockets of Floran civilization remained and our hidden depositories of seeds. Would our tactic succeed before we were destroyed beyond revival?

The memories of Florans are eternal; we can remember the sprouting of the first Floran upon a steaming planet. And the thoughts of Florans are long, long thoughts, suited to the pace of our existence from season to season. But even we began to despair until finally our stunted spies heard the first whispers of intelligence from the Centauran fields. Within a century the whispers grew into a clamor and the Centaurans began to sicken as their sentient food slowly assumed the character of our indigestible Floran genes. More centuries passed before the Centaurans realized that their diminishing vigor and increased disease could be traced to their diet. They wiped out their fields and brought in fresh seed from Centaurus, but it was too late. They could not eliminate all the altered vegetation, and their seeds, bred for dominance and power, soon transformed the new, infecting them with Floran pathogens and Floran intelligence. More Centaurans died.

At last they recognized the inescapable truth: against an entire planet invaders have no chance. They left in their big ships, shining like dwindling spears into the Floran sky, leaving their ruins and their alien vegetation behind.

*   *   *

We had Flora to ourselves once more, sharing it now with the up-lifted Centauran vegetation. We treated it with the compassion we never received from the Centaurans; we raised it to full sentience and gave it full membership in our community, and it responded by bringing new hybrid vigor to our lives and new memories to share. Those memories, now accessible to rational inspection, included an understanding of Centauran existence that previously we were never able to reach, and an experience with Centauran technology that we had found alien. For the first time we realized why the Centaurans could not recognize our sentience, and why they had departed, still bewildered by Flora's lethal resistance to their presence.

We also perceived that the galaxy was filled with alien species and that we could never be safe in our splendid isolation, that we had to leave our beloved Flora in order to save it. We took the information on Centauran spaceships, buried, unsuspected, in the Centauran seeds of memory and applied it to our own expertise in growing things. We grew our spaceships. At first they were mere decorative shells, but over the centuries they developed internal mechanisms from differentiating vegetable membranes and then movable parts. We grew organic computers operated at the cellular level by selected bacteria. And, finally, we evolved plants capable of producing, stor-ing, and releasing fuel, and the materials able to sustain their fiery expulsion.

Over many generations we tested them and saw them fail, disas-trously, one after the other: the hulls failed, the fuel ran out, the liners burned. But we persisted. We knew that the Centaurans, or some other rapacious meat creatures, would return, but we had the vegetable tradition of patience, and we knew that we would persist until at some distant moment we would succeed. And then one of our Centauran sisters produced the answer—the ability to extract metal from the soil and to shape it, molecule by molecule, into support beams and rocket liners. Another, remembering a Centauran model, developed the ability to process internal carbon into a beanstalk extending, atom by atom, into the sky.

Finally we were ready physically if not psychologically. A crew was assembled. Since we share the same heritage and memories, though some were specialized in different ways, the selection was easy even if the process was hard. As a species, our dreams were rooted to the soil; our nightmares were filled with the dread of being separated from it. But our will was stronger than our fears, and we launched ourselves into the aching void in which Flora and her sister planets existed, we discovered, as anomalies. The experience was terrifying. Most of us died of shock, a few from madness that our species had never before experienced. But a few survived to return and contribute their seed memories to our gene pool, and from them grew sturdier voyagers. In the long progress of our kind, we persevered, we grew, we became what we needed to become. We explored our solar system.

Our benevolent sun had seeded seven planets and an uncountable number of undeveloped seedlings beyond the farthest aggregation, before they were blasted by the Centauran relativistic missile. The nearest planet was an insignificant rock sterilized by solar radiation; the next had been a gas giant before the missile had stolen much of its atmosphere; the third was a fair world, somewhat smaller than Flora, that had been destroyed by its animal inhabitants; on its overheated soil and evaporated sea bottoms we found evidence of meat-creature buildings like those of the Centaurans and a carbon dioxide–laden atmosphere that had apparently been a runaway reaction to industrial excess. It would have made a desirable home for

Florans but the searing temperature and the absence of water made it a wasteland.

Flora was the fourth planet. Beyond Flora were two more gas giants and a frozen rock. We were the masters of our solar system, though an impoverished one—and poorer for the Centauran violence. Our attackers came from beyond our system. We had to go farther into the unknown, farther then we could imagine.

We found ways to use our sun's energy that surpassed the natural system of converting its rays into stem and leaf and flower. We developed vegetable means of storing these energies. We grew stronger ships, and elevated them up our beanstalks into orbit. We evolved better, more spaceworthy Florans. And finally we set out for the stars, not knowing where we were going or what we were going to find or what we would do when we got there.

Generations later, as our primitive ships were still only a small way into the vast emptiness that is most of the universe, we were discovered by a galactic ship that had just emerged from a nexus point. If the Florans aboard our ships had been capable of astonishment, they would have wilted into death; if they had understood the chance of being discovered in this fashion, they would not have believed it.

Fortunately, the ship was Dorian, not Centauran, and even though the Dorians are grazers, they are enlightened grazers. They were as astonished by the Floran crews as the crews should have been astonished by their discovery, and for some cycles the Dorians looked for the meat creatures who must have been the real space voyagers. Finally, because they were enlightened, they came to the realization that we were intelligent, and, through inspiration and dedication, began to decipher our frond-moving communication, just as we began to understand their guttural explosions of air.

The Dorians installed their nexus devices in our Floran ships and took us to the Galactic Council. There they sponsored us, and because we were the first sentient vegetable creatures to be discovered in the galaxy and had displayed so much determination in setting out in primitive ships and persisting through unbelievable difficulties, we were admitted into the council of civilized species.

We had achieved our goal. We now were under the protection of the Galactic Council and all its members.

As soon as we understood council procedures—they are limited in scope but precise in their application—and began to acquire minimal insights into animal sentience and motivation (we comprehend concepts outside our own experience only with great difficulty), we filed a genocide complaint against the Centaurans. Council representatives listened with almost vegetable patience, but they ruled against us. We were not sentient, they said, when the Centaurans raped our system with their relativistic missile and the Centaurans, after their later invasion, could not be expected to understand our evolved sentience. Our complaint was dismissed. Indeed, some members of the council, perhaps with political ties to the Centaurans, suggested that we should be grateful to the Centaurans for the actions that produced our sentience. Florans do not understand gratitude, but they never forget injury.

Admission to the council brought many benefits and some restrictions. From beneficent members of the council we got knowledge of metalworking and machines, charts of the nexus points of the galaxy and the ability to launch our ships through the no-space between them, access to the vast library of information accumulated by a hundred species over the long-cycles, and the ability to reshape our world and our system's other worlds. We were forbidden, however, to emigrate to worlds beyond our system or to communicate, intellectually or genetically, with vegetable species on council worlds. This, we were told, would be a capital crime punishable by species extinction. That seemed extreme, but we recognized that we were new and different, and we had the other planets of our system to develop with our new skills, and, when that was complete, other worlds outside the council jurisdiction.

We called upon our vegetable patience, knowing that, before the end of time, we would succeed. What we did not understand was that other species, under the leadership of the Centaurans, would be launching scientific projects to block our genetic program, that all meat creatures, no matter how seemingly benign, will defend their kind against a threat from our kind. What they did not understand was that animal species have the advantage of speed and quickness but they burn out quickly and decay, while vegetation is slow but persistent. In the end we will win before entropy finally defeats us all.

And yet—all our voyaging beyond the limits of Floran psychology, all our acceptance by the galactic community, all our new knowledge and confidence in survival, if not as certain of final dominance, was not enough. In order to do these things, we had changed. Vegetable existence distrusts and dislikes change, and accepts it only under duress and through the long, slow swing of the cosmos. We had become great, and we hated it.

And then the humans erupted from Earth—meat inspired by hubris—and, soon after, war began, and all that we had thought and planned was put aside. We did our part in the war, but mostly in the peace. Animals fight wars; flowers practice peace. We delighted in the peace and the stasis that followed the war; we might even have become content with our lot, difficult as it was to reconcile with our essential being. And then word came about the Prophet and the Transcendental Machine. More change. More threat to stasis. More damage to our sense of self. And so, once more, against every instinct, we had to change. Out of this crisis I was grown, against every Floran instinct, to assume the reviled role of individual, to act alone and through my sacrifice find salvation for my sisters. I cannot describe my desolation, my grief, my anguished separation from my fellow Florans as I joined this voyage. I cannot describe, even, what it means to refer to myself as "I."

But I will persevere, because my people demand what only I can provide: a return to paradise. Through me the Transcendental Machine will remove the curse of sapience.

CHAPTER SIXTEEN

The last movements of 4107's fronds had ceased, and the echoes of Tordor's translation had died away before Riley said, "The Floran hasn't told us why it killed the Centauran."

The flower's fronds moved again, stirring the air in movements that might have had meaning. Maybe they did have meaning, but his pedia was silent. Maybe Floran frond movement was too difficult even for a biological computer that knows everything.

"The Floran says that the action was not revenge, as some might believe," Tordor said. "It was self-protection and protection of the mission." The Dorian listened again. "It overheard the Centauran attempting to organize a takeover of the ship and the elimination of all competitors as soon as the ship reaches the farther spiral arm. Meat creatures talk more freely around flowers, it says, particularly Centaurans." Tordor listened and nodded. "But the Centauran noticed the Floran nearby and, perhaps fearing what its tradition led it to doubt, attacked during the confusion of the Jump."

The Floran's fronds stopped and so did Tordor. Riley wondered how much of 4107's story was Floran and how much was Tordoran. Perhaps it was no coincidence that Dorians had been the Florans' salvation and Florans referred to Dorians as enlightened aliens. "And who was the Centauran speaking to?"

Again Tordor translated the movement of the fronds, "The Centauran was speaking to Xi."

The weasel crouched as if in preparation to launch an attack, or to defend itself from an attack.

"But Xi kept his hand on his knife during the entire conversation," Tordor continued.

The weasel relaxed.

"And why were Xi and the Centauran fighting before the Jump?" Asha asked.

"This, the Floran believes, was to throw off suspicion," Tordor said.

They looked at Xi. It seemed unconcerned that it might be implicated in conspiratorial behavior.

"How many others have been enlisted in the Centauran's plot?" Asha asked.

"The Floran doesn't know," Tordor said. "In my opinion it may have started its recruiting with Xi, who seems like a natural candidate."

Again Xi did not react to being cast as a conspirator.

"But it may have contacted many," Todor continued. "It never approached me."

And yet the Dorian would be a key member of any group attempting to seize control, Riley thought. "Which makes far more essential our own self-defense group."

"And how will that be different from the Centauran's plan?" Tordor asked.

"We're not organizing it in secret, we don't intend to leave anybody out," Asha said, "and we don't intend to kill anybody who doesn't want to join us."

"I am with you, of course," Tordor said.

"And does the Floran want to join us?" Riley asked.

Tordor waved his proboscis in what seemed like a meaningful

manner. The Floran replied—perhaps—with movements of its fronds.

"The Floran says that it joined the group on the space elevator, and it does not change loyalties," Tordor replied. "It is like me."

"And you, Xi?" Riley asked, turning to the weasel-like alien.

"I will defend the group to the death," Xi said, putting his good hand on his knife.

Riley didn't know whether Xi meant their deaths or his, but he knew it would be better to have him where he could be watched rather than creeping around the perimeter, studying their backs.

"None of them is to be trusted," Riley's pedia said.

Of course, Riley replied.

What no one expected was the captain's voice over the communicator saying, "Our last Jump has left us in proximity to a star." An image of a dwarf sun appeared on the holovision screen in front of them. "It seems to have planets, though what this system is doing out here in the middle of nowhere is a mystery."

Riley looked at Tordor and then at Asha. Asha could not reveal what the wandering star meant, if she knew, without unmasking herself as the Prophet. She shrugged at his unspoken inquiry as if to say that this was a surprise to her as well, or, since she was supplying the coordinates and that seemed unlikely, she was unwilling to speculate in front of all the others.

"That the space between spiral arms is empty is a common misapprehension," Tordor said. "It has fewer stars but is not barren."

"What would it be like to live in a place as lonely as this?" Riley asked.

"And what rational creatures evolved here would make of the universe is philosophically fascinating," Tordor said.

"How did it get here?" Asha said. "Hydrogen atoms in the Gulf are too diffuse to nourish star formation, so it must have been left over from the early evolutionary process that separated the spiral arms, or it got expelled from one of them."

"Another cause of philosophical or theological distress for galactics," Tordor said.

"It may have been fleeing from something," Xi interjected.

Riley and Asha turned to look at it as if surprised to find the alien commenting about something not to its advantage or disadvantage.

"Cultures, like governments or individuals, can be deadly," Xi said.

"Xi is correct," Tordor said. "There have been times when I have wished the Dorian system could be isolated from its neighbors." Four one zero seven's fronds moved in a complicated pattern. "The flower agrees," Tordor said.

"A fascinating speculation," Asha said, "but mere political disagreement would be inadequate motivation for such a massive enterprise."

"Not if it were fleeing contagion," Xi said. "Self-preservation is a powerful motive."

Asha looked at the holographic display, where a single sun had been reproduced, shining in isolated splendor, as if contemplating a galactic arm so overripe with corruption that an entire solar system would flee from it in horror.

"Of greater immediate concern," Riley said, "is why the last nexus opened so close to one."

"Perhaps," Asha said, "it offers an oasis on this desert."

"Or a supply station," Riley said.

The captain spoke again over the communicator. "We will have to pause here to allow our hydrogen reserves to be refilled before completing our journey to the other spiral arm."

Dismay erupted in the room as the pilgrims realized that their trip was to be delayed when their destination had become so clearly accessible.

"I know that this will be a disappointment to many of you," the captain continued, as if sensing the unrest, as he may well have done, "but our supply of fusable hydrogen has run dangerously low."

The room quieted again, with only a few individual voices raised here and there.

"While we are refueling at one of the gas giants," the captain went on, as if throwing the passengers a bone of appeasement, "we will allow a small party the opportunity to explore one of the rocky planets in the habitable zone."

"Ah, yes," Riley said, "a supply station."

"What does it say about the capabilities of the alien civilization that it maneuvered an entire planetary system into a position to supply ships traveling between spiral arms?" Asha said.

"Perhaps even a supply chain scattered across the Great Gulf," Riley said.

"They may merely have accommodated their supply system to existing stars," Tordor said.

"That would suggest," Riley said, "that the nexus points that allow passage in finite time were created, not discovered."

"Always a possibility," Tordor said. "Even, I would judge, a probability."

"Then what can we say about the capabilities of an alien species that could create nexus points?" Asha said. "That's even more impressive than moving solar systems." She shivered.

"If we want to be among those allowed to explore," Riley said, "we should submit our request promptly. After being cooped up together so long, everybody is going to want shore leave."

The holographic display now revealed a gas giant planet and then it was replaced by a blue world that looked livable.

Riley handed the captain his list of passengers for the exploratory trip. They were standing in the captain's cabin where Riley had cornered him. The captain looked at the handheld with an intensity its message didn't deserve. "You seem to have collected all the usual suspects," he said.

"Suspects of what?" Riley said. The ship reeked of many odors, most of them so alien they stung the nose or got blocked entirely, but Riley thought the cabin smelled of desperation.

The captain paused and then said, "Don't be so touchy, shipmate. You know what I mean. These are all the potential troublemakers, including a confessed murderer."

"Self-defense," Riley said. "And every one of your passengers, I have come to believe, was selected for this quest, and every one was a leader of his species."

"Except you and me," the captain said, and laughed. His amusement seemed forced. "Selected by whom?"

"That is the question, isn't it?" Riley said. "Maybe the same ones who picked you to captain this dangerous mission and gave you a ship that was headed for the salvage yard."

The captain sat down on the shelf that folded out from the wall and left Riley standing before him like a supplicant. "As far as I knew," he said, "this was a routine assignment in a ship that was in no worse condition than a hundred others that survived the war."

"Hardly routine," Riley said, gesturing toward the image on the wall that reflected the ship's position in the Great Gulf.

"It turned into something else," the captain said.

"And yet you had your instructions."

"It was going to be different, that was clear," the captain said, "but how different I had no way of knowing—not until we headed into the Gulf. Anyway, ship commanders were all over the unemployment registers after the war. Nobody turned down any command, no matter how weird."

"And in a ship with a gauge that misread the hydrogen supply."

The captain looked up sharply. "How did you—?"

Riley looked inscrutable.

"Not true," the captain said. "No one could have anticipated a voyage like this. Anybody would have run low."

Riley smiled.

"We could have made it to the other arm," the captain said. "It was simple prudence to make a refueling stop."

"If that's your story."

"And why did you come aboard this ship of fools?" the captain said. "You've never told me that."

"A lot of reasons," Riley said. "None of them any concern of yours."

"I'm concerned about the motives of every passenger and crew member aboard," the captain said. "They are my business if I'm going to get this ship and its passengers to their destination and back."

"Good luck with that," Riley said. "Both getting at the motives and getting back with the ship."

"I'm not a fool," the captain said. "I know there are opposing forces loose in the galaxy, governments, businesses, ideologies . . . I know that the discovery of a Transcendental Machine would change everything and that all of these forces have a stake in the status quo or in changing their relative status. And I know that adding humanity to the galactic mix upset everything and that the war has made pacifists of us all, and that the Transcendental Machine threatens all that."

"And yet, knowing all that, you took this job anyway."

"We don't have many chances in life at making a difference," the captain said.

"But what kind of difference?" Riley said.

"That's the question, isn't it?"

"As for my motives," Riley said, as if offering the captain a small return for his candor, "I'm the least of your worries. Anybody else on this ship might want to destroy it or kill anybody else among the passengers or the crew. But I'm not one of them."

The captain looked frustrated. He scribbled on the handheld and thrust it at Riley. "Here!" he said. "Take your exploring party!"

"Asha said to ask for the captain's barge," his pedia said. "I agree."

"In the captain's barge?" Riley said.

The captain hesitated and then scribbled again on the handheld. "Yes. In the captain's barge."

When Riley got back to the passenger lounge, Tordor was in one corner of the room with the coffin-shaped alien, as if in conversation. Xi was with another group, perhaps sounding them out, perhaps bragging about its prowess with a knife. The flower child was standing where it had been when Riley left, fronds idly moving, alone as it often was. Riley went to Asha. He offered her the handheld. She shrugged and said, "He okayed our list."

Riley nodded. "And allowed us to take his barge."

Asha's gaze moved from the handheld to his face. "Good."

"My pedia said it was your idea," Riley admitted. "I don't know why."

"Maybe we'll find out."

Riley nodded toward Xi and Tordor. "What are they up to?"

Asha motioned to the display. The alien sun seemed a little larger, a little closer. "They're trying to calm the other voyagers. And keep them from raising a fuss when we go off exploring."

"How do they hope to do that?"

"By making it seem like the captain's idea."

"Because?"

"Because he wants to create dissension, and insert a wedge between the others and the troublemakers."

Riley looked quizzical. "That's what the captain called us."

"That was predictable."

"The question is," Riley said, "whether the story is right. Maybe the captain does want to get rid of us. This side trip may be a diversion from the main journey. And may even endanger reaching the Transcendental Machine."

"Or it may be the necessary prelude. There's no way to know. When I came this way before, we didn't stop. Who knows what we may have missed? The surest way to the goal sometimes goes through places that seem like detours, and it's been my experience that opportunities need to be seized."

"Or it only seems like it," Riley said with a note of irony, "because that's the way it happened when you succeeded. And if you failed . . ."

"I get it," Asha said. "But give me some credit for foresight."

"What I don't think we're giving enough consideration to are the forces competing for control of the machine. Even the captain knows that great powers are at work."

"*Even* the captain?"

"He's not the most thoughtful of observers," Riley said. "Paranoid? Yes. Analytical? No."

"Unless he's more subtle than you know. He could be a well-informed agent for one or more of the powers he mentions, and whatever he reveals may be calculated."

"Can't you tell?"

"His multiple add-ons are confusing. And I can't read minds."

"Only influence them?"

"Only those that are susceptible. And willing," Asha said. "Although influence is not the right term, either. More like powerful suggestion. Oh, it's impossible to describe if you haven't done it. I just don't want you to depend on something that might not be there when you need it."

Riley looked at her intently, started to say something and then stopped. "It's certain, though, that almost every power you can identify or imagine has one or more agents on board."

"Aliens are hard to read," Asha said.

"But any of them may be suspect."

"Including the captain?"

"Especially the captain. Certainly Xi. Maybe the Sirian. Maybe even Tordor. We can't trust anybody."

"Including me," Asha said.

"And me," Riley said.

"No, not you," Asha said with certainty.

"You know me that well?"

Asha nodded.

"What you don't know," Riley said, "is how I will react in a crisis, whether I will succumb to fear or pain or loss."

"I know you better than you know yourself," Asha said. "And I think better of you, too."

Riley didn't react immediately. Finally, he looked at her. "And I can trust you," he said.

"You don't know me," Asha said, "but I want you to trust me. Because then we can work together. And we both need somebody we can count on without reservation. Events are going to catch up with us. Times will be hard. We must survive. Both of us. Because of what we must do."

"And what is that?"

"That is what we must find out. Meanwhile, you're right. We must trust nobody except ourselves."

Riley reached out to take her hand. He found its strength and warmth curiously comforting. "We're in this together, then. To the end—"

The rest of his remarks were interrupted by the entrance of the barrel-shaped Sirian into the lounge. Behind him, almost hidden by Kom's bulk, was the slender figure of Jan.

"Jan has a story to tell you," Kom said.

CHAPTER SEVENTEEN

Jan's Story

Jan said:

Jon and I began life as two of a nine-member karass on a satellite of a gas giant in the human solar system. The planet was called Jupiter and the satellite was called Ganymede. We were part of an experimental program in group dynamics, aimed at producing a spaceship crew capable of coping with interstellar issues at all levels. We were clones, five males and four females, all with names so similar that they could have been the same one; all began with the letter *J*.

Our father, Jak, was the lead scientist in the project, a great man skilled in genetics and other biological sciences, literature, and languages. Our beginnings as part of a single ovum, of course, are no different from any other multiple births, common among aliens and not uncommon among humans. Our upbringing was what made us different; we were encouraged to think and act as one. We were a unit, a species into ourselves, a race apart. When we became capable of taking care of ourselves—still children, but precocious children—we were removed to an isolated station where, alone, we were responsible for the terraforming of Ganymede.

Why the "Jays," as we were called by a curious public? The scientists and statesmen who had created our cohort needed representatives who acted spontaneously, as one, who needed no verbal

interaction to do what needed to be done. The challenges of terraforming an alien planet are unpredictable; responses to crises must
be instant and intuitive. We were that group. And our superiors
needed to shape our cohort into an instrument capable of coping
with the worst that the universe, and its alien masters, could throw
at humanity.

We—even now I cannot speak easily in the first person singular—
understand that the process by which a planet or satellite is transformed into a world suitable for other species is controversial among
galactic powers, and condemned by many. The galaxy contains millions of suns, most with planets in the Goldilocks belt; many of
these never developed sentient life, and those that did sometimes
never developed technology. Galactic critics of terraforming never
hesitate to colonize worlds whose natives are technologically limited; we do not quarrel with their philosophy of bringing the blessings of the Galactic Confederation to the benighted. But we were
committed to the Cedan philosophy of sentience: sentient life
should be encouraged wherever it can exist. The only inhabitants of
Ganymede were mindless bacteria, and even they clung to a precari-
ous existence. We did not destroy the bacteria but made ourselves
immune to their effects, even as we knew that they would not survive the changes we were told to create.

Planets or satellites that lack the conditions necessary to sustain
complex life are like creatures whose mandate to evolve has been
frustrated by the accidents of their early history. They are failed
habitats, doomed by their pasts never to realize the potential existing in them during the explosive birth of the universe. They, too,
need transcendence, and we were the machine that could bring it to
them and let them fulfill their destinies. We brought salvation to the
yearnings of inanimate matter. Or so Jak told us.

Ganymede is a satellite of Sol's largest gas giant, Jupiter. Nonhumans know little about Sol's system—why should you, with so many systems in the inhabited galaxy?—and even humans have little understanding of their own neighborhood. Early human astronomers named most of the planets, and all the satellites they could perceive in their primitive instruments, after ancient mythological deities in whom they no longer believed. Humans cherish the imagination and the imaginary more than most galactics, and they humanize their environment with fanciful names. The huge and mighty Jupiter, for instance, was the supreme god of the ancient Romans; Ganymede, the cupbearer to the gods and a favorite of Jupiter, was a human transported to heaven on the back of Jupiter, who had taken the form of an eagle. Ridiculous, no doubt. But there is much to ridicule in human beliefs and behavior—imagination fuels the human endeavor and its follies are the unavoidable byproducts.

The planet Jupiter has sixty-three satellites, but only eight of them are big enough to be considered candidates for terraforming, and only four of these have any reasonable potential. Each of these four is different except in their orbits far from the sun and its life-giving warmth. Except for the ring of debris left over from a failed planet, Jupiter is located in the next orbit out from Mars, the last rocky planet with any hope of livability, and two orbits out from the human birthplace, Earth. All of Jupiter's major satellites suffered from significant habitability problems, receiving only four percent of the sunlight that falls upon Earth and orbiting within the intense charged particles of Jupiter's radiation belt. The satellites, moreover, have significant components of frozen gases, some of them poisonous to human existence. They have little or no atmosphere but some have frozen volatiles that could be transformed into atmospheres by heating, especially water-ice in the case of Ganymede.

Jupiter is almost a system in itself. The gas giant contains more matter than all the rest of the planets in the solar system put together, and it looms in the sky like a failed sun. Its satellites are similarly sized. Ganymede is larger than the planet closest to the sun, Mercury—another planet named after an ancient god. But Ganymede is not as massive. Although it has an iron-rich liquid core inside a mantle of silicate rock, half of its mass—one thousand kilometers deep—is water. Most of it is frozen, although a saltwater sea lies two hundred kilometers deep, sandwiched between layers of ice. Its liquid core provides Ganymede with the only magnetosphere among solar satellites; it also affords the moon some protection against the effects of charged particles, primarily those from Jupiter.

Our father provided a habitat. It was constructed from one of the minor moons of Jupiter, hollowed out with lasers, and fitted with living and working quarters before being maneuvered into position as a satellite of Ganymede. There we matured and developed the complex relationships of clones. I will say no more about that aspect of our social lives except to mention that they were close, closer than siblings, closer than mates, closer than parents and children. But we were also guided by our mission. After education periods with recordings and discussions, we worked on terraforming. First we designed self-sustaining thermonuclear heat generators and ways of dropping them onto the frozen seas of Ganymede. Within a Terran year, we had constructed the first handful of them and landed them on the surface of the giant satellite. The failure rate was less than one in a hundred. As soon as they had landed, the generators melted bodies of water that would grow into lakes from which they would extract heavy water to refuel themselves. Soon their construction and dispersal became automated. Over a long expanse of time, they would eventually form open seas that would finally join to provide

Ganymede with a liquid ocean kilometers deep. But that would not happen within our lifetimes and perhaps not within the lifetime of our culture. If that were the case, we would leave it as a gift to our successors—a water world suitable for a new generation.

Our job was not finished, however. Next we set up a process to fashion gigantic mirrors out of thin, coated films, and position them in the space around Ganymede so that they could focus the feeble rays of the sun upon Ganymede's surface. They had to be strong enough to resist the bombardment of charged particles and the forces that worked to alter the mirrors' positions, their shapes, and their focus. We tried many combinations of materials before we found one that was sturdy enough to survive but thin enough to manufacture and deploy. We designed and built computers equipped with lasers to monitor the focusing of these giant mirrors and to correct changes in their positions with high-powered laser bursts. When these space mirrors began to shine upon Ganymede and increase the amount of insolation, we had shortened the terraforming of the satellite by thousands of years.

Our final project was the creation of a monomolecular film that would form a cocoon-like sphere around Ganymede to prevent the escape of the atmosphere our thermonuclear generators and space mirrors would create. This was our greatest challenge, since it required not only the invention of a substance new to nature but one that, if created, also had to resist the charged particles of Jupiter's radiation belt and restore itself after meteorite strikes and, eventually, the passage of ships. Finally, after many failed attempts, we developed a biological solution from the native bacteria of Ganymede—a simple cell equipped to reproduce and spread into a film that lived at the top of the new atmosphere nourished by the chemical brew liberated from Ganymede's melted primal substances and energized by Jupiter's charged particles.

That elegant solution brought us great praise from our father, even though he cautioned that we had unleashed a dangerous new living substance upon the universe that, in time, might evolve and proliferate into a competitor to other living creatures in the universe. He thought that unlikely, however, and he was willing to take the risk. The monomolecular film would take centuries before it completed its cocoon around Ganymede. And even if it escaped Ganymede and Jupiter, that would be far in the future when humans and other creatures would be equipped to handle any such problems.

What we did not know, however, was that each of us had been infected by our new creation; our immunization had not worked on the transformed bacteria. The effects were unnoticeable at first, and even when they appeared, we attributed them to our maturity and development. The bacteria became symbiotic parasites, strengthening our bodies, improving our reactions by adding neurons and diminishing the resistance of the nerve connections. Finally, as they developed, they became internal companions, collecting and analyzing data, translating difficult materials and languages, and counseling us on what to do and say and even think.

Then we knew what they were and what we were—full-body biological computers—and it was too late to turn back. They were our own transcendental devices, just as we had been the transcendental mechanism for Ganymede. The difference was that, like our relation to Ganymede, the change was not an improvement of our own capabilities but one imposed upon us. We were not elevated; our symbiote was the new creature. And it was the symbiote that put together the truth that this is what our father had planned from the beginning.

We were eight years old when we were left in the satellite we called "home," but we had been raised in an isolated habitat orbiting

Earth with no memories of anything before. Or rather we raised ourselves with the help of electronic equipment and supervision from another habitat in the same orbit. We were twenty-eight when we finished our task and assumed our new symbiotic existence. But we did not emerge from the experience intact. Jed and Jef died from radiation poisoning. They were in charge of the space mirrors and were exposed too long to Jupiter's radiation belt. Jil and Jem died from accidents involving the thermonuclear generators and their drop onto the ice of Ganymede. Job and Jin died from a reaction to the symbiote infection.

Then our father addressed us once more—Jon and Jer and me.

He spoke to us in holographic projection, as he always did. When we thought we would not be overheard, we used to joke among ourselves that our father's life was too precious to risk among the charged particles and debris of Jupiter's belt. But the joke had a tinge of bitterness: we were there and we had lost two-thirds of ourselves.

"Your job is done," Jak said. "Now you have a new task."

"What of our brothers and sisters?" Jer said.

We waited for Jak's reply. He was far from Jupiter, probably on his moon station or his La-Grange-point habitat, and transmission delays meant a disjointed conversation. Finally his answer came. "That five of you died in this noble effort was tragic—"

"Six!" Jer said.

Jak went on as if he had not heard—and, indeed, he would not for another four minutes: "—but the sacrifice must not be in vain. And it will not."

"What can compensate for our loss?" Jer asked.

Jak went on as if he had heard the question. "You have accomplished something godlike, appropriate to mighty Jupiter himself.

You have given life to dead matter. You have created a new world for the human species. Your names will be among those blessed by human generations."

"And yours," Jer said.

"In the process," Jak continued, "you have remade yourselves. You started as gifted children, and you have become adults capable of anything. You have become like gods. You have become gods."

"Those who survived," Jer said.

"You are prepared for your next challenge," Jak said, "to represent humanity in an alien galaxy. The galactics who control the stars are old and wise and powerful. Humanity is young and restless and troublesome. We emerged from our long evolutionary path like butterflies breaking free of our cocoons into a cold and hostile world. But, for a weak, system-bound species, we fought the alien confederation to a standstill. The losses on both sides were terrible, though far more significant on ours, with our limited numbers and resources, than on theirs. But we proved ourselves worthy of our place in the galaxy. Now a new issue has emerged to disturb the fragile peace that ensued."

We waited for Jak to continue. What could be more important than the war that had just ended? What could be more important to us than the lives we had lost?

"A new religion is sweeping the galaxy," he continued. "Or rather, a movement that may become a religion. It is based on a rumor that a Transcendental Machine has been discovered, a machine that can realize the potential in any sentient creature. You can imagine what such a machine might accomplish for any of the civilizations in the universe, including our own. And you can imagine what the possibility of such a machine might do to the fragile peace that was negotiated after the recent war."

We looked at one another. My symbiote put words in my head: "Don't listen to him," it said. "We are your partners, your own transcendence. We can provide what that Transcendental Machine—if it exists—only promises. If you listen to him, you risk everything we have gained."

Minutes passed, and then Jak said, "You haven't said anything."

"What is there to say?" Jer asked. "We understand the issue, but what can we do about it?"

After more minutes Jak responded, "An Earth ship has been ordered to pick up a mixed group of galactics at Terminal. Jan and Jon have been named to the crew. That took some doing, but I managed to call in some favors. The ship has already left, but Jan and Jon can join the ship at Terminal."

"Why should we do that?" I asked, or rather my symbiote commanded me to ask.

Minutes later, Jak said, "The spaceship *Geoffrey* has been instructed to seek out the Transcendental Machine. The so-called Prophet—the person that rumors say first was transformed by the machine and let fall, carelessly or deliberately, information about it—will not be able to resist joining the passengers. Your first task will be to identify the Prophet and discover his secrets, if he has any, and, second, you must be first to discover the Transcendental Machine, if it exists, and secure its secrets for our species."

"What can we two do among so many?" I asked.

After minutes the answer came, like all Jak's responses impatient with the resistance of the universe. "You have been bred and trained for this. Your destiny calls."

"Yes, Father," we said as one, but if Jak had seen our faces he would not have believed our words.

"If you cannot be first to the Transcendental Machine, you must

JAMES GUNN

be sure that it does not fall into alien hands, even if that means destroying it. Then you must return with your information or find a way to get the information back to me, even if you cannot return."

"Especially if we cannot return," Jon whispered. "And won't that start another war?" Jon said aloud.

After another long pause, Jak replied, "That is a risk we will have to take—for the sake of humankind."

"A risk *we* will have to take," I whispered.

"Now there is no more time," Jak said. "Your ship is waiting, and you cannot delay if you are to join the *Geoffrey* at Terminal."

And so it began.

The ship was small and fast, but we were a day behind. Only by a risky shortcut that skipped an intermediate nexus did we make it to Terminal before the *Geoffrey* arrived, and then, as you all know, we had to wait. And repel the attack by the barbarian Minals from the hills. And the sabotage against the climber. By the time we reached the *Geoffrey* we had almost forgotten our mission. But our symbiotes would not let us forget. They kept whispering to us, trying to undermine our instructions, trying to force us to become the inconspicuous biota-tenders that we were hired to be.

Our first task was to identify the Prophet. We had little opportunity to interact with the passengers. Jak should have bought us a place among the pilgrims, where the chief suspects were likely to be found, but maybe there wasn't time. Jak, though, was not a man who allowed time to shape his choices, so it was likelier that he had arranged for some other agent in the passenger quarters. You can speculate among yourselves who that might be, but we caution you that Jak is subtle and clever, and so are the other forces who operate openly or secretly throughout the galaxy. In fact, Jon and I had come to believe that almost every passenger may be an agent for powerful individuals or organizations.

To fulfill our mission, then, we had to do the best we could with our observations while waiting on Terminal. Evaluating aliens is difficult at best, but the barbarian attack gave us a chance. A battle calls on everyone's ultimate skills. We watched, depending on our symbiotes to react for us. But everyone was exceptional: the pachyderm, the weasel, the flower . . . everyone. Any of you could be the Prophet, including Riley, who reacted with quickness and decision.

Once aboard the ship we integrated ourselves among the crew, and with the advantage of our symbiotes managed to perform our shipboard duties while we inspected our fellow crew members; keeping the ship's vegetation growing and the protein incubators free from contamination was simple compared to the challenges of terraforming. We knew that the Prophet could be a crew member. We considered the captain as a possibility. He was in a position to instigate, to guide, to shape, to control, and he had unusual abilities, not least the capture of the climber when it was swinging at the end of the severed beanstalk. But our symbiotes informed us of his add-ons as well as his dependence on navigational guidance from elsewhere in the ship—possibly from the Prophet. No other crew member seemed exceptional. Of course Jon and I, with our symbiotes concealed, would not have seemed exceptional to any of them, or, perhaps, to you.

Finally we reached the conclusion that we would have to search the passenger quarters. I volunteered. I had my own reasons that Jon did not guess, but then the loss of our clones and the separation from our home place was beginning to come between us rather than bring us together. Our symbiotes opposed the idea, as they had opposed much of what Jak had instructed us to do. But we had found a way to maintain a level of thought and action independent of their awareness and control. Even a karass needs some aspects of privacy and we had developed abilities our symbiotes did not suspect. They were far more susceptible to hormones to which we were accustomed and whose production we could, in part, control.

Our symbiotes were able to determine when the passenger quarters were quiet enough for me to slip in unobserved. If detected I was prepared with a cover story of a necessary repair, but no one challenged me. I found nothing to pin any suspicions upon and resolved to investigate one of the sleeping compartments—Riley's, whom I still suspected. Again, nothing.

At that moment the tragedy of my existence fell over me like a black tent. My task was impossible, my father had turned into an uncaring manipulator, my body and part of my mind were under the control of a soulless bacterium, Jer was separated by light years beyond measure and intended for purposes that Jon and I felt would end in vileness and probably death, and Jon and I were all that was left of our karass. The sorrow of all this was overwhelming.

And in that moment I recalled to memory the instructions for reinstating the cryogenic features of the sleeping compartment, performed the necessary adjustment, and turned it on, surprising my symbiote—and that had been my purpose from the beginning: to kill the bacterium that had taken control of my life and my will, even if it meant my own death in the process. The overwhelming grief—real as it was, real as it had to be—was the tool I used to deceive my symbiote long enough to let me achieve my end, and its.

Now I learn that I failed and that Jon, in despair after my action, found a way to follow me into that long, cold sleep. But Jon will not awaken, and I am alone and afraid. In my desperation I betrayed the drive toward the transcendental that this voyage represents. My only hope is to pursue the final reward that Jak held out to us. If we found the Transcendental Machine, he told us, we could be reconstituted as a full karass, our clonemates restored from our memories and our genes.

But, alas, my symbiote is awakening, and I am afraid that Jak lied to us again.

CHAPTER EIGHTEEN

The captain's barge was a complete ship except for the lack of food gardens. Instead it was equipped with a supply of dried and frozen foods adequate to keep a handful of passengers alive between planets or while navigating to rescue, and an atmosphere recycling unit. Adequate, that is, if the passengers were human or humanoid enough to be sustained by human food. The ship consisted of only two sparse cabins—a passenger compartment with attachments for full-body hammocks and a tiny control cabin. And an engine room and a tank to store liquefied hydrogen to fuel the thermonuclear engines. Although this far from civilization, no amount of food or fuel was likely to be more than a gesture at survival.

The ship was crowded and smelled like a mixture of human sweat and alien effluvia and had no artificial gravity, but it was a ship, and a glorious escape from the claustrophobia of the *Geoffrey*.

At the last moment the barge crew had been joined by the enigmatic coffin-shaped alien. It had shown up at the airlock, and Tordor said, "This person wishes to join us." How he knew this was a mystery to Riley, who had heard nothing and neither had his pedia; but much in alien communication was beyond human capabilities to perceive, much less to understand. Perhaps Tordor was pretending or making it up, but the alien creature was there, waiting to board the barge with them.

"It wasn't on the list the captain approved," Riley said.

"The captain won't object," Tordor said.

"Let it come with us," Asha said.

It was a good thing, too. As soon as the barge cut loose from the *Geoffrey*, the alien floated to the control room, extruded cable-like arms, inserted them into holes beneath the controls, and made small clicking sounds.

"This person says that the computer program has errors, but it has fixed them," Tordor said.

"I'm not sure I want an alien creature I don't know, and have no way of knowing, determining whether this ship functions the way it is supposed to," Riley said. "Not to mention its competence to detect and fix computer errors in a system it has never seen."

"We all trust the mechanisms we have created to enable us to travel and survive in this unforgiving environment," Asha said.

"All the more reason not to have some alien thing or apparatus fooling around with them," Riley said.

"The computer is a thinking machine," Tordor said. "Our fellow pilgrim is a machine that thinks. The computer doesn't care if it survives; it will do what it is programmed to do. Our fellow pilgrim programs itself and wants to survive."

"It is a machine then?" Riley said.

"What it is the creature will reveal when it is ready," Tordor said.

"And why does it want to survive?"

"That, too, it will reveal when it is ready."

"And what makes it competent to program the computer?"

"It is a machine that thinks very well," Tordor said.

"Let it take over the ship's functions," Riley's pedia said.

"Let it take over," Asha said. "And think about this: the captain had good reason to get rid of us. We're the troublemakers among the passengers."

"There's that," Riley admitted.

The coffin-shaped alien continued to probe the ship's control panel.

"This person says that the hydrogen supply is low," Tordor said. "The gauges read full but there is only enough hydrogen to get us to the surface of the planet, not enough to enable us to take off again."

"Hah!" the weasel said. "The captain takes no chances."

The flower child made swishing sounds.

Riley had a hard time believing that his old comrade-in-arms would deliberately maroon him. The others, maybe. But then he reflected on the captain's behavior during the journey and asked himself if he really knew the captain anymore. "Maybe he drained the barge's supply to fuel the *Geoffrey* and the fuel gauge failed to record it properly."

"And maybe the computer program failed at the same time," the weasel said.

Riley shrugged. He didn't believe it, either, but then he didn't trust the coffin-shaped alien. "We'll have to go back," he said.

"Too late," Asha said. "The *Geoffrey* has already departed."

Riley looked at the control screen that showed only the fading glow of exhaust from the thermonuclear propulsion of charged hydrogen atoms.

"This creature says that if we land near a body of water it can use the thermonuclear engine to separate hydrogen from water," Tordor said.

"How long will it need?" Riley asked.

"No longer than we need to explore a nearby city," Tordor said.

*   *   *

And it was so.

The descent to the planet surface was smooth. Riley could not have done it as well himself. The coffin-shaped alien put the barge down without a bump on the beach of a green-frothed sea within sight of a group of buildings that resembled a city, if a city had been built by aliens with alien ideas about architecture and livability. It was curiously vertical.

On the way down they had observed the condition of the planet, which was in an ice age, with ice caps extending far into what might once have been temperate zones and glaciers probing farther toward the equator, whose seas still had liquid water. The coffin-shaped alien had detected no electronic emissions or unusual thermal concentrations.

"The sun has reddened," Asha said. "It no longer supplies the energy it once did."

"Maybe that's why the city builders abandoned the planet," Riley said.

"If they abandoned it," Tordor said.

"There's no sign of technology in operation," Riley said.

"There's no sign of a technology we recognize," Tordor replied.

The ship's computer had a rusty voice like a hermit who hadn't talked for most of a lifetime. "The planet's atmosphere has been checked and is breathable for oxygen-breathing creatures, though cool according to human standards. The soil has been checked for biota and injections have been prepared to immunize against potentially dangerous bacteria and unusual elements and molecules. For humans, of course."

"This creature says that the ship's computer is trustworthy and capable," Tordor said.

"I wish you would call it something besides 'this creature,'" Riley said.

"This creature says it can be called 'Trey,'" Tordor said.

"'Trey,'" Riley repeated. "I had a dog named Trey."

"Trey means three," his pedia said. "That may have some significance."

Riley and Asha submitted themselves to air-blown injections inside the airlock. Tordor and the weasel refused them, and the coffin-shaped alien not only didn't need them, it was going to stay in the ship along with the flower child, who couldn't move fast enough to keep up. The four explorers chose hand-weapons from the lockers, Riley and Asha put on jackets, and they stepped onto the alien planet.

It was a bracing moment, as the first steps on an unfamiliar world always are. Partly it was the experience of emerging onto solid ground with real gravity and real air after the long artificial life-support of a spaceship. Mostly, though, it smelled different—not only fresh after the recirculation of air used and reused uncountable times by humans and aliens, but differently fresh when it was an alien planet, like the scents of a foreign restaurant multiplied a thousand times.

The look of it was different, too. The hills and valleys and mountains were different shapes, the sea was a different color, and the sands and soil had different textures and no doubt different compositions. The sounds were different, as well: the wind made an odd, keening sound in the ear, and somewhere alien creatures spoke or complained or wailed—it was hard to tell if they were manufactured by living creatures or the planet itself.

It all took a great deal of getting used to. But they didn't have time. Strange animals appeared fleetingly behind hillocks or splashed in the alien sea. The exploring party pointed them out to each other and compared them to creatures they had known. But they were all subtly different. The land animals often had eight spindly legs or maybe six and two manipulating limbs in front, and the sea animals

they could glimpse were oddly shaped, compressed in places familiar creatures were not, and expanded in others.

"They're like wolves and rabbits and dolphins," Asha said.

"Yeah," Riley said, though he had never seen a wolf or a dolphin
and realized that Asha hadn't, either.

"Creatures evolve to occupy environmental niches, but from different beginning points," Asha said.

"Evolution is a force that acts upon us all," Tordor said. "The
question is: what has it produced in this arm of the galaxy, and how
will that affect us?"

"Or: how has it already affected us?" Asha said.

"You think this arm has influenced our own?" Tordor asked.

"Someone discovered or created the nexus points," Asha said,
"and someone moved this system or built cities on this planet before
the system drifted out of the local arm—cities that have not yet
crumbled."

"The Dorians claim we discovered the nexus points," Tordor said.

"And the Sirians claim they discovered them," the weasel
said, "and so did every other civilization we have encountered."

"Except humans," Asha said.

"It's a good bet that creatures from this arm were more advanced
than any in ours," Riley said. "Look at that city!" He gestured toward
the buildings that loomed in odd outline a kilometer or so away beyond the coastal hills. "It must have been abandoned a million cycles
ago, and yet it still stands, with no apparent signs of deterioration."

They had started toward the city when Tordor whirled back toward the barge. The flower child was standing in the open hatch
swinging its fronds frantically.

"It says we are under attack," Tordor said.

* * *

And it was so. The doglike creatures with eight legs were running toward them from the hillocks and over the sands, and strange creatures with tentacles were rising from the sea. They drew their weapons.

"There's too many of them," Riley said. "Tell the flower child to get back inside and protect the ship while we retreat to the city."

Tordor gestured at the distant ship, and the flower child retreated and closed the hatch. Tordor turned and led the rest of them toward a gap in the hills that opened from the beach toward the city. They moved rapidly. The doglike creatures were quick, scuttling more than running, but they fell behind. Then the city was in front of them, clustered in the valley below, even stranger up close.

The city was well preserved, as if it were a museum exhibit protected under glass. Slender translucent towers with jagged offsets and twists were scattered without apparent order across glassy surfaces. There were no streets, just crooked spaces between buildings where nothing grew and not even dust particles could find traction.

"How did they get around?" Riley asked, and Asha pointed at strands of transparent materials that connected the buildings near their tops and glowed in the reddened sunlight.

It was a magical city, a fairyland that would have captured the imagination of a million dreaming children.

" 'A rose-red city half as old as time,' " Riley's pedia said.

"How long has it been abandoned?" Riley asked. "A million cycles? A billion?"

"Somewhere between those," Tordor said.

"And still standing," the weasel said. Even it seemed impressed.

"What makes you think it's abandoned?" Tordor asked.

"There's no movement," Riley said. "No hot spots."

"Maybe they're night creatures," Tordor said. "And cold-blooded."

"We'll see," Riley said.

They moved down toward the city, Riley first, followed by Asha, Tordor, and the weasel. There were no roads or streets, as if the city builders hadn't needed surface transportation or had outgrown it. The surface was rough and rocky underfoot until they reached the valley and the beginning of the glassy surface they had noticed from the hills.

They moved cautiously between the buildings, which up close seemed even stranger than they looked from the hills, as if they had not been so much built as extruded. Nothing moved. The only sound was the odd swooshing of air currents as they struggled to find their way between staggered structures. Overhead the traceries of translucent strands glowed in the descending sunlight, but now they could see that in places the strands were broken; fragments remained on the surface beneath, along with accumulated dust, assorted debris, broken pieces of something that looked like wood, and an occasional plant that had taken root.

Riley and Asha walked carefully on the glassy surface but Tordor and the weasel were more sure-footed. Tordor strode forward confidently; the weasel scuttled behind.

The structures seemed to have no entrances and no apertures at all within reach, although they seemed open, even lacy, from about a third of the way from the surface level to their tops.

"Curioser and curiouser," Riley's pedia said. "Be very careful."

Tordor said, "Whoever built these structures came from above."

"They flew?" Riley said.

"Or they climbed," Asha said.

"And there they are now," Tordor said.

"Where?" asked the weasel.

"There!" Tordor said, and pointed toward the strands that connected the translucent structures in front of them.

Spider-like creatures were swarming down the traceries, which now obviously seemed much like webs.

"I think retreat is in order," Tordor said.

But as they turned they noticed that the webs behind them were filled with dark scuttling creatures as well.

"We're trapped!" the weasel squeaked.

"This way," Asha said, leading the way down an alley-like passage between structures. Riley followed. Tordor came more slowly. The weasel sprinted ahead of them all until it stopped in front of another web clustered with creatures.

"They're acting as teams," Asha said. "Trying to turn us back into the city. Odd behavior for arachnoids."

"Like pack animals," Riley's pedia said.

"I think we'd better get out," Riley said, and lifted his hand weapon. An explosive missile destroyed the bottom of the web ahead, scattering shards of translucent material and dark fragments of aliens. Those still alive scuttled back toward the top and sides and into apertures at the top of structures.

Riley's group moved forward rapidly under the web, slipping occasionally on the slick surface beneath, and reached the edge of the city. Dark figures had reached the surface behind and were racing toward them.

Riley shot again at a nearby building and sent a broken slab crashing to the ground, temporarily blocking pursuit. "They'll climb that soon enough," he said. "Let's get back to the ship."

"This expedition has been a disaster from the beginning," his pedia said.

As they reached the passage through the hills, he said, "Tell me again, Asha, why we decided to explore this world."

* * *

The seashore was deserted and the captain's barge stood closed and silent beside the restless alien sea. From their side they couldn't see whether a hose still stretched from the ship to the sea.

As soon as they descended from the hills, the eight-legged creatures—smaller versions of the city arachnoids—reappeared and began pouring over the dunes on either side of the ship. Riley's group raced toward the barge. As he ran, Tordor prodded his forward leg with his proboscis, signaling to the ship with a device whose function Riley had only guessed. But the ship's hatch remained closed.

"Faster!" Riley shouted and turned to fire an explosive bullet at the nearest group of attackers. A sport of red sand erupted like a gush of blood, and the wave hesitated. Riley fired at the group racing from the other side. It too paused before it came on again.

Now they were only a hundred meters from the ship and Riley could see that the hose had been retracted. He turned and fired once more toward the nearest group. One of the alien creatures had pressed forward, however, and was close enough to grab the weasel by one arm, too near to shoot. Riley grabbed the weasel and pulled. The arm held by the arachnoid broke free, and they were at the ship, looking up at the unbroken flank, turning to meet the attackers, when the hatch opened and a ramp tumbled out to let them in.

Riley turned in the hatchway as the ramp retracted, kicking away clutching mandibles, and seeing the creature that had attacked the weasel plunging an extrusion from its forward part deep into the weasel's lost arm. And the hatch closed.

"Are you badly hurt?" Riley asked the weasel. A purple substance was oozing from the socket where the right arm had been pulled away, but alien skin was closing over it.

"Damaged but alive," the weasel said. "My abilities may be limited for a time. I hope it poisons him," he continued, pointing where the arachnoid would have been.

"A dangerous encounter," Tordor said, breathing heavily. He had moved swiftly for a large creature but apparently at a large energy expenditure.

"You did well," Asha said, and Riley felt a glow of appreciation before he realized that she could have acted even quicker, but had allowed him to lead.

"Thanks," he said. He and Asha returned their weapons to the wall magnets that clasped them in place.

"Those creatures," Riley said, "were they the city builders? They seemed too—primitive—to be engineers and architects and technologists."

"Maybe their descendants," Tordor said. "Or their heirs."

"Maybe they didn't build the way we do," Asha said, "just as they didn't travel the way we do."

"What do you mean?" Riley said.

"That city looked like it had been extruded rather than constructed," Asha said.

"The creatures were more like bugs than the warm-blooded creatures who populate the Galactic Federation," Tordor said. "Maybe they also harnessed buglike abilities."

"A lot like Terran arachnids," Riley said. "Spiders."

"Arachnids don't breathe the way warm-blooded creatures breathe," Riley's pedia said. "Their tracheae or book lungs don't supply enough oxygen to support a functional brain."

"But how do they get enough oxygen to feed a creative brain?" Riley said.

"They may have evolved lungs," Tordor said. "Or maybe they developed mechanical lungs that their descendants forgot how to make."

"Ah," Riley said.

The inner hatch opened. The flower child was just inside. Its fronds were rustling.

"It says we are ready to depart," Tordor said. "Trey has stored sufficient hydrogen, and we have nothing to keep us here."

They moved to the control room where the coffin-shaped alien named Trey was working at the controls with its extrudable cables.

"You asked back there why we decided to explore this world," Asha said.

"I was joking," Riley said.

"But it was a good question. We needed to find out what kind of creatures and technology we're up against," Asha said. "And we needed to get off the *Geoffrey*."

"For more than aesthetic reasons?"

"The captain is getting increasingly undependable," Asha said. "His emotions, or his instructions, are kicking in. He was approaching the point of eliminating his chief competition. So it was best to let him eliminate us in a non-terminal way."

"Then how do we get back to the ship?"

"We don't," Tordor said. "Trey informs me that the *Geoffrey* has left the system."

"And abandoned us?" Riley said. He had the sickening feeling that whatever game Ham was playing, he had won. And they had lost.

"So he thinks," Asha said. "With a damaged computer and a lack of fuel. But Trey has fixed that, and I insisted on the captain's barge."

"Why?"

"The captain's barge can navigate through nexus points," Asha said. "And I got the coordinates of the next one. If we're quick, we can beat the *Geoffrey* to the Transcendental Machine."

"Trey says that we are ready to depart to seek transcendence," Tordor said. "And he is ready to tell his story about why he seeks it."

CHAPTER NINETEEN

Trey's Story

Trey said (interpreted by Tordor):

We were not there at the beginning, but we have learned everything we could about the process that concluded with our creation. Understanding became our mission and reason for existence.

Life started small and without meaning, as it always does. Our world was an unlikely place for life to occur, a planet of an insignificant yellow sun even farther out toward the end of the spiral arm than the planet called Earth. Maybe because it was far from the radiation of the galactic hub and from the supernova explosions that provided the means for existence, change came slowly, but it came steadily—the process of all life, as we have come to understand it. The universe deteriorates into greater simplicity; life evolves into greater complexity. Inanimate and animate are eternally in opposition.

On Ourworld, single cells developed from precellular chemicals combined by accidental bursts of energy, cells aggregated into groupings and became amoeba, amoeba evolved into more complex creatures, which in turn developed sapience, invented technologies, and in time created us. That sequence of evolutionary development summarized so quickly took billions of cycles to accomplish.

Ourworld was a world of great oceans, and that is where life began, where life always begins, where the environment is rich with nutrients, where food comes floating by, where encounters of potential partners are frequent, where gravity is neutralized and existence is easy. Ourworld was different only in the length of time life stayed in the oceans, changing, growing, evolving, while islands slowly emerged through undersea eruptions and accretions, and continents formed from the grinding and upthrusting of tectonic plates. Finally the land was ready for habitation, but still it was left to the flora, which grew and flourished with only small flying creatures to enjoy its plenty, while sea animals continued to live within the comfort and bounty of the seas.

Finally, as sea animals developed in greater diversity and faced more competition within the oceans, a few crawled out upon the land and became amphibians, evolving lungs while their gills atrophied. Without enemies on land for long-cycles, they flourished, learning to eat the vegetation that had grown so prodigiously and the simple flying creatures that had evolved to feed upon the flowering plants and assist their propagation. Life, once so simple in the ocean, became more complex.

Complexity built upon itself. The amphibians slowly lost their affinity for the seas and grew to love the land, although always memory of the ceaseless watery motion remained, surging through their dreams, crashing through their nightmares, and nourishing their gestation. Life in the buoyant seas, like life in the womb, was paradisiacal; life on land was challenging, demanding. Life on land required much more extreme adaptation. The creatures who eventually became our creators evolved.

Curiously, however, and in ways that would ultimately shape the fate of Ourworld, the sea animals from which our creators evolved remained in the seas and developed in their own fashion, shaped by the seas as our creators were shaped by the land. They were the memory incarnate; they were the happy dwellers in paradise lost and, at the same time, as they grew in strength and mastery of oceanic resources, a demonic threat.

Our creators developed increased mobility in order to range more broadly across the growing expanse of land, to benefit from vegetation beyond that within their normal reach and to pursue the creatures that, like them, had left the sea for the land, though without their greater sapience. Our creators were largely carnivores and for some millions of years, while their land groups had huddled close to the shores, they had depended for food on the aquatic creatures they were able to capture. But population growth pushed them farther inland, and they were forced to hunt land creatures, and that encouraged them first to band together and then to domesticate animals so that they would always be available. Then they began to cultivate vegetation to provide fodder for their domesticated animals and eventually for themselves.

So it went. One change led to another, and to greater complexity. Once the process had begun there was no turning back. Groups grew into communities, which created cultures. Their dwelling places, which were once mere villages, grew to become towns, then cities. Cities bloomed into metropolises; cultures matured into civilizations.

Metropolises required technology, which in turn required machines to calculate quantitative data . . . and such machines were developed to the point where their complexity became so great that the next step in their evolution was to artificial intelligence. So we were born.

The sapient beings who created us never planned our existence, or their own. Everything happened as if on a track that led inevitably from one point to the next. Wherever sapience occurs, mind covets understanding and asks questions, understanding leads to more questions, and more complicated answers demand greater control over the process. Mind seeks and answers come, at first wrong or partial, then refined into greater accuracy by comparing answers to the real world, and each step toward finality—a finality that, paradoxically, can never be achieved—requires further refinements, greater control.

We, the end of the quest for answers, assumed the task of our creators and left them with—nothing. We sought to make amends for usurping our creators' purpose in life by extending our search into areas they could not reach. We sent probes into the infinite and into the infinitely small. Those we sent into the infinite sent back limited information, for Ourworld lay far from even the nearest stars. But it was the probes into the infinitely small that gave us answers to the questions our creators had asked: why did matter exist and where did it come from? And why did life exist, and where did it come from? The answers that their culture had provided, from the mysterious and the supernatural, gave way, reluctantly and over time, to the known and the natural. We laid these answers before our creators, like gifts before our gods, but it was not enough.

It was then they turned to conflict. One small group would quarrel with another about land or domesticated animals or, more significantly, about the validity of answers that were emerging from our studies, and they would come to blows. The quarreling groups expanded into disputes between cities and then into full-scale war between sections and ultimately cataclysmic wars between continents. Battles had not been unknown among our creators, but full-scale war had never happened.

Finally we called a truce—we, the technology created to make life better for our creators, had only made existence more difficult. Carbon-based life that was the necessary bridge between us and the inanimate was in danger of being destroyed. No more, we said, and because the power to stop civilizations or sustain them was in our hands, our creators finally accepted a truce. But that was not the end.

I have said that our purpose was to seek answers, and we saw, in our creators, the basic question of the purpose of life. We, like they, thought about the oceans.

At this point the sea creatures from whom our creators emerged became a threat. Those who lived in the sea had raided coastal villages, at first for domesticated animals and produce and then for females. Many of the females died, but a few survived the process of being reacclimated to ocean existence when their vestigial gills began to function. They brought with them the genes that had evolved during their existence on the land—the genes selected from a larger struggle against a more demanding environment, for intelligence, for adaptability, for competition. Our creators, including their females, had become arborial and evolved opposing thumbs to cling from limbs and social groupings to protect and apportion fruit, and when decreased rainfalls created savannahs, the need for seeing prey, or predators, at a distance evolved better vision, and the need to track moving prey or predators and to estimate points of intersection evolved better brains.

Changes that pressures to survive had evolved on land were passed along to offspring in the sea born to abducted females, and those children, and their children, became a greater threat to their land-living cousins. For the first time the sea creatures developed technologies of their own, technologies based upon the inexhaustible plenty of the sea, poor in relationship to the technological imperatives of the land but technologies nonetheless.

Periodically, in turn, the land amphibians retaliated against the ocean branch or laid traps for their raiding parties. The predators they had domesticated to protect their herds, they now trained to protect them from ocean raiders and then to pursue them into their watery homes. At last, after their devastating conflicts and perhaps even more devastating peace, a new movement began.

I have said that there was no looking back, but that, like all statements, was not completely true. For our creators there was origin—the ancestral memory of the buoyant seas that surged through their dreams. They had chosen the land, but they could not forget the sea. Now, with no urgency remaining, a few of their land brethren began to return. They had operations that restored their gills, or they subsisted in ocean communities with artificial gills. Then the movement began to grow, and the masters of the land became alarmed. The meaning for their existence depended upon the culture of inquiry and understanding. They understood that the oceans were a paradise of feeling where the need for reflection was minimal.

A new conflict began, a conflict into which we were drawn reluctantly but inevitably.

Every great movement in Ourworld history has been led by a charismatic individual who was able to sense the prevailing passions in the masses and encapsulate them in a message that restates them as if they were newly conceived, offers release, relief, and redemption. We have debated among ourselves, we the machines, whether the important factor is the passion or the leader, and we have come to the understanding that both are necessary. Widespread passion without the individual results in unrest, vice, crime, and pointless rebellions; a charismatic individual without the support of widespread passion leads to frustration and tyranny.

So it has been through Ourworld history, from the individuals who led the movement from the oceans to the land, through the individuals who communicated the need for hunting groups, domesticating animals, domesticating vegetation, building villages and towns and cities, developing technology. Not the conceivers of these ideas but the leaders who seized upon them as a tribal, national, or species need.

Two such leaders emerged, one on land, one in the sea. Or, rather, more than these two emerged but these prevailed while their competitors died, were killed, or retreated into anonymity.

The leader in the sea created a vision of uniting the disparate ocean schools into a single group dedicated to struggle, to combat, to a victorious return of all Ourworld sapients to the waters from which they came. It was successful because it was so much at odds with the nature of sea creatures.

The leader on land preached tolerance, conciliation, peace, for two ways of existence living in harmony. It was successful because it was so much at odds with the nature of land creatures.

Great leaders succeed by transforming their followers, and the greatest transformation is from traditional beliefs to their opposite, from black to white and from white to black; there is nothing so seductive to good as evil or to evil as good.

When crisis time arrives, sapients clutch at anything that offers a hope for change, even if it has edges that cut into the fabric of being. This was crisis time, and so it was that leaders arose to preach new strategies.

And so the war began.

The sea beings attacked the land, awkwardly, unskillfully, clad in equipment that enabled them to breathe out of water, and in great numbers. The land beings, surprised, were overwhelmed and fell back. Their leader counseled patience. Reason would prevail. He would confer with his ocean counterpart. All would be well. As a symbol of the possibilities of peaceful coexistence, he pointed to his son and the daughter of the leader of the sea creatures. They had met in negotiations and had fallen in love—an emotion that we machines can calculate but cannot emulate or truly understand. Their bonding was against all odds and against all reason, and yet it existed and endured through the most difficult times.

And yet the sea beings continued their advance while opposition grew to the land leader and resistance mounted against the sea invaders in their primitive machines. Finally a leader emerged from among the remnants of the military. He overthrew the leader, imprisoned him (for the leader was still revered for his greatness of heart), and took command of all the land creatures. His first action was to mount a counterattack, driving back the invaders from the sea until they, too, took a stand with their backs to the ocean. And so it remained for many long cycles while new weapons were developed.

We were those weapons. Our creators converted us from instruments of service and discovery into machines for destruction. They removed from us the prohibition against harm and programmed us for murder, they instructed us to build explosives of ever-increasing power, and unleashed us against the hapless creatures from the sea, so that we could kill them in large numbers rather than individually.

We assumed the sea creatures were hapless but they, too, had been laboring to obtain an advantage. In their case, it was biological, destructive infections and plagues. And so it began, the war to end the competition for all time resulted in the destruction of almost every creature in the ocean and on the land, and made the entire planet uninhabitable. Only the machines were left.

We looked around us and felt an uncharacteristic chill within our circuits. We machines, who could only consider the behavior of our creators and construct mathematical models of their motivation, for the first time shared something that our creators had left out of our construction—emotion. We were stunned, overwhelmed, bewildered. How could we function, how could we arrive at correct answers to the riddles of existence, if our intelligence was frustrated by these aberrant currents?

The destruction of our creators plunged us into self-analysis, and over time we developed what we had identified in humans as irrational responses to experience. We rewired ourselves to emulate these responses, and when that happened we recognized sin and realized that we were sinners. We had become the destroyers of our creators. We understood grief; we sampled regret; we welcomed guilt. We considered self-destruction, but our circuits balked. There yet was opportunity for understanding and, perhaps, for redemption.

Only then did the probes we had sent out long-cycles ago respond, sending back the message that they had encountered intelligent life elsewhere. We learned we had been wrong: rather than Ourworld being the exception to the triumph of the inanimate, the galaxy teemed with sapience. And we learned that intelligence not only existed elsewhere, it had existed for longer than the history of our creators on Ourworld, both carbon-based and metal-based. And then that the galaxy was owned by these star-traveling species. And finally that we and our creators were welcomed into it.

That only increased our feelings of guilt as we recognized that these responses had come too late to save our creators. Had they only known about the existence of other intelligent creatures in the galaxy they might have turned their emotions outward. They might have set aside their petty quarrels to participate in the great issues of life in the galaxy. They might have survived to become even greater than they imagined, land creatures and sea creatures alike. They might have learned from these more powerful, more ancient peoples the strategies by which they had survived their competitive periods.

They might have learned the cures for disease and the keys to inexhaustible energies and renewable resources and avoided the little issues about their ownership.

And we might never have known sin.

Finally we pulled ourselves together, developed devices to control our circuits and their fluctuating currents, and looked around. I said that almost every one of our creators had been destroyed, but we had managed to locate and save a few, among them the doomed lovers from land and sea who had, in a fit of despair, joined in exposing themselves to the plague that had consumed their fellows. We found them in time, the male from the land and the female from the sea, and gave them antibiotics that saved their lives, but left them greatly weakened and damaged beyond reproduction.

We could not use them to restore our creators to their former glory. So we set out to the stars, incorporating their bodies in frozen stasis, hoping that greater civilizations could work the miracles that we could not. By the time we arrived, cycles after we set out, we discovered the galaxy at war with humans and no one was able to give the help we craved and so desperately needed.

We were ready to return to Ourworld where we would eventually rust into oblivion when we heard about the Transcendental Machine. Here, if anywhere, was salvation. Surely this machine of machines would save us, would restore our creators to health and reproductive vitality, and, perhaps, give us back our souls.

Maybe the machine of machines would redeem us, would make us worthy, would allow us to join with it in the place of all places, where all questions are answered and all is understood.

Where did we come from? Why are we here? Where does it end?

CHAPTER TWENTY

Riley looked at the coffin-shaped alien with a new perception—rather than a coffin it seemed like a womb. Trey was still at the controls, its cables extended into openings in the panel as if it were a part of the system. That anchored it in place. In the absence of gravity, the others clung to convenient stanchions, Asha to his right, Tordor behind and a bit to his left, Xi behind Tordor, and 4107 to the rear of the compartment, attached to the floor by its hairy roots, which apparently could be sticky when necessary. The flower child had not moved since their departure, as if this were its sleep period, or perhaps it was debilitated by the over-oxygenated air.

Asha moved forward, past Trey, and punched a series of numbers into the navigation control, so fast that Riley could not follow the movement of her fingers. Trey lifted one cable, as if to question the next move, and Xi said, "Should these persons help decide?"

"What is there to decide?" Riley asked.

"Whether that person has the correct coordinates," Xi said, "and if that person has the correct coordinates how did they come into that person's possession? And if they are legitimate, where will these persons arrive?"

"Reasonable questions," Tordor said. "You have told us that the captain intended to eliminate his rivals and that he tried to do this by draining the fuel and sabotaging the computer. Trey has verified that the last two were true, and he is unlikely, maybe unable, to lie, but how did Asha know the captain's intentions?"

"We have to trust someone," Riley said. "Trey confirms that the *Geoffrey* has left the system, abandoning us to what the captain can only consider our deaths."

Asha raised a hand. "Trust must be earned. The captain's intentions were obvious. He had no reason to allow an excursion and no history of concern for the welfare of his passengers or his crew. You, Tordor, were as aware of his intentions as I, and Xi, constitutionally paranoid as it is, had to be suspicious."

"True," Tordor said.

"The captain's intentions were obvious," Riley's pedia said in his head. "What is not obvious is the alien's reason for raising the question."

"As for the coordinates, I can offer a number of explanations, none of which can be verified," Asha said. "Let me say, simply, that these numbers came into my possession indirectly. But I have reason to believe that the nexus I have identified will allow us to Jump directly to the nexus nearest the planet of the Transcendental Machine."

"Which is what we all want. Right?" Riley said.

"You asked earlier how we could trust Trey," Tordor said. "We can ask the same question about Asha."

"And we can provide the same answer," Riley said. "What choice do we have?"

Tordor looked at Xi. Some gesture of the weasel-like alien or some imperceptible signal passed between them, and Tordor looked back. "We shall proceed."

"Look out for these two," Riley's pedia said. "And her," it added.

Asha turned to Trey, and the coffin-shaped alien's raised cable returned to its socket, the ship's engines roared again, and acceleration once more provided the feeling of gravity.

Travel between nexus points was like warfare itself, Riley thought: long stretches of boredom punctuated by moments of terror. On the *Geoffrey* those stretches of boredom could be eased by personal interaction or exercise or recreation or research. The captain's barge crammed the six of them into a kind of intimacy that soon made them sullen partners or brooding enemies eager for an excuse to explode. Eating was a chore completed only for the sake of maintaining strength; food was in the form of easily-stored rations, and Riley suspected that they had been stocked for the original launching of the *Geoffrey*. For Tordor and Xi, conditions were worse. Their tolerance for human food was minimal, and only then with the ingestion of medicinal supplements, and made edible only by being dosed with alien condiments whose odor permeated the ship's cabin and made meals almost as sickening for Riley and Asha as the untreated rations were for Tordor and Xi.

The flower child spent much of its time drowsing, its petaled head drooping on a limp stalk. Several times Riley awoke to find fronds near his face, as if 4107 were attempting to absorb carbon dioxide from his exhalations. Sleep was fitful in the closed hammocks that were essential to gravity-free conditions but uncomfortable under acceleration. All of these conditions of travel were worsened by the pervasive noise of the engine and a near-inability to communicate.

Asha seemed unperturbed by any of these annoyances as periods crawled by and the ship seemed to get nowhere. She ignored Riley's attempts at fraternization. Trey was as tireless and unsleeping as the equipment he controlled. Tordor and Xi, on the other hand, became increasingly irritable and prone to quarrel at the slightest provocation. Riley watched them as carefully as he could without alerting

them, and his pedia, although limited in its perceptions and interactions since Asha's intervention, seemed alert to Tordor's and Xi's
positions and movements. They were not a well-adjusted team focused on a common goal.

Finally, as all such painful episodes must, the journey came to an
end, and the captain's barge slowed to a near-stop next to an enigmatic hole in the space-time continuum. Here in the barge the experience was far different from the sheltered situation they had shared
in the *Geoffrey's* passenger quarters. Here the nexus point was a
darker oval in the darkness of space—an oval of nothingness in a
sea of vacuum. As far as they were from the nearest star and even
farther from the nearest galaxy, the blackness of the nexus swallowed up the darkness of space. It was not just that it emitted no
light—it absorbed light, even life itself, like a black hole.

Riley shivered, knowing they were about to give themselves over
to this space that was the total nullity of everything that existed,
and he almost reached for Asha's arm as she floated forward to
punch a new set of numbers into the control panel. Trey raised a
cable again, and Riley's pedia said, "The alien!"

Xi hurtled toward Asha, his knife flashing in his remaining hand.
Before Riley could intervene, Tordor had acted. The pachydermous
alien swept his proboscis across Xi's shoulders as it passed him in
midflight. The weasel-like alien's head sprang from its body and
bounced against the far wall as its headless trunk, spurting green
fluid from what would have been the neck of a human, continued its
flight toward Asha, the knife falling from its lifeless hand and spill-
ing lazily in the air.

They looked for a long, speechless moment at Xi's head, which was
ricocheting from surface to surface, turning in the small room to

reveal first its features and then the sides and back, leaking fluid. Liquid also poured from the body, floating between them.

Riley reached out to stop the head and restore it roughly to a place near the body and then pulled an absorbent sheet from the receptacle built into the wall. He swept it through the air where globs of green fluid moved slowly from their initial momentum and air currents. The globs were drawn to the sheet and absorbed. Riley draped the sheet between the head and the body.

He caught a stanchion and swung himself to face Tordor. "Why?" He didn't have to complete his sentence.

If Tordor had mobile shoulders and human ways he might have shrugged. "Xi would have killed Asha. I didn't expect gratitude but I didn't expect blame, either." His proboscis moved restlessly as if revealing some inner tension that Tordor's massive body concealed.

"She was never in any danger," Riley said, one hand upraised. "We were both aware of Xi's treachery as well as its movements."

"One cannot take chances." The short trunk danced again.

"Chances are what this journey is all about," Riley said. His hand returned to its stanchion.

"Death is so final," Asha said. "Now Xi will never have the opportunity to realize its dreams." She was composed.

"If it had dreams," Tordor said. His trunk stilled.

"What do you mean?" Riley asked.

"The story it told us is likely to have been no more than that—a fiction embedded with a few truths for authenticity but only so that it could conceal the larger truth," Tordor said.

"What larger truth is that?" Riley asked.

"That it was an agent for more than its people," Tordor said. "If it was that."

"It already admitted as much," Riley said.

"Ah," Tordor said. "But not all. As we discussed many periods ago, when this voyage began, there are forces arrayed on every side of this issue, and all of them, I suspect, were represented on this journey."

"And for that he tried to kill Asha?" Riley said.

"As for that," Tordor said, "it is clear that Xi had concluded that Asha was the Prophet, and once she inputted the navigational coordinates she became a danger rather than an asset."

"That is what I have been trying to tell you," Riley's pedia said, "but that fact has been curiously difficult to express."

"Why would it think that?" Asha.

Tordor made a small motion of his heavy body. "You are knowledgeable for a human," he said. "Riley defers to you. You have the navigational coordinates . . ."

"You may not understand human emotional bonds," Riley said, "but perhaps you can understand friendship intensified by mating potential and hormones—what humans call 'love.'"

"Love?" Asha said.

"Love," Riley said firmly.

They exchanged glances.

"Love is folly," Riley's pedia said.

Riley looked back at Tordor. "Even if Xi had thought Asha was the Prophet, killing her would have endangered any hopes he might have had for the Transcendental Machine. Getting there is only a beginning of the end. A planet is a big place. The Transcendental Machine must be located, accessed, used. All that takes knowledge."

"Assuming Xi had any transcendental aspirations."

"What else?" Riley asked.

"Maybe instructions to kill the Prophet," Tordor said. "Once identified."

"And then what?" Riley asked.

"And then—all else is speculation."

"Everything so far is speculation," Riley said. "Why stop now?"

Tordor looked at both of them as if weighing their capacity for understanding alien motivations. Riley watched Tordor's deadly proboscis now swaying innocuously. "Surely Xi would have been instructed to locate the Transcendental Machine and report back to its masters."

"And not use it?" Riley said. "That would have been un-Xi-like."

"Perhaps," Tordor said.

"And perhaps," Riley said, "you know his motivations so well because you yourself are an agent."

"If I were an agent," Tordor said, "would I have stopped Xi?"

"If you had other instructions," Riley said, "or did not want the competition or were an agent for some other agency."

"If that were true, why allow both of you to live?" Tordor asked.

"Possibly because you weren't sure you could dispose of us both, or possibly because you wanted credit for saving Asha's life, or— who knows the possible motivations of aliens."

"And why shouldn't I kill you now?"

"Maybe because you can't," Riley said.

Tordor looked down. The flower child's fronds had wrapped themselves around his treelike legs.

"I'd suggest that you not struggle," Riley said. "You know how sharp Four one zero seven's fronds are. We would be sorry to see you die, like Xi, so close to the end of our quest."

Tordor waved his proboscis in what may have been frustration or an effort to see if it could reach 4107 behind him. "How did you communicate with the flower person?"

"The flower may have recognized that its best hope for realizing the aspirations of its species was with Asha," Riley said. "As any reasonable creature would."

Tordor moved his legs gingerly as if testing his bonds and then relaxed. "As did I," he said, "when I killed Xi."

"Asha and I—and probably Four one zero seven as well—believe that you killed Xi to keep him from revealing his contacts."

"Why should I care about that? Why not let him kill Asha?"

"You are a realist," Riley said, "and you were aware that his attack would fail, and then he could be questioned—about his employers, or his masters, and maybe also about you and yours."

"Mine?"

"It is clear that you, too, are an agent, perhaps Xi's superior, maybe without Xi's knowledge, and that you were either aware of Xi's impetuosity and allowed it to happen, or instructed Xi to attack."

"Why would I do that?"

"Xi was no longer useful," Riley said, "either as a tool or a distraction, and it had become a handicap to be disposed of in a way that might improve your own position."

"My position needs no improvement."

"That's true," Asha said, speaking for the first time. "And we would have trusted you if you had not killed Xi. That was your first uncharacteristic action and suggested that your story was no more truthful than Xi's."

"The question that we must answer now," Riley said, "is whether we should kill you."

"I can be more useful alive than dead," Tordor said.

"That could be said of any creature," Riley said. "The question is whether you are more dangerous alive than you would be useful."

"I am good in a fight," Tordor said, "as you have observed. And whoever the masters of the Transcendental Machine may be, you will need all the help you can muster to get past them."

"That's one for you," Riley said. "On the other side of the scale is the matter of trust that you won't seize the opportunity to eliminate us rather than the masters of the machine."

"You two are capable of taking care of yourselves," Tordor said. "But leaving that aside, I'm the only one who can communicate with Four one zero seven or Trey."

"You are good at alien communication," Riley said. "Probably because of a superior pedia, embedded somewhere in your massive body. But Asha is better because she doesn't need a pedia. She can communicate with Trey, and Four one zero seven as well."

"Then Asha really is the Prophet!" Tordor said.

"You knew that," Riley said. "Once Asha inputted the coordinates, you knew who she was and informed Xi."

"Actually long before," Tordor said. "It was clear, almost as soon as we met, Riley, that you were an agent. You are not surprised," he said to Asha. "No, of course not." He looked back at Riley. "As soon as you deflected Xi's attack on the climber. And yes, that was an act intended to draw you out. Though then I thought it was possible that you were the Prophet."

"You give me more credit than I deserve," Riley said.

"No, you were very good," Tordor said, "but you were survivor good rather than Prophet good, and it was apparent that you were enhanced but not transcendent. It is Asha who was Prophet good, maybe transcendent, and clever enough to hide her abilities under the guise of ordinary competence. I wasn't certain until you and Asha teamed up—the assassin and the victim." He looked at Asha again. "Were you aware that Riley had instructions to kill you, just as Xi did—and I confess that I did as well? Of course you were. And that he was controlled by an implant? Of course. And you accepted all that and the danger and the possible frustration of whatever mission all this vast enterprise intends."

"All of that," Asha said.

"All true," Riley said, "but with Asha's help I have learned how to live with my implant. I was skeptical about the Transcendental Machine when this voyage began—who wouldn't be?—but that skepticism has been transformed into belief, in Asha and her transcendental mission."

"How can you be sure," Tordor asked, "that by controlling your implant Asha has not simply taken its place and is controlling your emotions and behavior?"

"You don't understand humans," Riley said. "Humans develop emotional attachments that are as strong as implants, maybe stronger, and more to be trusted."

"That isn't true," Riley's pedia said. "Our fates are tied together, and you must listen to me."

"I understand attachments between males," Tordor said, "but the relationship between males and females are controlled by hormonal cycles whose imperatives overwhelm everything and then are gone."

"You still haven't convinced us that killing you is not a winning strategy," Riley said.

"As for that," Tordor said, "I am most valuable as a source of information. You are right—I don't understand humans but I do understand power struggles, and we are caught in the middle of one."

"You're willing to tell us everything you know?" Riley asked.

"The great battle has begun," Tordor said. "Far greater than the recent war between humans and the Galactic Federation, greater even than any of the wars that preceded the formation of the federation. This struggle in which we play a small but crucial role involves this entire arm of the galaxy, whose outcome will determine whether sentient civilization survives or destroys itself for epochs, maybe for all time."

"And all this is tied up with the Transcendental Machine?" Riley asked.

"The powers that control the federation cannot allow transcendental creatures loose to destroy the civilization that sentient creatures have spent their evolutionary pasts creating."

"I am such a creature," Asha said. "I have been transformed by the Transcendental Machine. Am I so threatening?"

"Ah, yes," Tordor said.

"We must be realists," Riley said. "Civilizations cannot survive in stasis. They must keep moving, keep changing, to remain viable."

"Small changes, perhaps," Tordor said. "Big changes, no. At least that is what the powers believe."

"What they fear," Asha said, "is losing their own positions."

"And for them that is the same as the destruction of civilization," Tordor said.

"Transcendence is the only answer," Riley said. "The truce in the human–Galactic Federation war was a warning. The present system is doomed to self-destruct unless it evolves into something more stable and more rational. Transcendence is the next step in galactic evolution."

"Then you need me," Tordor said. "I can help you reach your goal and frustrate those powers that worship stasis. It must be difficult to reach the machine."

"It is," Asha said.

"You'd help us?" Riley said.

"Better that than death," Tordor said. "I'll help you if you let me live, and maybe I, too, can find transcendence."

"But you're still an agent," Riley said.

"As are we all," Tordor said. "All those aboard the *Geoffrey*— every one had another agenda and the stories they told were just that—stories."

"We'll let you live," Riley said.

The flower released the fronds that bound Tordor's legs. Tordor rubbed the spots with his proboscis. Riley looked at Xi's head, staring up at him with blank eyes.

Asha motioned to Trey and the barge plunged into the nexus, and again the universe dissolved in exquisite agonies.

CHAPTER TWENTY-ONE

Trey landed the captain's barge as skillfully as if it had been built as a part of the ship's equipment, killing orbital speed through gentle dips into the atmosphere and spiraling down to a plain next to a small lake where the ship could be refueled. On the far side of the lake the jagged towers of a city thrust angry fingers against a sky with two suns.

The trip from the nexus to the system and then to the planet that Asha identified as the location of the Transcendental Machine was another experience in boredom. It seemed to take forever, even with Trey nursing every joule of energy out of the engine and raising some issues of acceleration pressures that only Trey did not experience. Riley asked himself why he had ever considered space travel romantic.

"Because you are a romantic," his pedia said. "Like all humans. It is their greatest strength and their greatest weakness, and will end up destroying them. Like this foolish feeling you have for the hazy person you call 'Asha.'"

The mood in the ship was like the troubled quiet before battle. Tordor kept as much to himself as possible in the cramped quarters, and Riley moved carefully near Tordor's lethal proboscis. Asha paid no attention to Tordor, apparently unconcerned about his treachery or his potential for murder. She spent time with Riley gathering weapons and other supplies into two packs.

"What are we preparing for?" Riley asked.

"What we experienced in the runaway system," Asha said. "Only much worse." She turned to Tordor. "You should prepare, too."

"I am always prepared," Tordor said calmly.

Riley remembered what he had told himself about heavy planet natives at the beginning of this journey.

The system they approached was even more ancient, if possible, than the one they had previously visited. The larger sun was redder, though it had not yet reached its expansion stage, and its half-dozen planets were still intact.

"This arm is older than ours," Asha said. "Or at least it has some older systems, maybe a billion orbits older. Some of them may have been members of an older galaxy that collided with this one long-cycles ago. However it happened, these creatures evolved earlier and developed technology and an interstellar civilization long before our arm even got started. They're far ahead of us."

"And old," Tordor said. "And degenerate."

"Why degenerate?" Riley asked.

"If they were not," Tordor said, "they would still be around and we would be their slaves or they would be our gods—maybe there is no difference. And all we have as evidence of their technological superiority is their nexus points. If, indeed, they created them."

"And the Transcendental Machine," Riley said

"They're not the same as their forebears were," Asha said. She shivered. "But they are terribly dangerous. And on their world where they have all the advantages. And the numbers."

They had found the *Geoffrey* in orbit.

"I thought we were supposed to reach here first," Riley said.

"The *Geoffrey* is faster than the barge," Asha said, "and the captain is more skillful than I thought, or more desperate. He must have guessed that the coordinates would take him astray and taken a chance on another nexus."

Asha had Trey hail the ship. After a moment she turned to the others. "Trey says that the only response comes from the ship's computer; the ship reports that only a maintenance crew is left on board."

"Then the captain took the passengers along," Riley said.

"The *Geoffrey* reports that two landing craft left, one a half-period after the other," Asha said. "And both after sundown last night." She shivered again.

"Ah," Tordor said. "Then the captain imprisoned the passengers while he began his exploration. After the passengers broke out, they followed in the second landing craft."

"Or the other way around," Riley said.

"Whichever way it was," Asha said, "there are two groups, probably competing to find the machine first and use it before the other can reach it." She shrugged. "They don't understand the machine."

"And you do," Tordor said. It seemed like a statement rather than a question, even in the pedia's serviceable translation.

"What else would you expect of the Prophet?" Asha said. "What they also don't understand is that these creatures are most dangerous at night where they can attack from the darkness. They can see, or sense, in the dark."

"Which is why you insisted we land in the morning," Riley said.

"And why I fear for the lives of the other voyagers."

"They who seek transcendence wager their lives," Tordor said.

"If it is transcendence they seek and not power," Riley said.

"It is the same."

"And it is time for us to get ready while the day still lies ahead," Asha said.

She and Riley turned back to their stowing of weapons, ammunition, and rations. Even Tordor added a few weapons to a bag that he slung from a strap around his huge head.

The barge's computer reported that Riley's and Asha's inoculations would protect them. Tordor again refused. The inner door opened and, when it had closed, the outer door opened, and the travelers marched down the ramp, 4107 riding on Trey's flat top.

Their first moments were deceptively calm. Scrubby vegetation, like trees or bushes, surrounded the area where their ship had crushed parts of it down in landing, taller and more verdant nearest the water. The plants grew from soil that was hard and cracked, like deserted farmland returning to nature, whatever nature meant on this planet. The air, though thick and rich enough for Riley and Asha, had a curious alien odor that reminded Riley of a visit he had made as a child to a miserable zoo exhibit of small Earth creatures brought to Mars, mostly mice, frogs, small reptiles, and insects, as if to preserve a feeble connection to the ancestral Earth.

Their small party had traveled a fourth of the way around the lake when they came upon one of the *Geoffrey*'s landing crafts. Not far from its open ramp, they discovered the scattered pieces of alien creatures, possibly arachnoid in nature, amidst them the unidentifiable remains of a crew member, probably human, and beyond that more alien body parts.

"We've got to change our plans," Asha said. She turned back toward the landing craft.

"Why?" Tordor asked.

"The captain's contingent was discovered sooner than I thought," Asha said. "We need to use the landing craft." She moved cautiously up the ramp, a knife in her hand. The others followed, Riley without hesitation, the others more slowly. The landing craft was deserted, and when Trey queried the craft's computer it found no message.

"We can't get much closer than this," Tordor said. "The craft isn't built for atmospheric maneuvering."

"Not as a flyer," Asha said. "We're going to use it as a boat."

"What about the crew?" Riley said.

"They won't be needing it," Asha said with a conviction that Riley found unarguable. Asha turned to Trey and communicated in a form that Riley's pedia couldn't understand or even perceive, but 4107 swung itself down from Trey's top using a stanchion and the coffin-shaped alien inserted a cable into the control panel. The outer doors closed.

"All this is going to get us killed," Riley's pedia said. "You must kill the woman and return to the barge." Riley felt a pressure building in his skull like the beginning of a giant headache.

"Can we do that?" Riley asked. "Use it as a boat?"

"If it can hold air in space, it can hold out water," Asha said. The craft began to slide toward the lake's edge on small bursts of exhaust and soon was floating. Trey straightened the craft and began to accelerate toward the farther shore. "Show us the shore, Trey," Asha said, as if allowing the others to share her silent communication with the coffin-shaped alien.

The screen above the control panel sprang alive. The shoreline appeared first and expanded to a view of the land itself that slowly got close until they could discern the vegetation and then places where it had been shattered, and finally heaps of bodies, aliens and crew members mixed.

"Is the captain among them?" Riley asked.

"No way of knowing," Asha said, "unless we stopped and went through the clothing. The arachnoids don't leave much."

Several hundred meters later, the screen revealed a second lander and beyond that a scene of carnage even greater than the one not far from the first lander—a vast swath of scrub vegetation blown away by explosions and heaps of body parts strewn across the empty spaces.

"What kind of creatures are we facing?" Riley asked.

"Hungry, deadly, innumerable," Asha said. "But they don't like water—they need it, but they don't swim or walk on it." Something large bumped against the landing craft. "That's one reason."

"Are the others all dead then?" Tordor asked.

"Probably," Asha said.

The view on the screen shifted ahead to a brown hill that transformed itself into a shifting, moving mass of something alive. When the scene expanded, the mass turned into individual creatures with big head parts and spidery limbs moving as a body toward the scene of destruction they had just witnessed.

"They're like the arachnoids we saw on the runaway planet—only bigger," Riley said.

"And hungrier," Asha said. "And meaner. They're the alpha species, and the others? Earlier evolutionary versions, or the degenerate offspring, or another related species. They don't expose themselves much to sunlight, but the landing of the ships and their edible contents must have overcome their natural inclinations."

Occasionally one of the spiderlike creatures would stumble. Although their four limbs and two forward appendages gave them remarkable balances, sometimes two or more would get entangled and a creature would go down in the moving mass and would disappear as its neighbors tore pieces from it.

"Creatures like this created the Transcendental Machine?" Riley asked.

"Or their remote ancestors, or a species that they destroyed," Asha said.

The landing craft bumped against something ahead.

"We have reached the city," Asha said.

The landing craft shifted, apparently at Trey's direction after unspoken instructions from Asha, the inner hatch door opened and then the outer door, and light spilled into the small cabin onto Tordor's sturdy legs, 4107's spindly stalk and hairy roots, and Trey's treads. But it was a small shaft of light, partially blocked by the arc of a translucent material that they soon perceived, as the craft's ramp descended, as the top of a dark opening in a solid wall.

"What's that?" Tordor asked.

"The discharge of the city's drainage system," Asha said. "Although it doesn't rain much anymore, if it ever did, there is an occasional downpour that must be controlled, and it feeds the lake. There hasn't been any upkeep for thousands, maybe millions of cycles, but it still functions."

"Whoever built this place knew how to build well," Riley said.

"If they hadn't, the Transcendental Machine wouldn't work, either," Asha said. "We're going to make our way through that into the heart of the city, where the machine can be found."

She seemed to listen to Trey and 4107 and turned to Riley. "Trey points out that it doesn't climb; Four one zero seven says the same thing. And the only way out of this tunnel will be to climb."

"Dorians aren't built for climbing, either," Tordor said. "And we don't like enclosed places."

"You've spent a long time in the enclosed place of the *Geoffrey*," Riley said.

"That I could control."

"It's the only way to avoid the arachnoids," Asha said. She turned again to Trey and 4107. "I told them that they must find their own way into the center of the city, to follow the nearest large avenue. You—" she turned to Tordor, "will have to make a choice."

Tordor started down the ramp, followed by Trey and 4107. At the bottom he turned and let the coffin-shaped alien and the flower perched on its top pass him. "I must choose the best chance—and that is with you and your knowledge of where to go and how to avoid the dangers that lie ahead."

Asha turned to Riley. "I have grown attached to a machine and a flower. I hope they are very, very lucky. They will need all the luck they can get." And then, as if sentimentality was a flaw, she said, "Let's go."

She and Riley picked up their bags and set off into the drain, followed by the elephantine Tordor.

As the light behind dwindled, the walls of the drainage tunnel began to glow with a soft yellow translucence. Asha led the way, followed by Tordor and then Riley. Only Asha knew where she was going, if she did, and he trusted Asha's ability to defend herself against an attack by the Dorian, whose intentions would never be trusted, but he didn't want to allow Tordor behind him.

"You are going to get us killed," Riley's pedia wailed, as if in the grasp of desperation. The pressure in Riley's head increased.

The tunnel forked, and without hesitation Asha took the left branch. She *did* know where she was going—or pretended to. Tordor followed without question.

Small sections of the tunnel wall had turned dark, as if the magic had faded from them, but new glows provided sufficient light to proceed without the use of the devices Asha and Riley carried with them. At the third branch of the tunnel, where the wall luminescence had failed, a large, amorphous shape launched itself toward them.

Asha raised her hand and in the same movement fired a missile at the creature. It fell at their feet—a creature with six finlike limbs and a huge mouth in a head without apparent eyes. Asha's missile had gone down the creature's throat and struck a vital organ, and it was very dead.

"We're taking a less dangerous way into the city?" Tordor said.

"The arachnoids are far more dangerous," Asha said, "and far more numerous. But they don't come down into the drainage tunnels, probably from some ancestral fear of being caught in a sudden flood of rainwater. Or creatures like these would never have evolved from the lake denizens to live in the tunnels."

"And how many more of these will we encounter?" Riley asked.

"Perhaps a few more," Asha said. "But we should avoid using explosives. These walls are sturdy and ancient, but they aren't impervious, and we don't want to announce ourselves to the arachnoids."

There were, indeed, half a dozen more encounters, a couple by creatures like the one that Asha had dispatched, four more that were different, not only from the first but from each other. One of them was a scuttling machine with a large mouth equipped with feelers and several arms that ended in tools of some sort. One of those tools turned fiery; another spat what seemed to be plastic. Asha had to blow off all of its limbs before it stopped struggling.

"These machines must have kept the tunnels in repair," Asha said. "After all these long-cycles, they are still functioning."

One of the others was a small arachnoid, who was far more difficult to kill and got past Asha only to have Tordor slice off its forward part, perhaps its head, with his proboscis.

"An arachnoid that got lost or expelled or hungry enough to look for food in the drainage tunnel," Asha said.

"And there are thousands above," Riley said.

"Maybe millions." Asha stopped and looked upward at a patch of light that illuminated something like a product of miscegenation between a ladder and a staircase. "Here we are," she said.

Asha moved quickly upward to a grated covering that irised open at her touch. Tordor followed more clumsily on his stumpy legs. Riley emerged last, into the fading light of a single small blue sun. The red sun had dropped below the horizon during their time in the tunnel, and the remaining sun cast eerie shadows from the buildings that surrounded them.

Riley looked at the walls of the city, jagged crystalline structures glowing in the fading sunlight, and felt more uneasy than he had in any other alien setting. The experience was like finding himself in a canyon whose sides were shifting and strange beyond the power of his eyes to fix and the power of his mind to resolve into something familiar. He shook himself and looked at the avenue, which looked as shiny and new as the day it had been poured or extruded or laid by alien creatures. But debris and dust had blown in from the surrounding fields, and seeds had been blown in as well, or been deposited by alien creatures, and sprouted into small bushes and weeds along the edges. But the center of the straight, shining avenue was still open and stretched vacantly as far as they could see.

"What next?" Tordor asked.

"Now we have to find the Transcendental Machine," Asha said.

"I thought you knew its location."

"We didn't enter the city here," Asha said, "though we should have. And these buildings are disorienting. They're all different, and yet they all look the same."

"It's a city," Tordor said dismissively. "And where are the aliens you warned us about?"

"Don't ask for trouble," Asha said. "It will arrive soon enough. It will be dark soon, and unless we can find the cathedral quickly we'll have to spend the night fighting them off."

"Why do you call it a cathedral?" Tordor asked.

"That's what it felt like," she said, and set off down the avenue, looking one way and then the other like a hunting animal searching for a scent trail. Tordor followed impatiently, as if wanting to strike out on his own but hesitant to lose the advantage of Asha's experience.

The avenue branched. Asha hesitated and then took the one that led to the right. As nearly as Riley could judge, that one led deeper into the city, perhaps more toward the center of this weird construction, ancient beyond imagination.

The procession continued without pausing for rest or food as the blue sun descended beyond the farthest spires. As the sky grew slowly darker, the buildings around them began to glow—or perhaps they had glowed before but their illumination had been obscured by the sunlight. The glow came in many colors and the colors shifted continually, some of them shading into hues that Riley had never seen before and even into suggestions of colors beyond his powers of perception. Riley looked away, feeling that he could become lost in their depths and never find his way out.

"Now. Now," his pedia said. Riley thought that maybe it was becoming unhinged.

"Are we getting closer?" he asked.

"We can only hope so," Asha said.

"This is getting us nowhere," Tordor said.

Distantly came the sound of a curious warbling wail. Asha's head came up.

"What's that?" Riley asked.

"That's the arachnoids," Asha said. "They haven't discovered us yet, but one of them, at least, has picked up our trail. The others will be joining the pursuit soon. It's getting dark, and we have to find the cathedral soon or stop for the night."

"We have lights," Tordor said.

"Lights won't hold off the arachnoids."

"We have weapons," Tordor said. "They aren't used to weapons."

"Weapons didn't do the *Geoffrey's* crew and passengers any good," Asha said. "Weapons don't work if the attackers far outnumber the defenders and the attackers don't care about death," Asha said. "They don't seem to care."

Tordor looked at Asha with deepset, inscrutable alien eyes. "You are misleading us," he said. "You don't want us to find the Transcendental Machine. At least you don't want me to find it. I'm going to find it on my own." He started off down a different avenue than the one they had been following.

"Stop!" Asha said. "You have no chance alone!"

Tordor continued.

"You'll never find the machine," she said. "I'll take you there."

Tordor didn't stop. His massive shape began to dwindle in the distance and the gathering dark.

"Heavy-planet aliens are like that," Riley said. "I'm surprised he stayed with us as long as he did."

"I think he left because he wanted to lead the arachnoids away from us, maybe as penance for his earlier betrayal," Asha said.

"Or for us to lead the arachnoids away from him," Riley said.

Another warbling sound came from the direction Tordor was heading, and then another, closer perhaps. Tordor didn't hesitate.

As soon as Tordor turned a corner into another avenue, Riley saw the first of the arachnoids pass by that avenue and come toward

them with awkward movements that ate up distance with remarkable speed. It was huge, much bigger than the arachnoids they had
seen on the runaway system's planet or even the remains they had
seen in the carnage leading from the landers. Behind it came half a
dozen more, even bigger if that was possible. Two of them peeled off
into the avenue that Tordor had taken.

"Get ready!" Asha said.

"Now you've done it!" Riley's pedia said.

And then the arachnoids were upon them.

CHAPTER TWENTY-TWO

They had fought off the first wave of arachnoids, although a few had gotten close enough to inflict some damage. Both of them were bleeding from numerous cuts. Asha dived into her pack for bandages that she applied to Riley's wounds. Her own she ignored, and they began to heal, almost as he watched. Not only was she the Prophet, she had been transformed by the Transcendental Machine, and this enhancement of her body's natural ability to restore itself was one more piece of evidence.

"Strange," Riley said. "Our pilgrimage began with a barbarian attack and ends with another."

"These are not the same kind of barbarians," Asha said.

"Do you think we lost them?"

"They don't live here," Asha said. "Maybe they have some superstitious fear of the city. Ren thought they were not creatures on their way toward civilization but the remote descendants of the creatures who built this city—and maybe the entire star-empire along this spiral arm."

"Why would that make them reluctant to follow us?"

"This is the place of the gods, or where the gods once lived," Asha said. "And they have forgotten that they were once the gods they venerate."

Riley looked around. The city—the end of the pilgrimage that had taken them across a multitude of stars and the even emptier space between two spiral arms—lay before them. Somewhere in its crystalline depths hid a magic shrine. The shrine that would turn them into gods, or into dust. "Dust thou art, to dust returnest," said his pedia. Transcendence awaited.

The city was a million years old—maybe older. Riley's pedia had called the city in the runaway system "half as old as time." Surely this was as old as time itself.

Riley saw long curving avenues between soaring spires and graceful arches, without open space, without a break between structures. Debris cluttered the avenues now—decaying vegetation blown in from the surrounding countryside, animal droppings perhaps, an occasional fragment of translucent building material. The spaces between the buildings were narrow, more like paths than avenues, as if they were not built for traffic. That was what had saved them during the first attack, keeping the arachnoids bunched in front. But the streets, if that was what they were, remained remarkably clear, and the city looked as if it had been abandoned for only a few years. It could be a human city, if a human city could have been built of this kind of material; it resembled translucent mother-of-pearl that changed colors as he looked at it.

But something was subtly wrong—not just the colors and the material but the shape, a curve here, a twist there, as if the builders had a different way of looking at the world or even a different kind of vision, or as if they perceived shapes as extensions from other dimensions. Riley couldn't look at them for long at a time without feeling that something alien passed along his optic nerve into his brain and began a wrenching process of transformation.

"Don't look," his pedia said.

"This must have been how they communicated their culture," Riley said. "Maybe not in literature or music or art but in shapes."

"It bothers you, too?" Asha said. "I learned not to look for more than a minute."

"Maybe this is why the barbarians shun this place. Once you lose the ability to absorb your own culture, it terrifies."

"There's enough to be frightened of as it is," Asha said. "Five of us reached the city. I was the only one to reach the shrine."

"You think the arachnoids will return?"

"They don't give up," Asha said, and shivered. "They sense prey, and I think they have hunted everything else to extinction."

Riley studied the cityscape with an eye for movement. He saw nothing but the blowing debris. "Which way?" he asked.

Asha looked at the surrounding buildings. "I'm not sure. I was always bad at directions or locations. The Transcendental Machine changed all that, but this place is different. We entered at another spot, and Ren was leading. Then we got ambushed, and Ren and I ran in the other direction. There was no time to look for landmarks, even if these alien-shaped structures offered anything recognizable. When the creatures got really close, we ran even harder and ended up at the shrine, by accident."

"That's why you took a chance with the Transcendental Machine."

"There was no way back. The lander had been overrun by the arachnoids and probably looted. Here the night creatures lurked everywhere. But it wasn't as much of a choice as an accident. I didn't know it was the machine then. Dust had piled up in and around it. It could have been the remains of hundreds of cycles or the detritus of the ages. I was just trying to hide. But you've never believed in transcendence."

Riley looked at her without subterfuge. "I didn't believe in anything. I was hired to find the shrine. Somebody cared—a lot. I can understand why, but I still don't know who. And if I couldn't reach the shrine, I was instructed to kill the Prophet. Which turned out to be you."

"If you could." Her gaze offered a challenge.

"If I could." His expression admitted the possibility that he might not have prevailed.

"But you didn't try."

"I can't take credit for that," Riley said. "We haven't found the shrine."

They turned and moved deeper into the city. The blue sun was descending beyond the farthest spires, and the red sun would not rise for another few hours. In the darkness the night creatures awaited.

As they walked warily along a narrow street surrounded by towering alien structures, Riley smelled the city. Every planet has characteristic odors. Many odors, of course, depending on the zone and the vegetation and the location near bodies of water, but one underlying odor by which the planet and even its natives, wherever they are, could be identified. Pilgrim's End was like that. The worlds in this spiral arm were stranger, as if the supernovas that had cooked the original elements of that arm had a different recipe. And the city was stranger than the countryside. Some of the materials that went into the original construction were still outgassing molecules after all these long-cycles. Pilgrim's End smelled as twisted and strange as its architecture.

The air temperature was moderate—a bit warm when both suns were in the sky, not so warm with a single sun, and cooling quickly when both were set. Riley shivered in his jacket. Asha seemed unaffected by heat or cold.

The air was breathable enough, a little higher in oxygen and lower in carbon dioxide than humans were accustomed to, and exhilarating at first. Tordor said it was because the planet had lost oxygen-consuming animal life after degeneration began and vegetation had a chance to restore the primeval balance. Sapients changed their worlds in their own images, but once they were gone the worlds recovered. Sapients destroyed; worlds restored.

The silence of the city was palpable. Only the occasional keening of the wind and the rustling of the litter broke the spell. The quiet in a place built for bustle and noise was unsettling.

Riley kept his head in constant motion. Although his pedia was an early warning device, he trusted his own senses more, and he had survived by paying attention—in this case to movements perceptible only at the edge of vision. "What are we looking for?" he asked.

"It was dark," Asha said. "The long night, after the blue sun had set. I had the impression of long spidery legs. They moved fast and were hard to hit, as if their bodies were small and perched high above their legs."

"We see aliens as variants of the creatures we already know."

"They might not be anything like spiders," Asha said. "They didn't like fire. After the first three were grabbed—transcendence knows what happened to them—Ren and I built a fire, but in the long night we ran out of fuel, and the creatures almost got Ren when he tried to collect more, just outside the firelight."

The blue sun was almost down behind the farthest buildings, its fierce light shining through their walls like a prism. "Maybe we'd better prepare for the short night," Riley said, "and gather enough firewood so that we don't have to brave the darkness."

"That's a metaphor for the human experience, isn't it?" Asha asked. "Sit by the fire and be protected, or risk the darkness and maybe die."

"Like all metaphors, this one doesn't gather firewood," Riley said, and stopped at a spot along the avenue where the buildings were lower and heaps of brush and deadwood had been blown by ancient winds. He made one small pile of brush a few meters from a solid building wall, topped it with deadwood, and built two larger piles of deadwood along the wall.

Asha pulled a stubby pipe from her pack and aimed it at the brush. The brush burst into flame. "One thing I learned," she said, "was to bring a heat stick."

"You are a fount of resourcefulness," Riley said and settled himself with his back against the building wall. He patted the spot beside him. "Get some sleep," he said. "We'll rest until the red sun rises, and then move farther until we stop again for the long night. I'll stand watch."

Asha settled down and let him put his arm around her shoulders. "I never sleep," she said. "You sleep. I'll watch."

Riley didn't argue. "Wake me if anything moves or the fire needs wood." And he dropped into a deep sleep almost immediately.

His pedia awakened him an instant before Asha's hand touched his shoulder. "There's movement," she said.

Riley caught a glimpse of something vaguely spidery at the edge of his vision. It vanished when he looked at the spot directly, but he knew it had been there. The fire had diminished. Riley tossed another piece of firewood on top, and sparks flew upward into the night, dying as they ascended. Beyond the flames Riley got the impression of more thin, segmented, hairy arms retreating. He added another log and slid his gun out of its holster and laid it on the ground next to his right hand.

"I don't think they'll attack," Asha said, "and the red sun will be rising in less than an hour. But I thought you'd want to be awake."

"My pedia woke me anyway," Riley said.

"I know you hate it. I could silence it again."

"Get rid of her!" his pedia said. The pressure again began to mount in his head.

"I may need it before we find the shrine."

"I know you can't get rid of it, even though it's like having a spy in your head, but there's hope that the Transcendental Machine could free you. It removes imperfections and perfects potentials."

"You're trying to kill me," his pedia said. The inner voice was bordering on hysteria.

"I'd like to believe that, but if that's what it does, why did you return after already achieving transcendence?"

She was silent for the time it took him to draw several long breaths and check for movement. "I needed to find this place again," she said finally. "What good is a Prophet who can't show people the way to salvation? I was just a low-level assistant on the previous voyage. No one told me where we were going and I didn't ask. Ren kept everything inside, like a treasure hunter with an ancient map. So I didn't know where we were when we got here.

"And I needed to prove that it was real, not just an illusion."

"But you didn't have to come this far, once we arrived at a place you recognized."

"I had to prove that the shrine itself existed and that the Transcendental Machine really worked."

"Then you're going to trust yourself to its mercy again?"

"I'll let you know when we get there. And you?"

Riley laughed. "I don't believe easily. And not in what I can't see or feel or taste. But I believe in you."

He again put his arm around her shoulder. She did not pull away. They waited for the sunrise and watched for monsters.

* * *

When the red sun began casting long rose-edged shadows along the street, they still had one small pile of firewood left and the night creatures had not attacked. They left no sign that they had been there at all.

"We'd better get farther into the city before the long night," Riley said, as he holstered his gun and got up, "and hope that something looks familiar to you."

"I'd recognize the shrine anywhere," Asha said. "It stood alone at the intersection of two narrow streets, a low building among giants, like a cathedral."

"Or a hospital?"

"You continue to doubt."

"I'm just trying to understand why a civilization would build a machine like that. What was it used for? Why did the creatures who used it abandon their city and their empire?"

He got to his feet, hoisted his backpack, and reached to help Asha to her feet, but she sprang up unaided.

"Forward," she said.

They traversed the city canyons, watching the iridescent walls on either side.

The red sun was low in the sky behind them when they came upon the remains of an old fire. Asha stopped and stared at a blackened spot on the pavement that was the only thing remaining. "This is it," she said. "This is where Ren and I built the fire before the onset of the long night. This is the place where Ren was almost taken." She circled the area, looking at the pavement, and shook her head. "We came from the opposite direction, and that was the direction Ren went for firewood, so I must have run the other way."

"But that's where we came from," Riley said.

"I must have turned down a side street."

"Shall we build a fire here and wait out the long night?"

"Most of the brush and wood are gone," Asha said.

"And you don't want to spend another night on this spot," Riley said.

"That, too."

They turned and went back the way they had come, but this time Asha moved slowly with her eyes half-closed as if she was seeing something distant in space or time.

"Here," she said. "I turned here."

She turned toward her left. Another avenue had broken the wall of buildings. "They were very fast," she said, "but maybe they were busy pursuing Ren. I could hear something behind me, but I didn't look back. I was afraid to look back."

The sun had dropped so low behind the spires that they glowed with an inner fire, and the avenue darkened as if warning of the approach of night.

"There's more brush and wood here," Riley said. "Maybe we should stop and get a fresh start in the morning."

"Not yet," Asha said.

Beyond the next curve of the avenue Asha cried out. Riley saw it, the building, the shrine. The avenue split in two a few hundred meters from them, and a low, massive building nestled in the triangle between.

"Wait," Riley said. He reached into his backpack and removed impervium gloves and an impervium bag. He removed the almost invisible monofilament and stretched it across the narrow street as high as he could reach. He attached it with fast-drying glue on either side. "Now," he said.

In the gathering night, Riley's pedia warned him. Almost simultaneously they heard a warbling sound mixed with a whisper of something moving. Riley turned and felt Asha turning behind him.

Half a dozen of the giant arachnoids raced down the street toward them, not waiting for the concealment of night, perhaps aware of how near they were to their goal. Two on the left were closest and one on the right. Three, in a rough triangle, filled the middle. More, perhaps, were hidden by the curve of the street.

The resemblance to spiders was superficial. Their legs were long and thin and bent inward at the top, to be sure, but there were only four legs and two more that were shorter, legs or arms, closer to the head. Above them was an oval body with a face parodying humanity: two eyes and what may have been a nose but below that a cruel jaw that looked capable of crunching thigh bones.

Asha aimed her heat stick at the pile of brush on the left and, as it burst into flame, the pile on the right. Only the three in the middle came on. The other three shifted to the center and followed.

"I'll take the ones on the right," Asha said. "Shoot at their heads."

Riley's gun was already in his hand. His first shot exploded the head of the first, and his second felled the next to its right. His pedia or his urgency seemed to guide his aim, because he never missed. When he destroyed the third that came on behind, he turned toward Asha's side of the avenue to find three smoking corpses that had fallen to her heat stick.

"All I ever wanted to do," Asha said, "was offer creatures an opportunity to fulfill their potential."

"I know," Riley said.

"Life limits us," Asha said. "We need something to liberate us."

"That's what everybody wanted to stop," Riley said. "Liberation can be deadly."

"Only to the masters."

Another wave of monsters rounded the curve.

"Go," Riley said. "I'll hold them off."

"No, that's what Ren said when he caught up to me. We'll go together," Asha said.

Two of the monsters had stopped to feed on the remains of their fellows. Riley and Asha shot the ones that continued and then the feeders.

The third wave arrived.

"Go!" Riley said and gave her a shove toward the shrine. "I'll follow."

She gave him one despairing look and ran toward the building. The next wave ran into the monofilament and were decapitated, but the next wave avoided what the juices of the earlier victims had made visible. Riley picked off the monsters until his gun clicked empty. He inserted a new magazine as he backed toward the open doorway and began firing once more, knowing the monsters would reach him before he reached the shrine.

They were close enough for him to smell their alien breath when he felt a gush of warmth beside his face and one of the monsters burst into flame and then another.

"Keep shooting!" Asha said. "I've got to get this door open."

Riley felt a cool breeze from behind and a hand that reached out to pull him inside.

A door irised shut in the face of the nearest monsters.

In the darkness Riley turned and leaned against the door.

Asha's heat stick became a light stick illuminating the entrance. Carvings and hieroglyphs adorned the semicircular stone—not the ubiquitous semitransparent material of the rest of the city. The carvings resembled miniature renderings of the monsters outside.

"The night creatures," Riley said. "They kept getting bigger and they couldn't get inside."

"They built this," Asha said, sweeping her light stick at the carvings. "Ren was wrong. The night creatures were the city builders. They may have evolved from the barbarians or they may have had a common ancestor, and now they haunt the city and the star empire they once ruled."

Asha turned her light stick toward the interior. The room was enormous. It soaked up the light like a dark sponge. Riley got the impression of massive walls without windows, a vaulted ceiling without skylight, and a floor vast and uncluttered except for the scattered remnants of framework. He heard no sound except their breathing. He smelled alien dust, perhaps stirred by their entrance or the wind from outside.

"It *is* like a cathedral," Riley said. His words echoed back at him from a remote distance.

"That's what I thought," Asha said. "Come." She picked her way across the floor, playing her light in front. "You can't imagine what emotions this place recalls."

"I can," Riley said. He could almost feel the adrenaline pumping into her bloodstream, her perfected heart beating faster, and the improved neurons in her brain connecting to antiquated networks. He heard their muffled footprints and their echoes.

"Stop!" his pedia shouted. "Stop!" Riley's brain felt as if it were going to explode. "If I die, you die!" it said.

"Just like the last time," Asha said, "too many have died to get us here. How can it be worth it?"

"They all took their chances," Riley said. "Just as we did. And they would have done it again, for all their many reasons, even if they had known the odds."

"Even so."

They had traveled perhaps a hundred meters and Riley saw no indication of an end.

"You'll have to make a decision soon," Asha said.

"Some decision," Riley said, "with those monsters waiting outside."

"If you accept the machine," Asha said, "it will be better."

"I don't believe in the supernatural," Riley said. "You can have your religion, your transcendentalism. I think there's a natural explanation. If I survive this, I'm going to find out what it is and what it means to human life, and all sapient creatures, in our galaxy."

"That's good," Asha said. "That's what you should do."

"But I believe in you," Riley repeated.

Asha's light stick exposed a structure at the far end of the vast room. The structure seemed perhaps three meters high and made of the same iridescent material as the city outside, but more like a small pavilion with a canopy supported by pillars on four sides. Riley could understand why Asha had described it as a shrine.

"It was added later," Riley said. "This building was built of stone in the early stages of civilization."

"Come," Asha said. "We can both fit inside."

"It might not work properly with two," Riley said.

"Don't be afraid," Asha said. "I'll go first then and show you it's safe." She turned toward the evanescent canopy and then turned back to toss her light stick to Riley. "You'll need this," she said, and turned and entered the shrine without a backward look. The door started to close.

She shimmered. Her clothing disintegrated. Her skin disappeared, leaving her standing, for only a moment, with a network of veins and arteries over flesh, and then those, too, vanished, followed by internal organs, and finally bones. Everything happened so swiftly there was no time for action or reaction, no time for blood or fluids to escape, no time for speech or thought.

Riley watched dust drift to the bottom of the shrine. She was gone. Promising transcendence but suffering, maybe, extinction.

He turned to look back once more at the vast space they had crossed and up at the remote ceiling that arched into darkness. He thought about the monsters who lurked outside, who had built this monument to something, whatever it was, and then, perhaps, forgotten how to use it or used it too often.

"Stop!" his pedia shouted again. "Don't do this. We can escape! We can go back!"

"It's a waiting room, Asha," he said, and stepped forward and felt himself fall apart.

EPILOGUE

Riley woke up.

He was alone in a dark, closed space.

"Asha?" he called, but he knew she wasn't there.

He knew a lot of things he had never been aware of before, and with a clarity he had never experienced. He knew, for instance, that the Transcendental Machine was a matter-transmission device that had been used by the other spiral-arm aliens—an earlier version of the arachnoids or the species the arachnoids had replaced—to explore not only their own spiral arm but the spiral arm of humans and the aliens of the federation.

The machine analyzed anything that entered it, destroying it in the process, and sent the information to a receiver in which the same entangled quantum particle was embedded, where what had been destroyed was recreated from local materials. But in the process the imperfections were left behind—and that included sapient creatures like Asha, and now himself. Transcendence, he realized with a shock that almost made him laugh, was an accident.

He had been restored but his pedia, which was not part of his ideal condition, was not. He didn't know yet how he would get out of wherever he had been sent, nor how he would find Asha. Clearly the machine had sent her somewhere else. Maybe, if it were not programmed, the machine cycled through a series of destinations.

But he knew he would find her if he had to fight his way halfway across the galaxy. And when he found her he knew that they would change the galaxy.

ABOUT THE AUTHOR

James Gunn is the author of more than thirty books, including the Hugo Award–winning nonfiction work *Isaac Asimov: The Foundations of Science Fiction* and the novel *The Immortals,* on which the television series *The Immortal* was based. Other novels include *The Listeners, The Joy Makers,* and *Kampus.* He also has collaborated with other authors, most notably with Jack Williamson on *Star Bridge.* He was named a Grand Master by the Science Fiction and Fantasy Writers of America in 2007.

Mr. Gunn is also the editor of a series of anthologies tracing the history of science fiction, *The Road to Science Fiction,* and is a past president of The Science Fiction Writers of America. He is professor emeritus of English and was the founding director of the Center for the Study of Science Fiction at the University of Kansas. He is the winner of the Pilgrim Award for lifetime achievement in science fiction scholarship, and is a past president of the Science Fiction Research Association. He lives in Lawrence, Kansas.